MARSHMALLOW MOUNTAIN

Big Boys, Small Spaces
Book 1

A.J. TRUMAN

M.A. WARDELL

To anyone looking for a big boy for cuffing season. Here's two.

A note from the authors

Marshmallow Mountain directly results from the friendship that blossomed between us. We hope the love, laughs, and affection for each other shine through in Data and Marsh's story.

This work is an open-door romance intended for mature audiences. The characters in the story are consenting adults, and there is explicit, on-page sexual content, explicit language, and adult situations.

Marshmallow Mountain is a sweet, low-angst story. Here are the content warnings if you need them.

A character is dealing with a parent with Alzheimer's, a character has asthma and experiences symptoms and asthma attacks, and a mild car accident.

For signed paperbacks, merchandise, more information, and updates, visit us at:

www.ajtruman.com
www.mawardell.com

Best always,
A.J. and Matt

<u>Chapter One</u>

Marshall

Some people hear the rousing guitar strums of "Lose Yourself" and get pumped. Some people get inspired. I get nauseous.

Queasiness overtakes my stomach as the familiar opening chords of Marshall Mathers's legendary anthem blare from my phone, which means it can only be one very specific person.

Bryce slowly turns toward me as he hears it.

"Are. You. Fucking. Serious." Bryce narrates my surprise with narrowed eyes. Even Bobo, Bryce's adorable Bernese mountain dog, looks up with his giant brown eyes and cocks his head, equally confused.

We stand on the stoop of The Bigby, our pre-war six story walk up, Eminem's Oscar-winning song blasting from my front pocket for all passersby on West 89th to hear. Eh, it's New York City. People aren't fazed by the Naked Cowboy or pizza rats. An early 2000s jam coming from my crotch is par for the course.

"Are you going to answer it?" Bryce raises his thick eyebrows, waiting for a response.

Am I?

The phone clangs around in my pocket, mimicking my heart in my chest.

Anthony bobs his perfectly coiffed head to the music, oblivious to my imperiled emotional state. He's like a piece of art in a hotel lobby: generically pretty, but easily blends into the background. Sometimes, I wonder how he and Bryce make their relationship work. But then I hear them in the apartment above me at night, attempting to crash their bed through my ceiling, and it all makes sense.

"I love this song. I jam to it when I do squats," he says. What the man lacks in brainpower, he makes up for with glute strength and (apparent) sexual stamina. "Who is it?"

"It's the ex," Bryce says with clenched teeth.

"Why is Marsh calling?" I can't move. The booming hook has me paralyzed.

"There's only one way to find out." Bryce gestures at my jeans.

"Yo, was it weird having the same name as your boyfriend?" Anthony scrolls through pictures of himself on his phone. "You guys are a *Wheel of Fortune* category."

"Were," Bryce corrects.

"We made it work," I say. A thickness coats my throat as I swallow. "We had nicknames for each other. He called me … "

Data. The name bounces off the inside of my skull like a pinball, searching for a target. "My Data," he would say, sometimes repeating it like a prayer, whispering it into my ear, sending goosebumps tiptoeing over my skin.

My heart tumbles in my chest.

"Data," Bryce tells Anthony. "Because Marshall's an accountant. For a comic, he's not very original," says Bryce, playing the best friend role and coming to my defense. "Time's ticking. Are you going to pick up?"

"Yeah, tell him you're glad you dumped his ass, then hang up." Anthony lets out a smarmy chuckle.

"He was the dumpee, not the dumper." Bryce rolls his eyes both at his boyfriend and the breakup dynamics.

"I shouldn't answer it, right? We haven't spoken in … six

months." Has it really been that long? "Or maybe I should. There has to be a good reason why he's calling after all this time."

"Enough with the indecision, you Homosexual Hamlet." Bryce wrestles my hand away and shovels his fingers down my pants pocket. Wanting to join in what he perceives as playtime, Bobo emits a single, booming bark, startling us both.

I swat at Bryce's wrist, but he's taller and stronger. The man is a professional dancer. If he really wanted to, he could gracefully toss me in the air. His buzz cut allows his blue eyes to shine and right now they're framed by a furrowed brow.

"Excuse me, you haven't even bought me dinner," I say.

"I'll buy you brunch."

"But Marshall usually pays," Anthony replies.

"Sweetie, we're not going to brunch, it's banter," Bryce huffs and pulls my phone out, trying to answer the call.

"Bryce, stop. Give it to me." He raises his eyebrows. "My phone," I clarify.

The ringtone relents, and Bryce finally relinquishes my cell. "Well, your dramatics paid off. You missed his call."

"*My* dramatics?"

As the phone stops ringing, my chest deflates a little, my heartbeat finally returning to normal.

"Why is he calling you?" Bryce asks as Bobo guides us toward Central Park for our Sunday stroll. "You know how I feel about Carly Rae Jepsen, but 'Call Me Maybe?' No."

"I have no clue." As a statistically minded person, scenarios formulate in my mind. Naturally, I begin with possible catastrophes. "What if it's something serious? Maybe his asthma. Or what if he's been in an accident?" My head becomes dizzy. "What if he's in the hospital?" Knowing Marsh, he probably still has me listed as his emergency contact.

"If he was in the hospital, then the hospital would call,"

says Bryce. Bobo stops to sniff a tree. "You're only smelling your piss from yesterday, buddy."

"Right. You're right." I sigh deeply, the tension momentarily leaving my body, knowing he's okay.

"Don't breathe a sigh of relief for that fucker. He doesn't get that from you anymore." Bryce shouts, projecting all the way to the East Side. He's spent his career on some sort of stage, and yet *I'm* the dramatic one?

"He must want something," Anthony says. "Maybe he forgot his Netflix password."

"You better have changed all your passwords the second he moved out," Bryce says.

"Or maybe he left something at your place. I used to forget my box of condoms at guys' places all the time." Anthony smacks his forehead and laughs.

"You carried a *box* of condoms around with you?" Bryce asks.

"Yeah. Costco sells a pack of forty," Anthony shrugs. "I like safe sex. And a good deal."

Bryce and I became fast friends when he moved into Anthony's apartment above me. I'd never really spoken much with Anthony, but when Bryce found me sobbing at the mailboxes, he insisted I come up for Rocky Road ice cream. Because the New York performing arts world is as incestuous as the gay community, Bryce was already familiar with Marsh from a stint as a backup dancer in Marsh's improv troupe's musical revue *I Left My Shart in San Francisco*.

I hope these two have better luck than Marsh and me, although each time Anthony opens his mouth, I become more doubtful.

Anthony pulls Bryce to him and kisses the top of his head. "You're the only one I want to have safe sex with, babe."

Bryce blushes despite himself. Maybe these two have a shot.

"What if … " Bryce bites his lip. "He wants you back?"

And there it is. The potential answer hanging over us. A dark storm cloud just waiting to explode with rain.

"I don't … think so." I take a deep breath. It's been six months, and I'm still processing what happened.

"Why'd you guys break up again?" Anthony asks, even though I'm sure Bryce has regaled him with my sob story numerous times. If it's not on his social media feed, Anthony doesn't pay much attention.

My stomach churns with the memory of that night.

"Marsh said he needed time and space," Bryce says.

Anthony scrunches his brow. "Is he a physicist?"

"That would make more sense. You don't tell your boyfriend of almost a decade that you need space." Bryce gives my hand a squeeze, a silent hit of support.

I still remember the night that changed everything between us. After years of hustling in dingy clubs, Marsh got accepted into the Laughingstock Comedy Festival, one of the biggest events for comics in the world. It was the big break he'd been working toward for years.

And then he bombed. *Hard.*

Thank goodness the festival had a no phones policy during shows.

It's a truly terrible feeling watching someone crash on stage, even more so when that person is your boyfriend of eight years.

Marsh became a different person when we got back to our apartment. Whenever I encouraged him to keep going or asked about his day, he would withdraw. His usual joyfulness was replaced with sullenness.

Marsh said that the worst part about bombing was when you knew you'd lost the audience and you still had to finish your set. That was how I felt during the final month of our relationship. Yet when he sat me down in our living room one night and gave me the break-up speech, I still found myself shocked. Eight years together, and this was how things ended?

We'd been there for each other through highs and lows. Why couldn't we get through this?

There's a reason math is the universal language—numbers make sense. And when they don't, there's always a reason for it.

The numbers of our breakup didn't add up. They still don't.

"Don't worry, Marshall." Anthony puts a consoling hand on my shoulder, and remarkably, the pressure provides a bit of relief. "It's not you. He probably just wants to fuck other people." Anthony cocks his head, and sometimes I wonder if Bryce has the patience for both a boyfriend and a dog. At least Bobo doesn't speak.

"I'll text him about those Costco condoms," I snark.

"Sweetie," Bryce says to his boyfriend, and I know what he's thinking. *At least you're hung.*

Bryce gasps when my phone vibrates. "He left a voicemail." He smiles, amused. "How 1998 of him."

"He left a voicemail?" I repeat. Between texting, voice-to-text, voice messages in texts, and social media DMs, there is no reason for people to leave voicemails. Voicemails are for parents.

"Maybe this *is* serious," wonders Anthony. Perhaps he has a point. My stomach resumes its ride on the What If roller-coaster.

What if Marsh is in the hospital, and it's a family member ringing to tell me the bad news? What if he's trapped some-where and needs help, and I am the person he's calling? What if he's driven off a bridge and the car is sinking and he's holding his phone up in a tiny pocket of air trying to call me?

"Should we listen to it?" Bryce's finger hovers over the play button.

I take back my phone. "I don't know."

"That's a yes."

"I'm going to listen to it. By myself." Nerves flicker up my spine and my shoulders shudder. Sure, I'm plenty upset about how he ended things, but I don't hate Marsh. I spent over one-fifth of my life with him. Loving him. He's infused into my bloodstream like oxygen. I could never hate him. And I definitely don't want anything bad to happen to him—like being eaten by sharks while holding his phone in a pocket of air desperately trying to call me.

"People only leave voicemails in serious situations, right?" I check with Bryce.

"Typically. You can read the text translation too."

If given the choice between mistranslated text and hearing his voice, I'd rather go with the latter, as much as it may hurt.

The voicemail stares back at me, daring me to press play. It would be the first time I've heard Marsh's voice since the breakup. The thought of hearing his boisterous baritone that's forever dialed up to the highest volume makes my head dizzy.

"Isn't that the place that sells vintage toys?" I nod toward the mint green sign on the next block.

Bryce's eyes light up like he's just witnessed the choreo to Britney's "Toxic" for the first time. Vintage Transformers are his kryptonite—the man spends an ungodly amount of energy scouring the internet and swap meets for originals. It's the reason I've been to more flea markets and back alley toy stores in the last few months than I'd ever admit to under oath. The man is smitten with his robot/vehicle boyfriends. He even convinced Anthony to replace his oven with a custom-made display case.

"I'll catch up with you," I say.

"Good luck." Anthony gives me a salute.

Bryce is more subtle, offering a reassuring elbow nudge. "C'mon, Bobo!"

At the sound of his name, Bobo tugs at the lead, and they're off toward overpriced plastic toys laced with childhood memories.

I glance in the window of a store selling crafts and trinkets, one of the many storefronts on this overcrowded island that somehow stay in business. A display table of wooden artwork, carved and lacquered into things of beauty, takes center stage in the window. My hands twitch at the thought of what I could whittle. Woodworking, once a passion, gradually transformed into a hobby, and finally faded into a distant memory as the grind of adulthood took over. I remember spending lazy afternoons with Marsh on the couch, him reading a biography of one of the great comedians hoping for inspiration, and me carving tiny treasures. He loved anything I showed him, even when I knew it was crap. My chest swells viewing the pieces on display. I'm flooded with nostalgia for our time together and I take it as a sign.

I take a gulp of air and press play.

"Hey Data. It's Marsh. Uh, been a while. I hope you're good. Listen, I've been doing some thinking, and there's a question I wanted to ask you." I hit pause and take a cleansing breath, as a flutter of excitement zips through me. This is it. I hit play: *"What would you say to selling the cabin? I know we talked about sharing it, but I've been talking to a real estate agent, and she says it's the best time to put it on the market. Strike while the iron is hot. I'm going up this weekend to get it ready in case we decide to sell. I really think we should. It'd probably make sense if you came up too. We can clean out our stuff and discuss next steps. Give me a call, let me know what you think. Bye."*

Not a word from him in six months, and now this? A request to clean out the cabin we co-own and *discuss next steps?*

Eight years together, and all I get is *bye?*

My entire body goes numb.

Why did I think he had any change of heart or regrets over the breakup? Why the hell did I let myself believe he missed me, missed us, missed the life we'd built together? My bruised heart pounds, reminding me what this all means. Marsh is doing just fine. He has one thousand percent moved on.

And you know what? I should too.

I'll drive up to Marshmallow Mountain this weekend—pack, clean, and sell it, and finally get Marshall Goldberg out of my system.

In fact, I cue up "Lose Yourself" for extra motivation, and jog to catch up with Bryce, Anthony, and Bobo.

Chapter Two

Marsh

Here's the thing you need to know about Data: he doesn't take surprises well.

I once surprised him with a new coffee table for our apartment—one that was round, not rectangular—and you'd think I'd smeared mud on the walls. It was gone by that night.

I can't imagine how he's taking my voicemail. I slip my phone into my pocket and brace myself for his reply.

"Question: is it funnier if I say my vagina is like a venus flytrap or like Audrey II, the creature in *Little Shop of Horrors?*" Preeti hunches over her notepad, tapping her pen on the paper.

A horrified, daintily sweating woman in pricey athleisure stops when she hears the question.

"I'll take your towel, ma'am." Preeti reaches for the gym towel the woman is holding. Ms. Athleisure hands it over, shoots Preeti one of those polite-but-disgusted smiles that rich people master in utero. "Thanks. See you next Tuesday!"

"You too," says the woman, a little confused.

No Cornell graduate wants to be working at a gym, but like all of us, Preeti's doing what she can to pay the bills in order to focus on pursuing her dreams. Her boss, who's straight and married, accidentally sent her a dick pic a few months ago, so he now lets me hang at the desk with her, no questions asked.

"Was Audrey II a creature or a monster?" she asks, studying the joke in her notebook.

"That's more of a philosophical question, don't you think?"

"Audrey II is a more accurate representation of my vagina because it's perpetually ravenous and demands constant human sacrifice, but 'venus flytrap' sounds better. It's less wordy." Preeti says the joke to herself, running it over in her head, same as I do with my material. "And what if there are people in the audience who don't know *Little Shop*?"

"The club is in Chelsea. They know *Little Shop*."

Preeti and I became fast friends on the comedy club circuit because we're both outsiders. Me, an extra-large gay man with an ample stomach, and her, an extra-large Indian woman with an ample bosom. Despite strides made in recent years, stand-up is still overpopulated with straight white men bemoaning that "women be crazy." We outsiders gotta stick together. The people deserve fabulous comedy.

We used to regularly perform together at a queer-owned comedy club, Pauline's, where at least we're mostly able to play to our home team. Preeti still performs there, while I'm on a comedy hiatus.

"Most of the guys in the audience probably think there's a flesh-eating monster in your pants, so you're good," I tell her.

"Thank you," Preeti says to another woman in pricey athleisure handing over her towel. "See you next Tuesday!"

"But I don't come on Tuesdays."

"Great!" Preeti says without missing a beat of enthusiasm.

The woman disappears into the locker room a bit unsure what just happened. Preeti turns back to me.

"I want every joke to hit for this showcase," she says. "How's your material coming?"

"I told you. I'm—"

"On a comedy hiatus. Well, your pause is officially over."

"It's for the best that I never go out on another stage again."

"Bullshit. You're doing this with me."

After getting sloshed at a party hosted by a comedian "friend" who was staffed as a writer on *The Tonight Show*, Preeti came up with an idea to organize a comedy showcase to get us more (or any) attention: an end-of-year revue called *Out with a Bang*. She corralled our favorite marginalized comedians and is putting the word out to every manager, agent, producer, casting director, and industry-connected person. I said I'd help with graphics and putting up flyers, but I won't be performing.

"Preeti—"

"Don't Preeti me." She taps my empty notebook. "I'm letting you live rent free. In New York. You owe me."

"Can't I just give you a vital organ instead?" I point to my rib cage area to entice her.

She is not amused. "So you bombed. It happens to every single comedian. It's a rite of passage. You dust yourself off, take a shot of vodka, and get back out there."

Everything she's saying makes sense, but she's never bombed on that big of a stage. Anyone with any power to hire me for a TV show or movie was in that auditorium. Four years of building a name for myself disintegrated in four minutes. Thinking back to that weekend and everything that happened after—everything and everyone I lost—sends a chill up my spine. What's the opposite of nostalgia?

"Have you performed anywhere in the last few months?" Her big, brown, chibi-esque eyes study mine. "God, even an open mic night?"

"I performed 'Born This Way' in my shower."

"It's my shower, and you were so offkey you made Lady Gaga cry."

I don't have the heart to tell her that my enthusiasm for

comedy has petered out. At a certain point, pounding the pavement loses its appeal.

"*Out with a Bang* will be your grand return." Preeti's an optimist at heart. She's only twenty-eight. Life hasn't destroyed her spirit yet. I was an optimist too, once.

My pocket vibrates, sending a current of tension through my body. Data. I collect myself with a deep breath and prepare for the response. An excited flutter shoots through my stomach at the thought of hearing his voice. When I pull my phone out, there's nothing. Merely the screen background of us at a pumpkin patch, which I haven't been able to change yet. Damn phantom vibrations. I shove my phone back.

"How's your stuff coming?" Preeti looks over at my notebook. A blank page stares back. In better time, I used to fill notebooks with jokes. "Dude, if we're going to work shitty jobs, then we need to take advantage of the downtime for writing." She hands me an Eclipse Fitness pen. She's using a branded pen from the soulless law firm where I had my most recent temp job.

Now my phone is buzzing. I swipe it from my pocket. Shoot. Just a *Times* notification about some company filing for bankruptcy. Blah blah blah.

I place the phone face down on the desk.

"Who are you waiting to hear from?" Her eyes light up.

"I called Data about going up to our cabin this weekend."

She leans forward on the front desk, instantly turning into a gossiping teen. "OMG. Yes! Are you two finally getting back together?"

"Not quite. I need to sell it."

"Sell it? But you love that place. You have so many memories there. You desecrated every square inch with your sweaty, gross lovemaking."

All true. The cabin was both an impulse purchase and smart investment made years ago when we were in a much different financial situation. I was on track to take over my family's business, until I went full millennial and decided to pursue my passion for comedy. We called the cabin and surrounding land Marshmallow Mountain because Data wouldn't let me call it Broke-My-Back Mountain. It was our bubble where we could leave the stresses of the world behind. My heart dips as a quick highlight reel plays in my mind. Sipping fresh lemonade after skinny dipping in the pond. Cuddling on the couch and watching the snow fall. Cooking grand feasts together in the tiny kitchen. And Preeti is correct: we really did desecrate every room.

"Property on the mountain is selling faster than Ozempic. It's probably being sold to people like your customers."

Another pair of Eclipse Fitness members, a woman and her gay best friend, fresh from a barre class yet not a hair out of place, toss their towels at Preeti without stopping.

"Thank you, see you next Tuesday!" she calls to them, but they're already gone.

"Do you only see them on Tuesdays?" I ask.

"No." She winks at me. "These are the same bitches who teased me growing up. Now I have to handle their used towels. I'm just trying to find joy where I can."

"Fair."

"See you next Tuesday!" Preeti says to another group of women handing over towels.

"We can get a lot of money for the cabin now. And unless you want me to keep sleeping on your couch, that's a good thing." Bless Preeti for taking me in after the break-up and bless the New York rental market gods for giving her a studio large enough to fit a bed and a couch.

"You're welcome to stay as long as you need. As long as you don't mind listening to the occasional bouts of lady-on-lady sex."

"I didn't realize there was so much slurping involved."

She snorts a laugh, a *huge* win among comedian friends. Currently, Preeti is in her lady era, although that could change at any moment.

"What did he say when you called?"

"I left a voicemail."

Preeti's face twists into lemon-sucking disgust. "Marsh. My grandmother leaves voicemails."

"It wasn't planned. I heard his voice on the message, then the beep, and my mouth started moving."

She shakes her head at my antiquated communication method, but moves on. "I still don't understand why you two broke up. You were like hashtag couple goals. You almost made me consider monogamy." She keeps the snarky grin on her face, but a hint of seriousness creeps in. "Really, why did you break up with him? Marshall's the best."

It's a question I keep asking myself, even though I know the answer. My insides twist with the familiar pain of being Data-less. And no matter how many times I remind myself it was the right thing to do, it still hurts.

On stage, I'm great at staying upbeat while bombing, and I use that same skill here.

"He *is* the best. But we're not the best for each other." I sound confident when I say it. Maybe one day, I'll believe it.

Because the universe is a master at comedic timing, at that moment, my phone vibrates with such a forceful text notification that it shimmies right off the desk and into the pile of used towels. It could only be one person.

I open the message. Preeti watches me like I'm about to announce who won best picture.

"It's just spam. The DNC hitting me up for cash."

She tips her head at me. Preeti has no time for customers who'd like to speak to the manager nor for friends withholding texts from ex-boyfriends.

I clear my throat and read the message:

Data: Okay. Makes sense. I'll meet you
up there.

No three bubbles to indicate more's coming. That's it. Eight words.

"Oh fuck," she says.

"What?"

"He still hates you. *A lot.*"

"You can never tell tone from text messages."

"Bitch, that text was so frigid, I need to run into the hot yoga room to warm up."

"Eh. A little wordy." I put my phone face down on the counter, avoiding the message.

"You're right. That text was so frigid it belongs at a Connecticut family Thanksgiving."

"Better," I say.

"If you come back from this weekend with a ripped-off scrotum, I won't be surprised."

I wince at her quip. Even joking about that can cause bodily pain.

"He doesn't seem that mad." I grab my phone and read the text again, trying to imagine Data's warm voice saying these words.

"Um. Read it again. And I don't blame him. You were together eight years, and then you just ended it."

"I didn't just end it."

"Sounds like you did. What did you say? You couldn't be together because you needed to wash your hair?"

"No. I said I had a lot going on."

"That's even worse."

I'm in no mood to relitigate this period of my life, but I obviously have to set Preeti straight. "Look, I was in a rough place after the showcase. This career I was building instantly crumbled. Plus everything going on with my dad got worse. It was a lot to deal with."

Our friendship follows *Seinfeld*'s mantra: no hugs. But Preeti briefly breaks from our banter and bows her head, her forehead creasing in concern.

"Ultimately, I couldn't give Data the attention he deserves."

"Isn't that what a boyfriend's there for? To lean on during the hard times?"

On paper, she was right. But things were more complicated than that. My life turned into an avalanche of shit barreling down a mountain. It was best to push Data out of the way before it clobbered him too.

"Marsh, it sucks what's going on with your dad. And it sucks that Laughingstock didn't go your way. And it sucks that we're not headlining tours and getting lucrative deals with HBO yet. But what you told Marshall is even more of a line than my hair excuse. 'I have a lot going on right now?' Too bad you didn't cap it with 'I think we need some space.'"

"Actually, I might've said that too." I hide behind my notebook.

"Fuck. I'm shocked I haven't ripped off your scrotum."

"Can everyone please leave my genitals alone?" I cross my legs to quell the pain, both for my balls and my heart. "Was it my finest hour? No. But I just … " I don't want to go down this path. It won't lead anywhere helpful. History can't be rewritten. The bottom line is that Data deserves a prince, not a pauper. He should be with a man, not a mess.

My delivery might've needed more tweaking, but the sentiment stands.

"You should go with the *Little Shop* monster punchline, not venus flytrap. The room will eat it up. The Rick Moranis thirst is real." I tap the line in her notebook, hoping it shifts us back to lobbing jokes at each other, not dissecting my crumbling personal life.

She crosses out venus flytrap in her notebook, then looks up at me.

"When are you going up?" she asks.

"This weekend."

"Good luck," she says with a sigh. "Marshall is a sweetie pie, but he seems like one of those people where if you get on their shit list, you never get off."

She's great at reading people, but I hope she's wrong here.

A woman in a designer headband shoves her towel at Preeti. "You need to replace these towels. They're too scratchy. Can you please relay that to your manager?"

"Will do," Preeti says with a wide smile worn by every fed-up service worker in America. "See you next Tuesday!"

Chapter Three

~~Data~~ Marshall

"What is it?" Bryce's forehead creases and Bobo sits, waiting like a good boy.

"Marsh wants to sell." Saying it out loud somehow makes it more real, and a sudden wetness prickles the corners of my eyes.

"Sell what? His collection of horrible nineties T-shirts?" Bryce glances towards the heavens. "Praise, Jesus."

"No." A heaviness falls on my shoulders. "The cabin."

"That hovel in Maine?"

"It's not a hovel. It's rustic."

"Rustic is a euphemism for dusty." Bryce arches an eyebrow.

"Oh, I love Maine," Anthony says. "Excellent maple syrup."

While it's true that movie star looks can make a strong first impression, they only carry you so far. Bryce turns to me and makes a stealth measuring gesture with his hands totaling a significant number of inches.

Men are simple creatures, aren't we?

"Wait," Bryce says. "You still own the cabin?"

"Yes, we still own the cabin," I say, returning my gaze to him.

"Why? Honey, you're broken up. Divide the assets."

"We did. I got the apartment, after all." Marsh didn't put up a fight to keep it. I wish he'd put up more of a fight … for anything. Maybe I should have too. "Since we broke up in the spring, we forgot about the cabin. It's a lot of work to sell a place."

I shift uncomfortably. Bryce has a superb bullshit detector, but I'm hoping it's defective at the moment.

"You should not be sharing anything with Marsh, least of all a homeowner's insurance policy. You mean to tell me you've been paying to keep up your 'rustic' cabin that you share with your ex and you don't use?" He crinkles his brow. "Huh. You're usually good with money."

Bryce is right. Mom and I were barely middle class. Money was tight, and I learned not to throw it away. But money is also extremely emotional, and my emotions won out here.

Keeping the place on Marshmallow Mountain meant holding on to the bittersweet memories of warm campfires, breathtaking views, and all the laughter and love we shared there. Getting rid of it would feel like cutting off a limb. A shallow sigh escapes my lips. I thought neither one of us was ready to let that go, but like so much about Marsh, I guess I was wrong.

Bobo leads us toward home. The gray, overcast skies suggest an approaching storm, but the drops of rain have yet to make their appearance.

"It's a lovely cabin. You've been. You had fun."

"One of those statements is true."

"You've been?" Anthony asks, tilting his head.

"Only once, sweetie. You were on set that weekend. And Bobo loves nature." Bryce pats the dog's enormous head. "I prefer the creature comforts of civilization."

"We have plumbing. And heat."

"Setting the bar high." Bryce rolls his eyes.

"Cabins in the area have gone up in value since we bought

it. The land alone is worth a pretty penny," I say, kicking myself for repeating anything from Marsh's voicemail.

"Then you should sell. Get back your investment. Treat your broke-but-hot dancer friend to a spa weekend." Bryce hooks my arm as we head down the street, leaving Anthony in our wake. "Maybe holding onto this cabin is why you haven't been able to move on."

I push back from Bryce, heat flaming up my cheeks. "I have moved on!"

"I live above you. I have heard no creaking mattress sounds of late. And while Anthony and I love Sunday brunches with you, it's always a table for three, never four."

I can't argue with brunch economics. Although after putting in eight years with Marsh only for it to end so weirdly, I'm not in a rush to get back out there. I have my job. I can get a dog, perhaps a succulent. I'll be fine.

"The cabin is your last connection to him. Cut the cord."

"But an entire weekend with him?"

"It's the perfect opportunity for you to move on once and for all." Bryce takes Bobo's leash, turns around, and hands him off to Anthony as we approach The Bigby. "I'll be up in a minute."

Anthony waves goodbye. I kneel and kiss Bobo on the top of his giant furry head. Before I pull away, he jerks his head up and licks my face with his wide tongue.

"He never kisses me like that," Anthony says.

"I'm your boyfriend," Bryce says, patting Anthony's arm, "And Bobo is Marshall's."

A smile scatters on my face because even though I know Bryce is teasing, Bobo and I have a special affinity for each other. Anthony takes my would-be husband hound up the stairs, leaving my best friend and me alone on the stoop.

We sit, breathing in the crisp late autumn air. The tree in

front of our building is bursting with fiery orange leaves. There really is nothing like late fall in New York.

"There's something else you need to do to close the loop with Marsh." His hand lands on my shoulder. "You need to have break-up sex."

My mouth drops open. The mere thought of Marsh and me and sex is enough to send a rush of unwanted heat up my neck. "Excuse me?"

He dips his chin and glares. "Marshall Kaplan. This is Relationship 101. In order to move on, you need to have break-up sex. Think of it as your fucking funeral." Bryce pats his hands together, attempting to wash away the life Marsh and I built together.

"Well, that is not happening."

"Why not?" Bryce asks.

"Because Marsh broke my heart."

"And now you can break his back."

I still can't believe he ended things with such a generic breakup. He needed "space and time." For what, exactly? In our relationship, we helped each other when the chips were down. But Marsh didn't want my help. He didn't want my love or support, either. He simply left. Not only was I heartbroken, but too confused to protest.

"He didn't just break my heart. He ripped it out of my chest, threw it on the floor, and stomped it out like the time you forgot a hamburger on the stove and it caught fire."

"Don't attempt to distract me with charred meat," Bryce says. "Just do it. Him. Marsh. One and done. Put the ex in sex. Then we can gossip about it on our spa weekend you're treating me to."

I shoot him a "get real" look.

"I'm a dancer! My body is perpetually sore!"

My head shakes profusely, having a mind of its own. "We are not having breakup sex. No way. Not happening."

"See how you feel when you're up in the mountains alone with him. Surrounded by nature."

Me. Marsh. Alone. Together. Another flush of unwanted heat hammers my neck.

"Nope. Nope. Nope."

"Fine. Suit yourself." Bryce raises an eyebrow, not unlike my mother's passive-aggressive stance whenever I dared leave the house without a jacket as a kid.

It's only one weekend. Two nights. Not even two full days. Go up Friday afternoon, leave on Sunday. Done. Technically, that's not even an entire weekend. I'll bring the cardamom buns from the French bakery as a distraction. He loves those more than off brand La Croix. I'll grab a dozen. We'll clean out the house. Quickly. I'll keep my distance. Avoid Marsh's adorable face and charm. Pack up and go. And who knows, given the time that has passed, maybe we can tie a prettier bow on the end of our relationship.

"Just stay open." Bryce slaps my ass and runs up the stairs. Before he enters the front door, he turns and shouts, "Love you!"

I pull my phone from my pocket and find a reply from Marsh.

Marsh: Cool.

Our whole relationship boiled down to one word.

I can do this—one last weekend on Marshmallow Mountain.

Fall is still in full force in New England, making for a beautiful drive up to Maine. At least one part of this weekend will be enjoyable. As I get closer to the cabin, more snow appears on the ground. It's a light dusting, flecks of flakes sitting precariously on fall leaves.

I pass the local store and pair of cute restaurants on the main road before pulling off onto the access road. It's almost two miles on the winding dirt path to the cabin. The GPS doesn't work on this old logger trail, and the first time we came up, we got lost for almost two hours in the unmarked turns. Now, even after being away for months, I navigate to the cabin easily, avoiding the many offshoots to abandoned wood piles, craggy cliffs, and the actual dilapidated, abandoned hovel.

And then it slowly comes into view—our cabin. The last item belonging to 'us' as I turn off the road onto our long dirt driveway. Cocooned by a thick blanket of pine trees and smooth boulders, the cabin reminds me of the miniature versions I made with Lincoln Logs as a kid. A half-rotten step leads to a slightly warped door frame—all items on my list to fix next spring. The wildflowers and tall grasses that typically line the access road to the cabin in warmer months are missing, and there's barely any snow on the ground—unusual for this time of year at this elevation.

The sight of our small woodsy oasis and all it means … *meant* … sends butterflies swarming in my stomach. In the back of my mind, I've clung to the idea that even if we never returned, if we didn't sell, there remained a sliver of something meaningful between us. Then, the sight of Marsh's 'classic' Toyota Corolla, with its plethora of bumper stickers and a side-view mirror held on by what appears to be fresh duct tape, greets me. He's here.

"Marsh?" I creak the unlocked door open.

The realtor informed us, "It's Maine. Nobody locks their doors." A loud whirring fills the space as I set my duffel down, and then I see him.

Marsh is vacuuming by the fireplace. In only his boxers. The ones with my face all over them. The ones I bought as a gag Valentine's gift years ago. His dirty blond hair has grown out a little, and the sight of his meaty thighs sends my heart racing. Old school headphone cans cover his ears, the thumping bass of another Eminem jam, "Without Me," pouring into the room. And my face, all over his plump ass, smiles back at me as he shakes to the music.

Lord, give me strength.

Chapter Four

Marsh

Here's the thing you need to know about Data: on top of hating surprises, he looks like a pond at sunrise when he's surprised—completely still. Not even his eyebrows move. The only tell that shock has registered in his system is in his bearded cheeks, which blush red at the top and puff out.

Like they are now.

"Hi," he says.

Those red, puffy cheeks make him look like a woodchuck. An adorable, mushy, fresh-baked muffin of a woodchuck.

"Hey." I pull off my headphones. I'm not sure what my surprise tell is, but I have to be wearing it right now.

I knew Data was coming. I asked him to. But still, the sight of him, his thick curves, his well-kept beard, his deep, watchful eyes that analyze life as one continuous Excel spreadsheet … it's a lot to process. My head feels light and I move toward the sofa to sit. Is it possible he's gotten even cuter since our breakup?

"You're naked." He shuts the door. Even with the cold air coming in, warmth washes over me.

"I thought you weren't coming until tonight."

"I left work early."

"You? Leaving work? Early? Is the earth still spinning?" I

handle this awkward situation with the best tool in my arsenal: my robust sense of humor.

"I wanted to get this over and done with."

Ouch, but not totally unexpected. Preeti was right: My ass is totally on his shit list. No need to check it twice.

"I mean, we have a lot of stuff here. There's a lot to go through," he says, softening his stance a touch. That's the thing about Data. If you saw him on the street, you'd think burly, no-nonsense bear. The man has heft. But underneath the grizzled bear is a sweet, little cub that few get to see.

"How've you been?" I ask.

"Good. Great. Really, really great. Busy, but good."

"Great. And the spreadsheets are ... spread?"

"Yep. Work's great. Really great, but ... "

"Busy."

"Busy. Exactly." Data's nose was permanently affixed to the grindstone of the big accounting firm that has him under their thumb. When we were together, I tried to be the supportive boyfriend asking him about work, but when he started talking about flux analysis and journal entries, my eyes glazed over despite all my efforts to stay engaged. "And you? How's the comedy world?"

"A barrel of laughs," I deadpan. "Y'know, the hustle never stops. We're only one show away from our big break. Got a lot of irons in the fire."

Note to self: come up with a cliché of the day calendar, because apparently, I can pump them out like it's nobody's business.

"That's good. I'm glad you're getting back out there."

"Yeah, we'll see."

"What does that mean?" he asks. It breaks my heart a little that he's still interested, that a touch of hope lines his voice when it comes to my comedy career.

"Nothing." I wave it off. Now is not the time to get into this.

Or ever. Because as an ex, he's under no responsibility to listen to my woes.

Data's eyes drift south to my boxers before he pulls his head up and dear God please let my dick be soft. "Um, could you put on some clothes?"

"You don't like them?" I snap the waistband of the boxers taking a quick peek. Flawless and flaccid. "You got them for me."

Our first Valentine's. He damn near tore them apart getting them off me later that night.

"That was a long time ago. You shouldn't be naked."

"I'm not naked." I run my hand over Data's faces on my ass. "And why not?"

"Because we're not dating. We're exes, and not the type exes who turn into great friends—we're not lesbians. We are back to being acquaintances, essentially. And you wouldn't prance around in nothing but boxers around an acquaintance."

"Depends." I flash him a smile, finding a perverse turn-on in his discomfort.

I can see the tension on his face about how long he can check me out without it being weird. And honestly … same.

"Sorry," I concede. The sudden rush of blood to my groin signals it's time to stop teasing. "I didn't mean to make it weird. I'll put pants on."

"And a shirt."

"Jesus, is this a restaurant?" I ask in a kidding tone. I hold up my hand to block another rebuttal. I pull my sweatpants and T-shirt off the loveseat. "I was getting overheated," I explain.

When I throw my clothes back on, I give him a pose with jazz hands, as if I'm waiting for him to give me a gold star.

"Thank you." He cracks a hairline smile. "That's my T-shirt."

I look down, Fire Island scrawled across my chest in blazing orange letters.

"No, it's mine. I got it when we went that one summer."

"You bought the blue Fire Island shirt. I bought this one at that bodega—"

"Because you forgot to bring an extra T-shirt for the beach." I smack my head with the realization. Data always brings a fresh shirt to the beach in case the one he wears gets sand in it. No wonder it was a little tight. "Should I give it back?" I start to take it off again, and his eyes flare up before he shakes his head no.

"Keep it."

And then the most awkward thing of all descends upon the room: silence. There's only so much surface level chitchat two exes—now acquaintances—can exchange. This is going to be a long weekend.

I take another look at Data and my pulse races. His full face. His Pooh Bear belly. I'm about to tell him he looks good, really good, but I hold back. Breaking up with someone and then showering them with compliments is no bueno.

Data takes his duffel bag and walks behind the couch, avoiding any physical contact with me. The living room, like all rooms in this cabin, was built for smaller people and smaller furniture. Two enormous, floor-to-ceiling bookcases bought from a library renovation sale, an oversized coffee table, and a wood stove in the corner take up most of the space. Ironically, the only piece of furniture right-sized for the room is the loveseat, which barely fits both of us.

I watch him open the guest room door and place his bag on the bed, another sober reminder of our status. In better days, Data would run to our bedroom and collapse backward on the bed as if falling into a pool. And then I would collapse on top of him, smothering him with kisses and touches, which would escalate to more physical, naked activities, the bed squeaking to keep up with us. It's an unspoken rule that no trip to Marshmallow Mountain could officially commence until we rolled around in the hay—or in this case, our West Elm bed.

Well, it was.

The guest bed lets out a pitiful squeak at his duffel hitting the mattress, a stark reminder of the present that sends a pang of regret banging against my ribs.

"You can have the main bed if you want," I say.

"It's okay. Guest bed is fine." He returns to the living room. Whatever feelings that were dancing on his face are gone. Data is all business. "So what's the plan?"

"The plan?"

"The plan. For packing up all our stuff and clearing out the cabin."

Data loves plans. He would get fingercuffed by plans if they had dicks.

"I mean … we pack up our things, load our cars, and go?"

"Uh, it's slightly more complicated than that. Have you taken inventory of everything in here?"

"Inventory? This isn't a store. We know what we have."

"We haven't been here in months. Or at least, I haven't," he says, his eyes darting around the room. When we broke up, we didn't talk about who got custody of Marshmallow Mountain. I think we both assumed that we could share it, each take weekends here and there. But I never had the desire to come up by myself or with anyone else. Somehow, it seemed disrespectful to Data, like blabbing a secret.

"I haven't either," I say defensively.

"Where are the boxes and tape for packing?"

"Over there." I point to a pile of flat boxes splayed out on the floor with a roll of tape lolling beside it. "See, I think ahead, Data."

"You have one roll of tape. One roll? For all those boxes? For this entire cabin?"

"It's really strong tape. I splurged and got a name brand."

He stomps in front of the bookcases, overflowing with books we haven't read but look pretty. Why did we keep buying new ones when there's so many unread? "There's a lot of stuff here. Knick knacks and tchotchkes. Did you bring paper to wrap them in?"

"I think there's an old *Entertainment Weekly* on top of the can."

Data returns to pacing. He rubs his forehead, his mental spreadsheet scrolling out of control. "What about all the furniture? We don't have a moving van with us."

"The real estate agent I talked to said we could keep the furniture here for staging. She can come up early next week to take pictures and put together the listing."

"Oh. She moves fast." His jaw tightens.

"Well, she smells money." I crack a smile.

"Yeah. Okay. Wow," he stammers out. "Well, you shouldn't be making financial decisions without me. Both of our names are on the deed." Data's voice cracks.

"I know that."

"I didn't realize you were in such a hurry to get rid of the cabin." His eyes find mine.

"Just trying to be efficient," I say, hoping that the answer pleases him and that he doesn't dig further into my current cash situation. "The agent says this place will go quickly once we get the listing up."

Data opens his mouth to say something, but nothing comes out. He shakes off whatever cat has got his tongue and goes back to panic mode.

"Well, if it's going to sell quickly, then there's even more of an imperative to get packed up. We can't just wing it this week-end. We need a system for determining who keeps what, what to throw away, and what to donate. And how to attack room by room so that we're not scrambling on Sunday. And there's the attic. And the basement. Lord knows how much stuff is still socked away. Did you consider *any* of this before you texted me out of the blue saying you wanted to sell this place and that I had to come this weekend to clean it out with you?"

I don't know the proper protocol for calming an ex who's not a friend but merely an acquaintance. So I go with my instincts and rub my hands down his arms, same as I did to pull him from the brink when we were boyfriends. He lets me hold him for a beat, and my soul settles as our skin makes contact. It's as if the past six months didn't happen, as if I didn't make the heartbreaking-but-necessary decision to let him go.

"It'll be okay, Data. We'll get done."

I love that I'm a couple of inches taller than him and can experience those big eyes peering up at me.

"And that's another thing. Stop calling me Data."

"But it's your nickname."

"*Was* my nickname." He steps back. Apparently, using nicknames belongs with walking around half-naked in the category of *Things We Don't Do Anymore*. "This weekend better not be some long con to get us back together, because you're just wasting your time. You made it unequivocally clear that you don't want to be together anymore. And I've realized that the feeling is unequivocally mutual." Data's chin trembles, which either means he's angry or hurt and right now I'm not sure which serves me better.

His statement is a javelin through the heart, and one I should've been better prepared for. Holding onto the cabin for so long after our breakup is only sending mixed signals. I just need to get through this weekend. We'll sell the cabin, I'll pocket some badly-needed cash, and we'll sever the final link that's connecting us. I made my bed six months ago and now I have to lay in it. Without Data.

He digs his hands into his pockets. "You should get your coat and shoes on. We need to get to The General Store for tape and newspapers before they close."

I'm about to say something, but whatever cat was pestering Data now has my tongue.

"What?" he asks.

I struggle to fill the silence. "You look good, Marshall."

Oof. On stage, my timing was rock solid. Here, it could not be worse. I study Data's face, not sure what reaction I'm hoping for, yet it remains a block of stone.

I didn't give him the nickname Data because of his affinity for numbers and spreadsheets. That's just the story we told our friends. Data is actually short for 'dat ass,' because his is spectacular. Big and round and puffed out like the perfect loaf of Sourdough bread. He's self-conscious about its size. I think it should be carved on Mount Rushmore.

And after six months, his ass still looks fine, even as I'm watching it march away from me, likely for one of the last times ever.

Chapter Five

~~Data~~ Marshall

One roll of tape. No newspapers or packing supplies. He thinks we can pack the entire cabin with an old *Entertainment Weekly*. And it's the one with Darren Criss on the cover. As if we're going to rip that punim to shreds to pack our crap. I should've asked about supplies. No, I should've assumed Marsh wouldn't be prepared and stopped myself on my way up. This is what I get for not making a list. When we were together, I would've shared the list with him. Given directions. Notes. Assigned tasks. Made a checklist with boxes for him to check off. But now? Now, I'm grateful he put clothes on.

Marsh. In those damn boxers. His almost hairless body, with that round tummy, barely falling over the waistband, like the foam on a latte hugging the brim of a mug. He said he wasn't expecting me until later, but he was most definitely shaking his junk at me. Marsh knows how his package flops in those loose boxers and wanted to put on a show. Taunting me. Tempting me.

Headed to The General Store (North Central Maine, you couldn't come up with a better name for your store?) in my Prius, I'm reminded that despite its gas efficiency as a hybrid, the internal cabin space is sparse for two men who don't resemble a new up-and-coming pop star twink. Much like our personalities, Marsh and I never quite fit in either of our vehicles. He wanted to sell them both and buy something bigger, more hefty, more butch. A truck of some sort. Despite ditching traditional horse for pony power, I still have a deep affection for my Prius.

"Ah, the ole General Store. We had some good times there." Marsh has his legs splayed open as wide as possible because, much like his mouth, he's incapable of keeping them closed. As the car jostles over the bumpy road, his knee brushes against my hand clasping the gearshift.

"Shopping? Yes, a laugh riot."

"We did. Remember when I found that jar of red pepper flakes that had expired in 1987? Or when you accidentally knocked over that stacked display of soup cans?" Marsh breaks into an actual laugh riot next to me. I can't help cracking up at the image of cans splaying out across the floor in the most dramatic fashion thanks to my poor grocery cart steering. My stint as a pasty white Steve Urkel wasn't my finest hour.

But I'm not the only one in this car with an embarrassing story to tell.

"Don't forget the time you made apples tumble off their display, and you tried catching them in your shirt."

He breaks into another laugh. The hearty baritone of it gives me a warm, yearning feeling, which I try really hard not to enjoy. I shouldn't be sentimental this weekend.

"Why did you insist on taking an apple from the bottom of the pile? Everyone knows you're supposed to take from the top," I say.

"My public school education didn't teach me proper apple retrieval etiquette." A slight wheeze and cough caps off his laughter.

"Did you bring your inhaler?" Half of my job as Marsh's boyfriend was reminding him to bring his inhaler.

He pats his coat pocket, and his mouth draws into a straight line as he bites at his lower lip. "Shit. I'm sure it's back at the cabin."

"Do you need a refill?"

"Nah. It's at the cabin. All good. You don't need to … care."

The downside of not hating him like I should is that I still find myself concerned for his health.

"Of course I care. I don't want you passing out in the middle of packing because then I'll have to pick up the slack."

"Good one." A half-smile perks up his face, and I force myself to focus on the road rather than the way his smirk melts my insides.

The General Store looks like it was carved into the wilderness. Massive mountains serve as a dramatic backdrop for the small building. The G in the neon sign still flickers, forever on its last legs. It's weird to see the parking lot without a bank of plowed snow taking over half the spaces.

"You know, since we're reminiscing … there was also that one time here … in the bathroom. After the cabin closing. You couldn't keep your hands off me." A different kind of grin takes over Marsh's face.

Oh, that. A lifetime ago. That Data—no, *Marshall*—was a different person. I was under Marsh's spell. His damn charms. His jokes. His beautiful cock. If you conducted a study of the most perfect dick in existence, Marsh's would be right there at the top of the list. Fat. Just long enough. The head a beautiful rosy pink when he's excited. "I must have blocked it from my memory."

"Well, I'm happy to remind you. You were insatiable." His eyebrows lift as he jogs his own memory. "The tight quarters, while challenging, only made things hotter. For me. I'm not trying to project."

Marsh's knee rubs on my fingers. There's no reason for me to keep my hand on the shift. The car's an automatic. It has a computer. And cameras. If you veer even slightly out of the lane, it beeps obnoxiously. There's no need for my palm to grip the stick, yet I'm unable to remove it.

I jam the gearshift into park, my hand brushing across his knee. I'm hit with a flash of his panting breath on my neck as he bent me over the sink and drove into my ass. Insatiable, just as he said.

Put the ex in sex. Bryce's dumb advice bounces around in my head. Sex complicates things. It provides zero clarity, and definitely not closure.

"Anyway, besides tape and newspaper, what do we need?" I ask, the feel of my tongue heavy and dry in my mouth.

"I don't know. Food?"

"That's glaringly specific. Yes, food. But what?"

"Snacks. Lots of snacks. Packing is a serious snacking activity."

Remembering my surprise, I say, "I brought you cardamom buns." I motion to the backseat, where the box sits on the floor.

"Oh fuck," Marsh gasps, in the same blissed-out tone as when he would … do other things. "Data."

"Marshall."

"Sorry. Marshall, you didn't."

"I did." A smile pokes through—my peace offering a success. He truly adores the deliciously piney, minty flavor combo.

"Literally my favorite buns in existence." Marsh reaches back, grabs the box, and shoves one in his mouth. "Present company excluded."

Marsh's green eyes glisten, that magic sparkle surfacing as he chews half the bun in his mouth.

"Mmmm. Heaven," he moans with a full mouth.

Please don't moan, I want to tell him.

"Coming up here always reminds me of cardamom buns, so I thought … " I'm not exactly sure why I brought them. It was more of a subconscious reflex. The sugar from the cardamom bun shimmers on his lips like copper glitter. "And the General Store's stock is … "

"Cardamom bunless," Marsh finishes for me. He pulls the uneaten half of the pastry from his mouth and puts it in mine. It happens so quickly, clearly a subconscious reflex, and I go with it.

He's gentle, and I take a bite, the explosion of carb-filled peppery flavor making my taste buds come alive. After swallowing the first mouthful, I take the bun from him. We're not boyfriends. It's not prudent to be feeding each other. We chew silently, but a few more moans escape Marsh's upturned lips as he savors the flavor.

"Let's go." And I'm out of the car so fast, the cool air providing much-needed relief. I beeline to the store and grab a basket.

I roll my eyes, hoping Marsh catches it. Our fingers touch when he takes the basket from me, the familiar sensation of his skin on mine creating a tiny spark, and I pull away quickly.

"You grab the boring stuff like tape and boxes. I'll handle the important stuff: food." Marsh scratches at his little seedlings of stubble, which for him, could easily be two days' growth. "I have some recipes floating around in my head."

"No recipes. No cooking. We're packing up our kitchen. Keep it simple." The last thing I need is to get seduced by his home-cooked feasts.

"And snacks."

"Yes. And snacks," I say.

"Great. I'll grab the essentials. Cookies. Popcorn. Twizzlers."

"Chips."

"Chips!" Marsh smacks his forehead. I begrudgingly smile. "Of course! You can't spell snacks without chips. Doritos?"

"Too much orange stuff. It'll wind up everywhere."

"Cheetos?"

"Even messier."

"Fritos?"

"Just right." My stomach growls in agreement. "And of course … "

Marsh's face absolutely lights up. "Mallomars."

Gaahhh, exes are not supposed to banter. I am showing as much resolve against Marsh's charms as I am with my New Year's resolutions. And I haven't had a salad since January.

"Go get food." I point my finger away, into the aisles.

Marsh straightens his back, juts his chest out, and salutes.

I head off for my items, which are fortunately at the opposite end of the store.

"Data? Is that you?"

Maddi, the sweet clerk, comes out from behind the deli counter, lifting her glasses to her weathered face—her use of my nickname a reminder even this place belonged to 'us' at one point.

"I haven't seen you in a spell. Where ya been?" Maddi's thick Maine inflection, with its dropped "r's," could easily be mistaken for a Boston accent, but there's a distinct ruggedness to it.

"Oh, we haven't been up in months." I poke through the sparse box inventory.

"Where's Marsh?"

"He's here. Getting—"

"Mallomars! I remember what you boys enjoy. I just saw 'em on the shelf. With that storm coming, you should stock up."

"Storm? What storm? I checked the weather before I left the city and it was smooth sailing through early next week."

"Well, my chickens say otherwise. Squawking and pecking for nothing this morning. That's Nor'Easter behavior. You listen to your fancy city weatherman. I'm listening to my birds."

Maddi's insistence on the impending mystery storm makes my stomach twirl. But Todd Carson, WRMV's weatherman, wouldn't steer me wrong—not with that chiseled jaw and movie star smile.

I grab a three-pack of tape off the shelf. Maddi watches this and clocks the boxes in my hand. Her face falls. "Are you boys moving?"

"Uh, yeah." I feel like parents having to break the news of divorce to their small children. "We're selling the place. We're not together anymore. We actually broke up a few months ago. So … yeah."

The statements cause my stomach to dip. They seem to shatter Maddi.

"Oh," she says quietly. "I'm sorry to hear."

"It's okay. It was amicable," I lie. "We're still friends." And there goes another. A pained expression overtakes her face. She's taking the breakup worse than I expected.

Her spirits lift just enough to give my hand a squeeze. "You know where I am if you boys—you and Marsh—need anything."

She leaves me to shop in peace.

Spotting Marsh near the back corner of the store, I head over to check on his progress. His forehead wrinkles like a pug as he scrunches to read the bulletin board outside the single-user bathroom—the scene of the hot crime from long ago. Why does he make that face when he's concentrating? It's ridiculous. And endearing. But mostly annoying. He always found inspiration for his material in the community listings.

"Ready?" I ask.

"Did you know Hank Foster will 'clean your pipes out' for only fifty bucks?" Marsh points to a handmade sign on the board. "Sounds like a good time. I'm jotting his number down."

Steadying myself with a deep breath, I do my best to remain calm.

"Did you get everything?" I ask.

"Yup." He holds his overflowing basket near my face, and I take a step back.

"What's this?" Under the bags of cookies, chips, pretzels, and popcorn, I spy two large containers of broth, carrots, celery, onions, garlic, and eggs.

"I found an old box of matzoh ball mix at the cabin when I was wiping out the pantry. I thought it might be comforting if I made soup."

"Comforting? We don't need to be comforted." My jaw tightens as I ponder warm soup … in front of a warm fire … warm bodies cuddling …

Put the ex in sex, Bryce chants in my head.

"We need to pack. And quick. There's a storm coming."

"Storm? No, the weather looks fine for the next few days." Marsh takes his phone out and starts tapping.

"Maddi and her chickens disagree."

"Maybe I should invite them over for soup."

"That's not funny."

"I mean, not for the chickens."

"Can you stop joking for one second?" I unzip my coat, the blasting heat in the store getting to me. "We have to pack. A lot. All of it. And I'm not getting stuck up here … with you. Which means we have tonight. And tomorrow. I've got to head back on Sunday. We don't have time for soup."

"There's always time for soup. Soup is cool."

"Soup is not cool. It's hot," I spit back. Marsh's face twists into that half-cocked smirk he gives when he knows I'm annoyed. The man gets off on riling me up, and my irritation literally makes him hard. He's insufferable. My face burns hot.

This is what Marsh does. Makes light of everything. The packing. Selling the cabin. Soothsaying cocks. Fuck, I mean chickens.

"You're hot," Marsh says.

"It's the store. It's like a damn sauna in here." I tug my hat off and shove it in my coat pocket.

"I feel fine."

"Of course you do." I narrow my eyes at him.

"I'm usually the one who gets overheated." Marsh's eyes twinkle and I avert my gaze.

"I'm not overheated." My hands pull at the neck of my sweater, desperate for relief.

"Are we bantering?"

"Fuck you."

And I'm on him.

Chapter Six

~~Data~~ Marshall

We stumble back onto the bulletin board, papers scattering under Marsh's frame. Like a shiny nickel to a magnet, my lips find his. Marsh's fingers comb my beard, and his tongue juts into my mouth, and fuck, I've missed this. Not him. Not his jokes. Not his teasing. His tongue. His lips. His stubbly jaw. His lips on mine.

Marsh's hands migrate to my waist, and he backs into the bathroom, pulling me along, the door flings open with a loud slam before it clicks shut. My heart thumps so loudly I'm sure he can hear it underscoring my temporary lapse of judgment. His overflowing basket lands with a thud, and in a flash, the General Store bathroom, with its glaring fluorescent lighting, toilet, and sink, comes into focus—it's all coming back to me now. Fuck, I'm in the middle of my favorite Celine song.

"God, you're sexy when you're pissed." Marsh's thumb traces my bottom lip. I've always loved being a few inches shorter. As he stands over me, my body catches fire as my resistance wanes and I desire nothing more than for him to take control. For once, be the grown-up and boss me around.

"I'm not pissed," I say.

"Shhh." His hand covers my mouth. "Don't ruin it."

Remembering Bryce's advice I shoo my inner voice of reason away. Marsh needs to jam his ex into my sex before rage and lust swallow me whole. Perhaps not the ideal time or place, but beggars can't be choosers. My hand grabs at Marsh's sweats. His cock, already half-hard, throbs in my palm, and yup, this is happening. Operation Breakup Sex. Once and done.

"What? How? Where?" I mumble as he nips at my bottom lip.

"Dat ass. I want it. Need it." His fingers fumble with my belt. "Only you would wear khakis and a belt up here in the fucking woods."

"I came straight from work."

"You and your business casual attire." He gets the buckle undone, and my pants are open as his tongue darts back in. He's pawing at my butt, my pants falling, and I'm not exactly sure what he wants, but I'm ready.

Pausing the kiss, Marsh takes my face in his hands, rubbing my beard with his thumbs—my jaw softens along with my resolution. He knows what that does to me. Jerk. He dips in, kisses me softly on the lips, and whispers, "Bend over."

When he's direct, my skin simmers. There's no option but compliance. Marsh spins me around to face the sink, and I do as I'm told. His cool hands, warming from the activity, yank my pants and briefs down in one fell swoop. "Dat ass. Dat ass. Dat ass." He smacks a cheek, and the satisfying sting of contact sends my torso over the sink to wait for his next move.

"Cardamom buns have nothing on these." Marsh kneels and each word from his lips lands on my ass, causing my breath to hitch.

"So fucking delicious." Marsh spreads me open and buries his face. There's no pretense or manners. His tongue simply dives into me with the fervor and passion of a man who knows how to eat ass. Not just any ass. My ass. Like an explorer mapping uncharted lands, he's studied it carefully—he's dedicated himself to perfecting his craft through rigorous practice.

"Marsh, umm, yeah, uhhh, ohhh." Words hard. Complete sentences impossible. This is what he does to me. In an instant, I lose control, my thoughts racing and my body trembling. My ass, now under Marsh's spell, relaxes and opens. His stubble prickles every nerve in the area and the wetness from his mouth enhances the already damp conditions brought on by the kissing and palming of his dick. And now I'm thinking about his cock and what I'd like to do with it, but alas, I'm confined to my position, hunched over the sink.

"You like that babe?" he says, his cool breath on my wet hole dispatches shivers over my body. Babe. In an instant, we're back to babe and I widen my stance to allow him easier access.

"Uh-huh." It's all I've got.

"Your hole is so horny." He spits, then uses his thumb to spread the saliva. "Do you want me to fuck you?" His thumb enters me, priming his work surface. "Can I? Please? Pretty please? I want to fuck dat ass." He dispatches a soft kiss on my ass cheek and shivers disperse on my torso. "I haven't been with anyone else."

My heart melts a tiny bit at his confession, and I wonder why he hasn't dated. But now isn't the time to ask. We're in the public bathroom of the General Store. Maddi is dishing out deli slices twenty feet away. Once we had the monogamy chat, we stopped using condoms. But it's been six months. And there's no lube. He's right about my ass. I'm so open and ready for him. His tongue. His cock. But without lube, it's going to be rough going.

Before I can answer, Marsh's tongue juts back in. He's going to fuck me one way or another, and if it's only with his tongue, so be it. "But? We … " Speechless.

"I was a boy scout," he says, grabbing at the basket near the door. He procures a tiny bottle of lube from under a sack of onions. "Always be prepared."

"You were buying lube?" I ask, my ability to speak momentarily repaired by his presumptuousness. "For what?"

"Listen, do you want to argue about why I threw the only bottle of lube being sold in a seventy-mile radius into my basket, or do you want me to fuck you?"

"Fair," I say as I bend over more, bracing myself on the sink, which thankfully appears to have been recently cleaned. I haven't eaten since breakfast, other than the two bites of the cardamom bun. Fuck, I'm so ready. The bottle clicks open, and Marsh's fingers quickly apply a generous amount. When I hear the bottle hit the floor and his slick hand palming himself, I take a breath. It's been six months since we broke up, and since our split, I've been focusing squarely on work. In other words, he may find cobwebs down there. I hope he's gentle, but not that gentle. Strike that. I hope he fucks me into oblivion.

The sign under the mirror pulls my focus. *Employees must wash hands. If an employee is not available, please do it yourself.* I snicker at the joke, wondering if Marsh could do better, as he's pushing his cock against my hole. Even after all these months, the sensation of him about to rail me comes rushing back. With a heavy sigh I relax, my body desperate for the connection. Marsh's fingers grab my waist, holding me steady. "Fuck, Data. You're going to kill me."

Heaviness washes over me. That would be a major boner killer. "Wait, you're kidding, right? You don't have your inhaler."

"Data, I'm trying to be sexy. I'm fine."

"I'm fine isn't an answer to my—" Marsh's fingers dig into my side, a jolt of lust making me lose my train of thought. All I want is Marsh's train tunneling into me.

"And now, gimme dat ass."

He slides in, and the familiar sensitivity of his thick cock inside comforts me. Near the end, our time was consumed by tension and silly squabbles, wasting precious time that could have been spent doing this. I suppose that's the point of the breakup sex.

"You good?" Marsh asks. He's all the way in, balls to the wall, waiting for my signal to begin banging.

The room settles into stillness. Only the sound of our breathing fills the space, and Marsh's question reminds me, underneath all his bravado and swagger, he's a kind, gentle soul.

"Pound me." So much for gentle. After eight years, he knows what to do. Marsh takes my cue and, gripping me with one hand, slaps me hard with the other.

"Yes, sir." He pulls out, leaving only the tip inside, and then thrusts, pulling me back toward him. My ass slaps against his thighs, and the familiar clapping noise of our bodies making contact soon occupies the bathroom as he finds his rhythm.

He leans over, his lips nipping at my ear. "God, I've missed this. That ass. Your ass." He takes my earlobe in his mouth, sucking before his hot, damp breath whispers, "I've missed this, Data. Me. You. Us."

Did he say he missed me? My stomach flips as he pummels me. Each jolt of his cock reminds me of what we once were. Before the rupture. Raw. Passionate. Connected.

With another thwack on my ass, Marsh's hand reaches around, grabs my cock, and jerks me, matching his strokes to his fucking. When I reach down to take over, he pushes my hand away. "I got you, babe." His words fill me with a mix of relief and triumph. He wants to do it all, and this is the one area I allow him.

"Data. Babe, I'm going to come soon. Okay?"

What if I said no? It's not okay for you to come. Sorry, but please stop. This was a terrible mistake. Breakup sex is a joke and not the funny kind. The kind where you're up on stage, a crowd of people watching, and it's crickets. A big bomb of a joke. Like when they play the rattlesnake noise on

Drag Race. But he said he missed me. Us. He called me Babe. Fuck.

"Fill me up."

Marsh's hands return to my hips, anchoring me in place, and I can feel him coming. His cock pulses, each thrust stronger, and he's grunting over me. Somehow, he makes grunting cute.

Staying inside me, Marsh rests on my back, his sole focus now on me. "Now," he says, kissing my neck, "it's your turn."

Like unloading the dishwasher, getting myself off since we split has been more of a chore than anything. With the looming month-end reports, working overtime, and thinking about this weekend, I haven't jerked off in weeks. Luckily, Marsh knows how to elicit my orgasm quickly. He prides himself on it. With every stroke, his thumb lingers, only for a second, on the tip, rubbing precum and sending a vibration of pleasure through my core with each pass.

Marsh's warm breath on my ear makes my cock throb in his grasp. "My Data."

And that's it. The exquisite sensation of his lips on my neck, his hand stroking me faster, never forgetting the tip, all while his cock pushes against the walls of my ass—I'm done for.

"I'm close. Keep doing that."

"There's my Data. Come for me, babe. I got you." His left arm squeezes me, pulling me toward him, ensuring his dick stays put, his sweaty hand matting the hair on my stomach. I gleefully unravel. My orgasm rips through me, my entire body vibrating, but Marsh never lets go. He does his best to catch it all, but with such a build-up, I end up painting the bathroom wall like a sticky Jackson Pollack. Oops. I grab a threadbare paper towel and wipe it off quickly.

"Fuck, Data, you needed that, huh?"

I nod because, apparently, I did. Marsh always knew what I needed. He had a way of forcing me to relax, rubbing my shoulders and nipping at my neck, the stress of life melting away under his touch. Still hunched over my back, he kisses my neck again and then moves up to my ear. "Dat ass. Still does it to me."

"We needed this," I say, scared of how easy it was to fall back into intimacy with him, a man who wants to move on. I remind myself that Marsh pulled the rug out from under me once before, so even in a state of post-coital euphoria, I have to keep my guard up. "Breakup sex. We didn't do it six months ago. We needed to close the loop."

"Close the loop?"

"Close the loop," I repeat, hoping that like learning someone's name, the more times I say it, the more likely it will stick.

"Oh."

Cleaned and dressed, we take our items to the checkout where Maddi rings us up. She gives me a look. Can she see the sex written on my face? Can she smell the afterglow?

"Good seeing you, Maddi," Marsh says. "Give my best to Duffy and the chickens."

She mumbles something under her breath that sounds like, "Not together my ass."

Marsh leads us out the door. The bell rings on the hinges as it swings open.

Maddi is right, though. We're not together. We came to Marshmallow Mountain to move on. Close the aforementioned loop. Go our separate ways. Space. Time. That's what Marsh wants, what he thinks is best for us.

This was break-up sex, meant to signal a definitive end to our relationship. And yet it's only made me crave more of something I can't have.

Chapter Seven

Marsh

Here's the thing you need to know about Data: when he's tense, he drives with his hands at ten and two like a model automobilist. They could use him as a model in driver's ed manuals. But as he gets more relaxed, his hands slink down the wheel to a chill six-thirty. Once in a blue moon, like on our vacation in Palm Springs three years ago, he'll even drive one-handed.

Currently, his hands are at about four thirty-eight. Low, but not as low as I'd hoped. There is a needle of tension lingering in our haystack. I supposed that's to be expected post-breakup sex.

I can't believe I just had breakup sex with Data. A dullness settles in my chest. I wish I'd known it was breakup sex. I really would've pulled out all the stops. Maybe kept my heart in check and stopped myself from confessing how much I missed him, which obviously isn't a reciprocal feeling. Perhaps stretched a little beforehand.

I didn't take Data for the cum-and-go kind of person. Perhaps he isn't the same guy from six months ago and he really is moving on.

Despite being in the same small save-the-planet car we took to the general store, our knees never touch.

"I suggest we start with the closets. Clear out linens, towels, old junk stored away. First thing tomorrow morning, we can dive into the kitchen since that has the most fragile items. The closets and kitchen are the two most high-density parts of the cabin. If we can knock those out first, then it should be smooth sailing for the rest of the weekend."

"Aye-aye captain." I give him a salute.

A beat of silence hits the car, the staticky sound of the local radio station fills the void appropriately with "Comfortably Numb."

Data glances over at me quickly, then back to the road.

"What?" I ask, knowing full well when he has something on his mind.

"Nothing." His voice rises slightly as if part of him is asking a question.

"I think it's something." Being in a long-term relationship is like being a PhD student doing research for a dissertation on your significant other. After eight years, I can translate any tic, any eyebrow raise, any grin.

Data scratches at his beard. It was recently trimmed, which means the hairs are extra-prickly. And explains the reddish burn on my cheeks that I clock in the sideview mirror.

"Out with it," I command.

"Back at the store, you said you haven't been with anyone since … is that true?"

"Yeah, I wouldn't lie about that." I shift in my seat.

"Were you just talking about sex?" His hands climb up to nine and three. "Sorry. It's none of my business."

"I haven't. For the record." I went on one date, grabbing coffee with this recent NYU grad who wanted to "pick my brain about comedy." That statement was a dick softener right off the bat. He was so skinny, one hardy sneeze would snap him in half, and even worse, he didn't know who Chris Farley was.

"Oh." Data's mouth stays in that O shape for a moment. "Because I thought … "

"What?"

"Nothing." His gaze stays focused on the road.

"I know you don't do bits, but this feels like a bit."

Data turns off the main road onto the unassuming access road marked only by a reflective circle. It will be another few miles until we reach Marshmallow Mountain. The cabin lives way off the map.

"I thought that's what you wanted. To play the field," he says.

I know he doesn't mean it as a dig, but I can't help but feel a sting.

"You think that's why I ended things?" I ask.

"Well, your reasoning was a bit nebulous and … steeped in cliché."

Oy. I feel myself blush with a kind of shame different from the run-of-the-mill Jewish shame mixed with the classic gay shame. I once temped with a Tony-nominated playwright. I should've asked her to script a better break-up speech for me.

Sure, the break-up wasn't my most eloquent moment. But did he think these were excuses and that I just wanted to fuck a bunch of new people? What if his question was really a reverse psychology trick to get me to ask this question and he was about to spill that he's dating some hot guy named Evan who's an ear nose and throat doctor with a corgi named Maxwell?

"I take a Willy Wonka approach to sex, Marshall," I say. "I want to make sure a guy has the golden ticket before I give him the keys to the chocolate factory."

"Somewhere in heaven, Gene Wilder just threw up in his mouth."

"Nah. He and Gilda are having a good laugh."

Data chuckles under his breath, and it soon turns into a full honking cackle echoing through our small car.

We met when I was doing a play called *Glengarry Glen Coco* in some dingy basement theater. I'd leave Harmony Pianos and schlepp into the city for a ten o'clock show. Me and other gay comedians were performing David Mamet's *Glengarry Glen Ross* as characters from *Mean Girls*. Groundbreaking stuff. (Not to brag, but my turn as Regina Roma received positive notices.) Data was the only person in the crowd laughing, and I couldn't take my eyes off him. He had the cutest laugh I'd ever heard— it was manly, but also soft, like caramel. I had to know who this person was. I had to know everything about him that led to him having this beautiful laugh. It was like his body was one big magnet and the laws of physics would not let me turn away.

My heart thumps in my chest. I truly don't know how I went six months without getting to hear his laugh. It dawns on me that once this weekend is over, and the final link is severed, I'll never get to hear it again.

We pull up to the cabin. I clap my hands loud, silencing the dread pooling in my stomach.

"Let's get packing!"

Chapter Eight

Marsh

As per Data's plan, we start with the low-hanging fruit. Closets, cabinets. Things that can easily be shoved in a box or thrown in the trash. Data takes the attic while I clean out the linen and storage closets on the main floor. We decide to put everything salvageable in a storage locker that we reserve online and determine who keeps what once we return to the city. It's funny how the most random things make me sentimental. An old receipt from The General Store. Even that old *Entertainment Weekly* with Darren's face smiling at me. I probably read that on the couch with my feet on Data's lap on a lazy, snowy afternoon.

Even though we take on different parts of the cabin, our paths keep crossing:

Data climbs down the ladder from the attic to get more tape, and he smooths pieces of lint off my chest.

Data climbs back up the ladder to the attic, and I blatantly stare at his ass, a part of me wishing he'd fall right on my face.

Data climbs back down for more chips, and our bodies smush against each other as we pass one another in the narrow hallway.

Before I know it, a few boxes are packed, and my dick is hard.

We pack for about two hours. Time surprisingly flies. Data

comes down from the attic, and once again, I watch those perfect cheeks bounce up and down.

"How're you doing?" I rub his shoulders, his tense muscles relaxing under my familiar touch. "Ready for some dinner?" I smell his neck. "You smell stale, like an attic. Sexy."

Data squirms out of my touch and beelines to the kitchen, reminding me that packing is not foreplay. "I'm going to heat up some frozen dinners. Sound good?"

"Sure." The cabin doesn't have a microwave, and even though we could've easily bought a small one, I like not having the convenience up here. "Or I could cook us up a delicious meal." In happier times, I would spend hours preparing intricate spreads for us to eat by candlelight. Our normal city lives and tiny city kitchen never allowed us to cook proper dinners.

"Why create extra work for ourselves cleaning kitchen appliances we'll be packing tomorrow?"

"Right." It's all very logical, yet still, my shoulders slump. Watching Data moan over my cooking is almost as gratifying as watching him moan over my cock, which he did mere hours ago. During loop-closing, breakup sex. Fuck—the bad kind.

I thought I could handle a weekend with Data, but sex has poured water all over my internal circuit board.

I follow him into the kitchen and watch him take two frozen dinners from the freezer and preheat the oven. Speaking of ovens that are preheated, I readjust myself in my pants.

"How long do they need to bake?" I ask.

He checks the back of the package. "Eighteen to twenty minutes."

"Perfect." I pull him to me, his touch turning me to fire as my cock pokes at him through my tented pants. "Then we have more than enough time."

"For what?"

"Another round of breakup sex? To fully, truly, absolutely close the loop."

Data steps back. "We are not doing that again. That was one and done. Done." He turns toward the oven, but pauses. "And don't check my ass out when I put these meals in."

With a sigh, I face the fridge as he inserts the meals into the oven. I'm a gentleman, but I don't enjoy it.

"We could have a rule. What happens in the cabin this weekend, stays in the cabin." We could let this relationship go out with multiple bangs. A twenty-one cum salute.

Data leans against the counter, arms crossed. Not a good sign, unless he's playing bossy bottom.

"Unless you're seeing someone … " I say, my stomach stirring at the prospect. "Which I totally respect."

"I'm not," he says as he continues studying me. I can see the wheels rolling in his head, but I'm not sure what for. Oh crap. Is he planning to murder me here? Wait. Maddi saw us, so someone knows I'm here. Wait. He could easily murder her too. And the chickens.

"On the count of three, let's say if we're planning to murder the other. One, two—"

"Did you mean what you said in the bathroom at the store?" Data's lips part slightly. "Do you miss me?"

Fuck. Beads of sweat prickle my brow. Sex takes over the part of our brain that controls language. Lust pushed the statement out of my mouth with the same force that I pushed into Data. I hoped the sounds of his heavy breathing would've kept him from hearing my admission, especially since he intended our bathroom tryst as a one and done.

"Or was it something you said in the moment?"

"It's been six months since we saw each other. I hadn't seen you in a while, and it was nice to see you again. Without pants on." I grin, showing all my teeth.

"That's different from what you said. You said you missed me, Marsh. You've been flirting with me since the moment I walked in this door. It's a 180 from how things ended, and I'm just … " He shakes his head, his adorable forehead wrinkling. "I work with numbers. Numbers are black-and-white. I'm good with black-and-white. But things with you are extremely gray, and I'm confused. Did you mean it?"

Every cell in my body clenches so I can push out my response. "It was just something I said in the heat of the moment. Of course I didn't mean it."

His face changes the moment the words leave my mouth, hardening, a door firmly being closed.

"Good to know," he says, jaw tight. "You know what? I really should head back to the city in the morning. You can finish packing. Feel free to throw out anything of mine. I don't care."

"Data." I reach for him.

"Marshall," he says, his voice shaking, before brushing past me out of the kitchen.

Being good gays who want to support the economy, we splurged on the mattress in our main bedroom. It's garishly plush, like sleeping on a bed of puffed marshmallows. Tonight, it might as well be a block of cement. I toss and turn, catching zero winks.

Here's the brutal truth: I am still hopelessly in love with Data. Of course I miss him, so badly my heart hurts.

I loved him from the second I heard that laugh in the audience of my show. I loved him every day we were boyfriends. I love him now, and I'll love him years in the future. I love him in any past life we shared, in any multiverse we find ourselves, in any permutation, any scenario.

But I can't be with him.

See, I have this nasty habit of ruining the lives of the people I care about most.

My dad built a once-thriving piano manufacturing business from scratch. He didn't have a spec of musical ability, but in his twenties, he scored a ticket to Carnegie Hall one night and watched Leonard Bernstein in concert. Dad couldn't play, but he wanted to help other musicians reach their potential.

If you were a suburban New York kid in the '90s forced to take piano lessons, chances are you practiced on a Harmony Piano. He worked his ass off to send my brother Albie and me to medical and business school, respectively. "My right-hand man," he called me. He pinned his hopes on his MBA-toting son taking over the family business and bringing Harmony Pianos into the twenty-first century.

Dad never expected his right-hand man to leave the business to be a (gulp) stand-up comedian. Sure, there were signs, like the fact that his son stayed up to watch every single SNL episode when he was young, or that he graduated from business school with a C average, or that he woke up every day for ten years in a cold sweat at the thought of another fourteen-hour day trying to eek profit amid ever-shrinking margins and dealing with a sprawling network of suppliers, distributors, and vendors.

Once I left the business, Dad's mental capacity began going downhill. He'd forget names, forget to show up to meetings. I thought it was typical old age stuff. Then two days before my showcase at the Laughingstock festival, I got a call that Dad had wandered into a nearby high school. The principal found him in the locker room in his underwear. Dad thought he had gym class.

When I went to pick him up, I found him sitting on the bench, his pale, small body hunched over, his eyes gloomy with confusion and embarrassment, like a little boy who'd gotten lost. The sight ripped me up inside. He begged me not to tell anyone. Not Albie. Not Data. And watching my father—the strongest man I've ever known—stare up at me, tears filling his eyes, my world seemed to be crumbling around me. If I couldn't stop the impending collapse, not telling anyone about the incident at least seemed to help me pretend it wasn't happening.

The doctor assured me Dad developing Alzheimer's wasn't because I left the business, although she admitted the condition was exacerbated with stress. Like the stress caused by trying to run Harmony Pianos on his own, and the letdown of not getting to watch his son take over. Maybe he could've retired earlier if I'd stayed. Maybe Albie and I wouldn't have to be discussing full-time in-home care for him, which costs a fortune —another reason why I need to offload the cabin ASAP.

Having my mom die of cancer when I was eleven broke my heart. Watching my dad suffer with Alzheimers is like having my heart break over and over.

Because of me, dad's business is crumbling. After years of doing dingy sets for drunk tourists and barely making ends meet, I squandered my big break. I'm on the verge of quitting entirely and to do what? I don't know. I'm almost forty and have no clue what to do with my life. Data doesn't deserve that. He deserves Evan the handsome ENT with the adorable corgi named Maxwell. Maxwell probably has more Instagram followers than me.

Data deserves a good life. The best life.

Remember in *Titanic* when Jack didn't share the door with Rose, and he froze to death so she could live? People may have proven that he could've fit on the door with her, but what if Jack was right all along? What if he would've caused them to drown? He couldn't do that to Rose. She skipped out on the lifeboats to be with him. Data sees such potential in me, potential that I can't live up to. I can't face watching him drown.

So I made the heartbreaking choice to put the love of my life on that door and sink into the ocean. Alone.

At 6:00 a.m., I call it quits on trying to sleep. White light glows through the window. A new day. One day closer to Data being completely out of my life.

With heavy limbs, I creep into the living room. Data stands by the big window that overlooks our front driveway. My soul screams to be close to him. I would give anything to wrap my arms around his torso, rest my chin in the nook of his shoulder.

"Morning," I say.

"Marsh, we have a problem." He steps aside, giving me a clear view out the window. The scene jolts me awake faster than morning coffee.

There is no driveway. No access road. Only snow. A mountain of powder, a flat surface of white burying every inch of asphalt.

"We're snowed in," he says.

Chapter Nine

~~Data~~ Marshall

Trapped. Staring out the window, I can't help but feel a pang of frustration, knowing that the beautiful snowy mountain now simply means I'm stuck. With Marsh. Who most definitely meant nothing he said during the mind-blowing breakup sex. The sex Bryce assured me would help me move on from the eight years Marsh and I spent together. He said he missed us. Me. "My Data." Why would he say all that? My ass isn't that magical.

When Marsh broke my heart six months ago, he told me he was in a rough place. Between the news about his dad's declining health and the struggles with getting his standup career to ignite, he "needed time and space alone to figure out his life." Weren't we building our lives together?

He insisted we'd be "better as friends," but his evasive behavior told a different story. Marsh may be a hilarious comedian, but he's no actor.

Why would I expect anything different from him now? It probably isn't wise to take his words to heart. Especially when he uttered those words with his cock thrusting inside me. He "needed space" from me. And now we're stuck in the seven-hundred-square-foot cabin. How's that for space, Mr. Space Man?

"Shit." Marsh stands behind me, his stale morning breath reaching my neck.

"I guess the chickens were right," I say, recalling Maddi's warning.

"Fucking chickens." Marsh steps closer to the window. "We're definitely making soup now. We can feast on their relatives."

"You think this is funny?" I point out the window and turn toward him.

"It could be worse. We could be straight."

"Everything's a joke to you."

"It'll be fine. It snows here all the time." Marsh scratches his stomach.

"I've never seen this much snowfall at once." I get a sinking feeling that this won't be a blizzard easily cleared away by the afternoon. Thank goodness we recently replaced the roof.

"On the bright side, this means we can focus on packing for the next few days."

"Few days?" More snow equals more time snowed in with the one person I can't be in close quarters with, Mr. Space Man. "I need to get out of here, I mean, leave by tomorrow at noon."

"Hmmm." Marsh glances out the window again, cringes with the bad news. "I may not be Todd Carson, but I'm predicting a Sunday departure won't be happening."

I used to love the coziness of the cabin, that no matter where I was, I could always feel Marsh's presence cocooning me. The coziness is quickly curdling into suffocation.

"Data." He takes my hand and his palm slowly brushes up my arm, back and forth, his standard method to settle me. For a moment, I allow myself to savor the familiar touch of his fingers on my skin, feeling a sense of calm wash over me under his care. God, I've missed him. But then I remember his words last night. *Of course I didn't mean it.*

"Marshall." My hand jerks away and I move toward the door. I'm not falling for his shenanigans again. It is my job to keep the loop closed. "You dragged me up here to sell the cabin. Our cabin. And now this." I nod toward the snow covered window.

"You think I caused a surprise snow storm?"

"No, but you're probably giddy at the prospect of being stranded here."

"Data slash Marshall … " Marsh moves toward me, but I evade his attempt to soothe.

"Don't." I shake my head. "Just don't."

The light vacates Marsh's eyes, but he did this. This tension between us is on him.

"The snowblower. I think there's gas in the tank," I say, grabbing my coat. "If I can get to the access road, there's a chance it's cleared."

"The snowblower doesn't work."

"Yes it does," I snap back.

"No, it doesn't. When you yank its chain, it makes some noise, shakes around a little, and then craps out."

"Sounds like you." I flash a victorious smile at my zinger.

"Marshall Kaplan, we both know that's not true." Marsh shoots me a wink overstuffed with the confidence of being right.

Damn him. Damn that sexy wink. Must not think back to bathroom tryst.

"Why don't we call a plow company? That's why God invented money. To pay people to do things for us," says Marsh. Tell me you were raised in a cushy suburb without saying you were raised in a cushy suburb.

"I can get the snowblower to work. We both know I have the magic touch." I say every prayer in my head that it will turn on. At this point, I'm more motivated to prove Marsh wrong than to clear our driveway.

"Okay." He holds up his hands. "I'll come help. Well, first I'll make a pot of coffee. Then I'll assist."

"It's a one-person job."

"Miss Geist, I want to help."

"Your asthma, though. You don't do well in frigid temps for long." Despite my current frustration at his mere presence, I don't want him to die in the snow. His shoulders slump under his T-shirt, my statement on his asthma is the zinger that finally cut through. I soften slightly. "Stay here. You can help clean off the cars once I'm done."

All geared up, I use the shovel by the back door to carve a narrow pathway leading to the small shack behind the house. Although the snow isn't too heavy, the sheer quantity of it requires significant effort. It's up to my thighs, at least two feet —maybe more and still snowing. In a bid for efficiency, I simply push the shovel, occasionally scooping up the fluffy powder out of the way.

Without a garage, the small building serves as storage for the snowblower and various gardening supplies. There's no need to mow up on the mountain, but Marsh has a blast with the weedwhacker. Had—past tense. There'll be no more whacking—weeds or otherwise. The tank on the snowblower shows only a quarter full. I grab the gas can and slosh it around. Thankfully, it sounds at least half full, so I fill the blower and pull it out.

Inserting the key from the zip tie it hangs from, I check the throttle and pull the cord to start the blower. It makes the familiar rattling noise, turning over the moment I release the handle. Typically, it takes three to four tries, and I sigh, resolving to get the bugger going. I glance up and find Marsh watching from inside, coffee in hand.

I will get this snowblower to work. I don't care if I have to give it mouth-to-mouth.

On the second try, I yank harder, channeling my frustration with Marsh into the hunk of metal and rubber.

The fucker is still watching, thinking he's right. His lips curl into an amused smile, not unlike when I flung myself at him in The General Store.

Marsh said he missed me.

Yes, he was fucking me when he said it, but I know him. Despite his usual tendency to make light of things, his tone lacked any trace of playfulness. There was an eagerness. He meant it. Or I think he did.

Another forceful rip of the cord. Nothing.

Marsh's plump lips nipping at my neck. Goosebumps fanning over my skin under his hot breath. Whispering "My Data" in my ear.

I look to the window, glaring at my ex-boyfriend with a determined scowl. He thinks he knows this snowblower better than me? Which one of us has actually used it? Marsh's idea of DIY is lusting after HGTV hosts.

Get ready to be proven wrong, Space Man.

My jaw stiffens, and I pull the cable with all my might. The snow blower kicks hard and vibrates to life. Success! I turn toward the cabin and give him a big, fat thumbs up.

Just as I'm about to do a victory lap, the snowblower's engine makes a weird gurgling sound. The vibrations get stronger and erratic before morphing into full-on shaking. The snowblower has gone from piece of machinery to little girl possessed by the devil. The shaking and noises go full-tilt crazy. I grab the handle to steady it, and it goes haywire, letting out a mechanical shriek. The force of its jolt knocks me to the ground.

Shit. It's going to blow up. I'm going to be killed in a horrible snowblower explosion, and even worse, Marsh will have been right. I crawl away from the ticking bomb, shielding my face from the inevitable blast.

But just when I think the snowblower is about to go kaboom, the shaking slows to a rattle. It lets out what I can only describe as a pathetic burp before plumes of black smoke leak from its sides, its mortal coil being shaken off in the most theatrical way possible.

"Fuck!" I scream, louder than I ever thought possible. Anger and orgasms produce the same response in me, apparently.

Marsh is probably laughing his ass off from the cabin. I grit my teeth and sit up to face his reaction, but he's not inside.

He stands over me and extends a hand. "Mallomar?"

I swipe the treat from his gloved paw and jam it into my mouth before I can let out another expletive.

"RIP snowblower," he says. "Did you want to say Kaddish, or should I?"

"I told you to stay inside." The words mumble as I chew my consolation cookie.

"I heard the … commotion." Marsh removes the key, and one last pitiful puff of smoke escapes the snow blower, headed for the sky. "Are you okay?"

I check myself. No cuts or bleeding. Nothing's injured. Just my pride. I nod that I'm fine.

"Good." Joy radiates on Marsh's red cheeks as he helps me up.

"Our snowblower is dead. We can't clear our driveway. I was almost blown to bits. Why are you smiling?"

"Because I was right." Marsh shrugs his shoulders all the way up to his ears. "That almost never happened when we were together. And I was right about something with *machinery*. I wish I could bottle this feeling. Would you mind if I did a little dance?" He clocks my fury and dials it down. "Sorry." He breaks out a few quick running man moves. "Okay, I'm done. Wait, can you say 'Marsh, you were right about the snowblower,' and let me record it?" He reaches in his pocket for his phone.

The daggers I stare at him could tear through metal. And yet, a tiny, pea-sized sliver of delight blooms in me at Marsh being his old, silly self. It makes me want to turn those daggers on myself.

I push past him, grab the shovel from the shack, and head for the access road. "If the access roads are plowed, we can get to the main road and flag someone down. Do you have your inhaler?" Even if I want to wring his neck, I'm concerned about Marsh's well-being. He may be the biggest baby in existence. He may have broken my heart. But I still love him. The way you love a sad puppy on the side of the road you have no intention of rescuing, taking home, and cuddling with. No intention. Ignore the sweet face and bulging eyes.

"Yes?" He pats every pocket in his puffy coat before finding his inhaler in the back pocket of his sweatpants. "Yes! I mean, yes sir."

Marsh salutes me, and nope. He can keep that cuteness to himself.

"If we walk to the first clearing," I point toward the cluster of deciduous trees about a quarter mile away, "we can at least see the access road, which should be plowed."

"I doubt it's plowed. They usually wait until the snow stops."

"Not when it's this much snow," I counter. "Well, maybe we —or I—can shovel it enough to reach the main road."

"That's a lot of shoveling."

"The snow is soft." I begin to hesitate, mostly because I don't want to see him do another victory dance.

"Ready to follow, sir," Marsh barks. He knows his submissive soldier shtick annoys me. He also knows it turns me on.

I screw my face into my best scowl and push the shovel in front of us. I can do this.

Taking the lead, I alternate between pushing and shoveling, determined to carve a path through the snow. For once, Marsh is quiet. Only the sound of the plastic shovel on the ground pierces the soft silence of the falling snow.

When I turn to check on him, for a brief moment, I see, well, just Marsh. He's at his cutest when he's not trying to perform. He's wearing his purple beanie with the enormous ball dangling on the end, bouncing as he lumbers to keep up. In his green jacket that almost hits his knees, he resembles Shrek. A much more fuckable Shrek. Which either makes me Princess Fiona or Donkey.

His eyes flick up and catch me checking on him, and that goofy half-smile spreads across his face. A sharp pain slivers in my chest. How could someone so adorable be so callous? Like many neurotic New York Jews, he was never shy about talking about his current emotional state when we were together. And yet he ended things on such an abrupt, vague note. It takes a lot of energy to stay mad at him, and he's not making it any easier looking so precious and tasty.

"Okay, the road is right over … " The entire world appears to be blanketed in white, the snowfall getting more forceful.

"Where?" Marsh sidles up next to me. "Which way?"

"There?" I point through the few trees without leaves. "Or maybe there?"

Instead of finding a nicely plowed access road, all I see is white. The snow is so high I can't tell where the road should be. Behind us, the driveway I just shoveled is filling with a fresh layer of snow.

"We should head back before we can't find our way home," says Marsh, worry flashing on his face.

"It's got to be here … maybe a little bit farther."

"Data, we need to go back," he says a bit more forcefully.

I keep searching, trudging through thigh-high snow, the

cold seeping through my pants, hoping to see the cleared access road in the distance, a way out of here.

Marsh's gloved hand takes mine, pulling me back toward the house and the unfortunate reality.

I think I hear him wheeze and watch his chest, checking for any shortness of breath, but his breathing seems regular. I look down at his hand holding mine, and my free hand resting on his chest, and it's all too intimate.

"You weren't right," I say, taking back my hands. "I was just inaccurate in my assessment."

"Sure."

I motion toward the cleared path back to the cabin. It's best that I hang behind him in case his asthma acts up. "After you."

"You'll make any excuse to stare at my ass," Marsh teases, twerking in his coat, doing his best to grab my attention. Reluctantly, I follow him as he trudges back to the cabin.

My eyes definitely do not glimpse the two perfect globes swaying back and forth in his pants under that thick jacket. Nope. Nothing to see there.

Chapter Ten

Marsh

Here's the thing you need to know about Data: He can be rugged AF. Don't let the number-crunching, pencil-pushing, retentive-analing fool you. That's Data's Clark Kent side. He can go full Paul Bunyan like it's nobody's biznatch. (Preeti would call out my mixed pop culture metaphor, but I stand by it.)

He crams the shovel into the wall of packed snow blocking our front walkway. Since the driveway and road are a shoveling bridge too far, and he refuses to let the snow accumulate, he insists on clearing the front steps during a lull in the blizzard. A flush of red creeps up above his beard as his piercing eyes study the expanse of white. Each time he heaves the shovel into the snow, he lets out a grunt, as if he's a tennis player lobbing the ball back over the net. Or fucking me senseless. My groin shudders as I watch the process over and over again, finding a peacefulness to the repetitive nature.

In our relationship, Data was the handy one, the one who could repair things, fix things, paint things. I was the pretty face —although I once changed a light bulb he couldn't quite reach thankyouverymuch. Being the only child of a single mom made him the de facto man around the house at a young age. He regrouted their bathroom tile when he was in high school, and I only learned what regrouting was like five years ago. From him. He admitted to me years ago that when he realized he was gay, it motivated him to be more handy and to step up his DIY knowledge at home. Yet another item in the endless list of ways gay sons try to prove to their parents we're still men, all in the hopes that they'll still love us.

I watch Data furrow his brow with determination, wishing he could grip me like that shovel's handle. One of the many difficulties with ending a relationship is that your ex can still be drop-dead sexy after the breakup. Especially when he's being all butch.

"Why are you just standing around?" he asks.

"Don't you need a spotter?"

He cocks his head, and pulls his lips in.

"I can help," I say. "My lungs are fine."

"They're fine until you're huffing and puffing and calling out my name."

My tongue goes thick in my throat. Did he just …

"Calling out my name for help because you can't breathe." Right. The not-fun type of huffing and puffing. "People have heart attacks and die from shoveling snow."

"Old people." Before I remember that I'm closer to fifty than twenty, Data plunges his shovel into the snow.

"Since we're here to pack, maybe you should … " He waves his hand, trying to pull the answer out of me.

"Pack?"

Data gives me a round of applause. I give him the finger. A gentlemanly, we're-totally-platonic finger.

"Fine. But if you die of a heart attack, I'm taking back those Prada loafers I bought you for Hanukkah that you never wear." I shrug my shoulders and retreat into the warmth of the cabin, which isn't as warm as I'd like. This isn't the time for our HVAC system to crap out.

I put on an extra zip-up hoodie, grab a roll of tape and a box, and get to work. We're already behind schedule on packing, and me standing around lusting after my ex-boyfriend isn't helping. I have to keep my inappropriate thoughts at bay for the remainder of the weekend. I have to resist the ease of being around him. I made the hard choice to let him go, and I can't play with his heart by flirting with him. Maybe there's a chance we can be friends in the future, and for that to happen, I have to be on my best behavior this weekend. A total ex-boyfriend diplomat.

I march back outside and keep my eyes firmly fixed above his neckline. "We're running low on large boxes. Rather than save those boxes for packing heavy items, I'm going to use the medium boxes. Heavier items in smaller boxes will make them easier to transport, thus cutting down on loading up our cars on Monday. The larger boxes can be used for clothing and lightweight personal effects. You hadn't mapped out recommended box usage in our agenda, but I think this is the optimal course of action."

Data blinks at me a few times. "Uh, sure. Whatever you think best. As long as we're out of here by Sunday night or earlier if the streets get plowed."

His itching to leave sends tiny daggers diving into my heart.

"I'm going to tackle the living room. Even though it isn't as dense with items that need to be packed, it should provide a psychological boost to have our largest space all packed up, providing further momentum for the weekend."

"Okay … sounds good."

"Splendid, Marshall." I straighten my spine, turn on my heel, and return to the cabin.

Yep. A total baller of an ex-boyfriend diplomat.

To my surprise, packing up the living room does provide an emotional boost. It doesn't take long to fill boxes with books and our vast assortment of tchotchkes accrued over eight years and countless antiquing trips. I start with the paintings that we picked up on trips to galleries, where gallery owners with chunky glasses and pencil skirts smooth-talked us about the intelligence of investing in art. Data has a better eye than me, and he was better with investing, so he can keep these.

Sprinkled on the shelves are little wood carvings Data made during lazy afternoons. I would watch his hands move dexterously across the wood, shaping it and carving it just right. Little figurines of the both of us, a little model of The General Store, one of a deer that loves to frolic by our septic tank. Each one crafted by his fingers with crisp details, with the surface sanded to a flawless smoothness, like freshly poured cream.

Data's woodworking output slowed to a stop over the past few years. He said he was too busy, but he happily let his job consume him. A job that he rarely talked positively about, another life choice made in the hopes of making his mom proud.

On top of regular Jewish mom guilt, Data suffers from The Best Little Boy in the World syndrome that afflicts many gay men. It's an unquenchable drive to be successful, in the hopes that your professional and financial success will offset the shame your parents feel about having a son that takes it up the ass.

Taking a moment to appreciate the figurines up close, my mind is blown away by the sheer artistry. I can't believe I got to be with someone this talented.

Technically, these should go to him since he made them, but I slip the two figurines of us into my pocket. Little Marsh and Little Data. Together in some universe. If he wants them back, he can trade me the loafers.

My phone rings on the coffee table. DAD pops up on the screen. I put it on speaker so I can multitask and stay efficient, something Data would appreciate.

"Hello, Sir Dads a Lot!"

"Hey bud. How are things shakin'?" he says in his nasally New York accent that always sounds like home to me.

"I'm keeping busy. I, uh, have a show coming up next month." After leaving him in the lurch with the business, I don't have the heart to tell him I've failed at something else. And technically, I am helping with graphics for Preeti's show.

"Show? Is that what they're calling it nowadays?"

"Performances, I guess."

"Performances? What a weird thing to say. I hope you don't call it that in front of your patients."

I pinch the bridge of my nose as a familiar lump grows in my throat. "It's Marshall, Dad. The son who isn't a brilliant surgeon."

"Right, right. The reception isn't that good." He coughs, attempting to clear the confusion. "Where are you right now?"

"I'm at the cabin this weekend. But I can come back if you need." If Dad needed me, I'd trudge through a zillion feet of snow in a heartbeat.

"Say hi to Other Marshall for me." Hearing Dad's nickname for Data sends a flutter in my stomach. After months of never being sure how to differentiate us, the "Other Marshall" nickname stuck. I'm glad he hasn't lost all of his inside jokes.

"How did you know Other Marshall is here?"

"Why wouldn't he be? He's your companion."

"Uh, yeah. We're not together. Remember?"

"You never told me." Of course, I did.

"We broke up a few months ago." I feel my whole face crinkle into a cringe. It doesn't get easier having to jog Dad's memory, especially about the state of my pitiful romantic life.

"Oh. You did? That's too bad. But even when you think it's over, there's still hope. I remember when your mom and I once had a fight about … something. You and Albie were toddlers. Your mother bursts out of the house, gets in the car, and drives off." He chuckles to himself as he's telling the story, and I imagine his eyes getting brighter and that childlike smile peeking out. "You immediately started bawling. You were always more of a mommy's boy."

"That tracks." I'll gladly take a burn from Dad. It reminds me of all the times we joked together when I was growing up. My sense of humor and love of comedy came from him.

"I run out in my gatkes and chase her car down the street like a maniac. I'm screaming after her, and I can tell she's not going as fast as she could be. I think she enjoyed the spectacle."

I'm losing it thinking of Dad in his underwear running down our street, his gut flapping side to side. Our neighbors probably rolled their eyes regretting letting Jews move in.

"Did she stop?" I ask Dad. "How far down did you chase her?"

"She stopped at the stop sign, but then she turned right. I think if she had turned left, we would've been in real trouble. I run after her, and then I finally yell out as loud as I can … "

"Yeah?"

"I yell out … " He says again, this time confused. I can hear the struggle in his voice. "I yell out … "

"Miriam?" I say softly.

"Goddamnit!" he snaps. "I know her name! I don't need your help." His tone changes on a dime, his words cloaked in a helpless anger.

I should be used to this by now. I'm not.

"I scream out 'Miriam' and she stops the car," Dad says, finishing the story out of obligation rather than enthusiasm. "Couples fight. They get back together."

"Yeah. Well, Marshall has already seen me in my gatkes, so we're halfway there." I cling to humor like it's a life preserver. It's best not to dwell on things we can't change. "What's up with you?"

"Did you know your brother has been talking to people about buying Harmony Pianos?"

I clamp my eyes shut. Fucking Albie. He never had any patience.

"He mentioned it to me." I pace in the tight quarters, rubbing my forehead. "He has a friend who does mergers and acquisitions, and he found a potential buyer for the company."

"I can't believe he's been talking to people about selling," Dad says, horrified. "Did you know about this?"

"We … discussed it." Even as a full-grown adult, I can't convincingly lie to my dad. Because even with Alzheimer's, he'll know. "Albie jumped the gun in telling you."

Once Albie showed an aptitude for science, Mom and Dad steered him toward medicine. He doesn't have the same connection to Harmony Pianos. He only sees it as a burden, not a legacy.

"Why would I sell the company? I built this company from nothing, Albie!"

"It's … Marsh, Dad."

"That's what I meant. Albie shouldn't be talking to anyone about this."

"He was trying to help."

"I don't need help. We're in contract with a hotel group to provide pianos for their lobbies."

"That deal happened five years ago." My stomach churns with anger and hurt and sadness that I can't ever let come to the surface. He can fall apart, but I have to stay strong.

"They want more. They're expanding." Desperation hitches in his voice. "So we're going to sell the business to some private equity jerkoffs who are going to strip it for parts?"

That might be the most lucid thing Dad has said so far and one of my big hesitations about the deal.

"You can finally take it easy."

"I don't want to take it easy," he barks.

"I've tried talking to you about this. You can't … running the business is becoming too much for you. You rejected candidates to take over the company. Now would be a good time to pass Harmony Pianos off." My heart thumps in my chest with each word. I'm a tightrope walker taking each step carefully.

"I don't want outside candidates!" He exhales a voluminous sigh that crackles in the phone. "Harmony Pianos is supposed to stay in the family. It's supposed to keep that personal touch with its craftsmanship and its customer service. My son was all set to take over. He went to business school. He worked alongside me for years learning every inch of the business. And right when I was about to hand over the reins, he quits! He throws it all away because he wants to be a comedian." Comedian comes out with a mix of confusion and disdain. A shiver crawls up my spine. "Maybe it's dumb, Ira, but I'm still holding out hope that he'll come back. Working side-by-side with Marshall was my dream. I have to tell you, it was one of the best times in my life."

Wetness dots the corners of my eyes. I don't have the heart to tell him I'm not his lawyer. I barely have breath in my lungs to respond.

"Ira, you still there?"

"Yeah. Uh, we can discuss later." Tears pool in my eyes, and I use superhuman strength to hold them back.

"You sound funny."

"I'm fine. My bagel went down the wrong pipe. I have to meet with a client, Joe. Talk to you soon."

I hang up and press the phone hard against my chest, feeling so alone it hurts to breathe. Even the wittiest humor can't ease the depth of certain pains.

And then, a hand on my shoulder. Tentative, but warm. Pulling me out of this dark hole.

"I'm sorry." Data's voice is softer than it's been all day.

All I want to do is follow his hand to his arm, to his chest, let him wrap his arms around me in a comforting Data cocoon. Breathe in his scent, let his support blanket me. But an unexpected rush of embarrassment comes over me, a white-hot flame singeing my chest.

"Can you, uh, chop us some wood? I'd help, but … " I pound my chest, " … bum lungs and all." I wipe the tears from my eyes so fast it's like they were never there. "It's still cold in here. Either the heater is busted or Elsa really went for it when she 'Let It Go.'" I pull the corner of my lips into a smile, each joke another rung in the ladder up to the light.

"Marsh." He squeezes my shoulder.

I pat his hand, then in the gentlest way possible, push it off. "I'm good." I sniffle quickly. "At least I don't have to feel bad about forgetting to send him a birthday card anymore."

I grab my coat from the couch and head outside. The crisp air helps calm me.

Falling apart is something you do in front of boyfriends. Not acquaintances. Not diplomats. Not people whose hearts you've broken and whose trust you've lost.

Chapter Eleven

~~Data~~ Marshall

Being an accountant by day, everyone assumes I'm a meek mouse. But when the situation calls for it, I can be a burly bear. Something about the mountain, being immersed in nature, brings it out in me. And as a city boy, my hands used tools in a smaller, more restrained manner. Out here, I'm able to wield giant saws and axes with wild abandon. It's glorious.

Our woodchopping station is just outside the back screen door. It's next to a fire pit where, on better nights, we'd sit enjoying the fire under a starry sky with hot chocolates in hand. Marsh would always give me extra marshmallows. "Extra sweetness for my sweet," he'd say.

Currently, he sits in his folding lawn chair, watching me chop but also staring off, a million thoughts crisscrossing his face. His dad. The business. His body may be on the mountain, but his mind is far off.

"You don't have to stay out here with me," I say. "I'm almost done. You can start bringing wood in."

He gives me a nod acknowledging that words came out of my mouth, but that's it.

Trying to get his attention, I add, "This wood is really thick and rough. Duffy delivers it raw, but it's never been this raw."

I wait for him to take the bait and shoot back a zinger. I'm hoping for it. I've wanted Marsh to wipe that cute-but-annoying smile off his face since the moment I arrived, and now that he has … I want it back as soon as possible. The left corner of his mouth lifts into the tiniest morsel of a grin before going flat again.

A few months before we broke up, his dad began to have episodes. Calling Marsh Albie. Forgetting where he was or why he was there. It looked like the initial stages of Alzheimer's to me, but Marsh was in denial. He tried his damnedest to use humor to keep up his family's spirits, like when his mom died, but his dad's health couldn't be fixed with a joke. Some nights, I'd hold him in my arms as he cried himself to sleep. I was the one person he didn't need to perform for. He shouldn't have to go through this alone. Why did he choose to go through this alone?

Heaving the ax over my head, I slam it down on a piece of wood from the pile. As the metal crashes into wood, a flush of heat creeps over my face.

"I'm sorry," I say.

He looks up and crinkles his brow in confusion.

"I should've reached out to see how your dad was doing."

"What? It's okay. Really. You didn't have to."

"I should have. I've known him for eight years." It was longer than I knew my own father.

"You were right. He has Alzheimer's," Marsh says. There was no victory in being right this time.

My heart breaks all over again for him, for Joe, for the inevitability of what's to come.

"You officially got confirmation?"

He nods yes. "The day before Laughingstock."

"Marsh." Shit. Things I wish I knew months ago.

"He had a really bad incident. Wandered into a high school locker room and … yeah, it was bad." He nods again, his jaw painfully tight with the memory. "How's that for timing?"

My heart drops realizing how bad things were and how I wish I'd known. Is this why he withdrew from me? Fuck.

"Marsh … I'm here if you ever need to talk." My body longs to go to him. Hold him. Console him. I know this weekend is about severing our relationship, but I can't leave him like this.

"I appreciate that, but thinking about your ex's parents isn't your responsibility."

"I love him, too, Marsh."

Nobody warns you that when you're in a long-term relationship, your partner's family becomes yours. And when things end, suddenly you're without family members you've grown to care about. I put a fresh piece of wood on the chopping block, but I can't raise the ax. My chest tightens with memories. Post-dinner chats with Joe about ways to reduce his company's tax burden or think through ideas for expansion. Going to Yankee games together when Marsh was out of town. Watching him get so into the game that I found myself cheering with him despite finding baseball boring—sexy tight baseball pants aside. Every time he called me Other Marshall with an impish wink, the crater my dad left in my heart felt a little less hollow.

When you break up with someone, you don't just mourn that relationship, but the relationships you had with everyone else in their family, for better or worse.

"I'm sorry this is happening."

"Thanks. I hate when people say, 'I hope he gets better.' He's not. This disease only goes in one direction." Marsh heaves out a breath.

"Hey." I hold the ax out to him. "Why don't you chop this last piece?"

He perks up. "You serious?"

"Yeah."

"Because in all our time of coming up here, you hogged the ax and chopping block."

He's not wrong. "I didn't want your asthma flaring up. And … I'm better at it."

"Or so you think." Marsh gives me a crooked grin, and my chest swells with relief—grateful his signature smile has returned.

"I figure you have some frustration to let out. And I've already let out all my Marsh frustrations on our woodpile." I nod at the stack of wood by my feet.

Watching him cheer up sends a fuzzy spark of warmth fluttering through my chest. He bolts from his chair and takes the ax from my hand, almost dropping it.

"Shit. That's heavy."

"Ya think?"

Marsh gets a grip and steadies the ax. Now that he's holding it, he seems uncertain of what to do next. "So I just lift and drop it down?"

"That's the idea." Realizing that he could very well lose a finger or hand in this endeavor, I figure it's best to help him out.

I stand behind and put my arms around him to reach the ax. Our hands touch as I slide mine down to a free part of the handle. And everything else of ours is touching too. His body heat, his aroma of ocean-scented shampoo mixed with Mallo-mars and something all his own, threatens to make me deliver wood of my own.

Marsh shimmies his butt, presumably to get into chopping position but maybe also to fuck with me. There's a weapon in his hands, so I have to ignore the one growing heavy in my pants.

"Um, so you lift the ax over your head," I say. A bolt of heat chokes my throat as he shifts his position to raise the ax—another shimmy. Even with a thousand layers of clothing between us, I can make out the faint valley of his ass.

Yeah, though I'm close to the valley of Marsh's crack, I will fear no boner, for thou art a mature adult who can hold in bodily urges.

"How's this?" Marsh asks.

"Good. It's good." I lower my hands to support his arms, which I feel flexing under his jacket. I want nothing more than to bury my nose in his hair and sniff, but with an ax over us, our heads are literally on the chopping block. "And now you throw the ax down as hard as you can."

His body tightens, and he lets out a grunt as he hurls the ax onto the log, two halves spitting off the block into the snow.

That grunt. Oh, how I missed that damn grunt.

Marsh jams the ax into the block. He picks up the log halves and holds them like a fish he just caught. "You're right. That did help me feel a little better. Thanks."

I give a nod, feeling embarrassed even though Marsh is none the wiser about my bodily urges.

"If it makes you feel better, Dad still asks about you."

I smile, grateful to still have a home in Joe's fading memories.

He picks up logs to carry inside. He opens the screen door. "Question."

"Yeah?" I ask, picking up the rest.

"Do you always get a boner when you chop wood?" Marsh flashes me his cute-but-annoying smile and heads inside.

Chapter Twelve

Marsh

Here's the thing you need to know about Data: he was the cold one in the relationship. Not cold as in unloving, but literally chilly. The one who always needed a blanket, the one who kept turning down the A/C, the one who remarked "It's freezing in here" when we went to the movies. You'd think with all that cozy body hair, he'd be the warmer one.

So when he says that it's really cold in the cabin, at first I think it's just Data being Data. But when I take off my coat, even I notice it's draftier than normal.

He loads the wood-burning stove with logs. It sits in the corner of the living room. Despite its meager size, it has the power to provide ample heat. It's a grower, not a shower.

I can't help but notice the goosebumps starting to form on my arms. Has the temperature dropped in the short time we were outside?

"Is it cold in here?" I ask, giving credence to Data's icebox tendencies. "I need an afghan."

"It was working fine last night. I'm going to check the furnace." He trudges into the basement, the one room I don't want to venture into. It's where we threw everything we didn't need. Can we leave it for the new owners, pretend that we forgot to clean it out?

I warm my hands by the burgeoning fire, the burning and

smoky aroma reminding me of all the cuddling we did in this very spot.

"Furnace seems to be in order. I didn't notice any problems," he says when he returns. I take his word for it. "Basement almost seems a little warmer than up here."

He shivers a little as he warms himself by the fire.

"Here." I rub my hands up and down his arms. Unlike Data, I am my own furnace. I hug him to me, passing along my body heat as well as other heat. He smells like snow and wood, but I make sure not to take a deep sniff.

The good news is it's too cold to have sex. Although who am I kidding … men can get hard in any temperature, any climate. The propagation of the species depends on it.

Data heads over to the thermostat. "It's set to seventy, but only at sixty-four."

The furnace was never that efficient. It's why we had the wood stove installed. Once we get it cranking, the stove will spread its cozy heat throughout the entire space, pushing the thermostat to a toasty seventy-three or four. Warm enough for us to lie around naked.

Maybe we should leave it.

"Sixty-four. What a boring number. If we're going to freeze our butts off, at least go up to sixty-nine to make it interesting." I wiggle my eyebrows at him. Despite the obvious corniness of the joke, he smiles.

If an ex still smiles at your corny jokes, then maybe it's a sign that they don't actually hate you.

Data shakes his head, erasing the warm expression on his face. Back to business.

Diplomat, Marsh, diplomat. He's not a mouse in a cat's mouth. He shouldn't be played with.

"We can call a maintenance person when we get back to New York," I offer.

"Or if the roads are better by tomorrow, which they should

be, we can get one to come out then," he says. "This is a good thing. It's even more of an impetus to finish packing and leave ASAP. For now, the stove can keep this place well-heated, as long as we supply it with a steady stream of wood."

I snort a laugh.

"*Firewood*. For the fire." Data makes his cute stern face.

"Good thing this wood is, how did you put it before? Thick and rough and really raw."

"I swear, sometimes you're a twelve-year-old." Despite his efforts, Data smiles again.

"Ahem." I cross my arms. "We should be packing, not bantering, Marshall. I hate to have to be the taskmaster *as always* but," I tap the nonexistent watch on my wrist. "time's ticking."

"Okay. Then let's get started." He heads down the hall. I tell myself we can be friendly and make the most of the weekend. I don't know if we'll leave Marshmallow Mountain as more than acquaintances, but we can at least have some (clothed) fun while we're stuck here.

I follow Data, keeping my eyes away from his derriere. He walks into the main bedroom and stops at the bed. I stop at the door.

"The bedroom," I say, feeling awkward as hell.

"We should cross it off our list. Packing-wise," he says, awkwardness in his voice too.

The bed stares back at us, with plans of its own. My stomach flips with nerves.

Data spins on his heel. "We can pack this room up on Sunday, right before we leave."

"Good idea."

"Let's do the basement." He scoots past me, making sure our bodies don't touch. Quick as anything, he's walking down the hall.

The basement. The dreaded basement.

"Ugh," I groan, and not the sexy kind. Nobody ever wants to sort through what's been thrown in their basement. It's where you store crap you'll deal with later, like extra folding chairs and dead bodies.

I dart to the kitchen. I'll need backup. And by backup, I mean Mallomars. I grab the shiny yellow box off the counter.

"The only way out is through," Data says before descending the creaky staircase.

I follow again, and this time, I do check out his beautiful ass. I need the pick me up.

Time seems to slow as we survey the dank, musty space. Piles of junk and memories sit on the floor. Some are in boxes … which are soggy and moldy. Some are laying in the open, forming a lean-to of crap. Old skis, old furniture, old receipts, old bedsheets. The flotsam and jetsam of life.

"As I said before, ugh." I stand on the bottom step, not wanting to enter the junk dungeon.

"Do you know how to eat an elephant?" Data asks.

"No. But if you hum a few bars, I can fake it."

He rolls his eyes because he's heard my Elvira bit a million times, but she's really one of the great underrated comedians of our time.

"The answer is, one bite at a time," he says, brushing dust off a box.

Data wades into the mess and picks at random objects, but his heart isn't in it either. Still, it has to get done. I dragged him up here, I might as well make this as enjoyable as possible. (Again, with clothes on.)

I waltz into the center of the basement and breathe in the musty air. Then I clap my hands together, an optimistic can-do attitude lighting me up. "I have an idea."

"If it involves not cleaning up the basement—pass."

"Why don't we make a game of it?" I reveal the box of

mallomars from under my arm, holding the box above my head like a trophy.

"Where did those come from?"

"Well, when a graham cracker, a marshmallow, and melted chocolate are in love, and they want to express that love—"

"Marsh."

"I brought them from upstairs." I flip open the box. "There are eighteen cookies left. Everytime one of us packs up a box, we get a Mallomar. We keep going until this box is empty. Whoever eats more Mallomars wins."

The stakes could not be lower, and yet, I know Data, and his competitive urges. Our relationship might not have lasted, but our adoration of Mallomars is eternal.

"Deal. But each box must be sufficiently packed. No cutting corners," he says.

I give him a little salute. We go upstairs to get the boxes and tape. When we're back in the basement, we split the supply in half and put the two stacks in opposite corners.

"The Mallomars will remain on the steps, a neutral zone." I place the box oh-so-carefully on the steps and give it a tap. We go to our sides.

While my feelings for Data are complicated, my desire to win is not. My adorable, fuzzy, human icebox is going down.

"Ready. Set. Pack!" I pretend to fire off a gun, and we're off.

Chapter Thirteen

~~Data~~ Marshall

The pile of stuff almost seems insurmountable, but then I remind myself of the platitude I uttered to Marsh: one bite at a time. I'm definitely the faster, more efficient packer between us, but it wouldn't be fair to have this fun game be a complete blowout.

I start a box and leisurely fill it with half-burned candles. I suppose I could throw them out, but they still smell good. I do love a quality handmade candle. Underneath them, I find a familiar Moleskine notebook with Marsh's name inscribed on the cover. His first joke journal. A present from me for our first Hanukkah together.

He used to jot down ideas on scraps of paper and then hoped he didn't lose them. I encouraged him to consolidate. He carried it everywhere, as it fit in his back pocket. I'd find him around our apartment and the cabin, smiling to himself as he scribbled something down. A first step to a new career. It would be a colossal waste of time to go down memory lane seeing as we're in such a time crunch to pack. But some treasures demand our attention.

His penmanship resembles a fourth grader's and to make it worse, he insists on writing in all caps. As I flip it open, I notice the pages contain a plethora of ideas for jokes and sketches. He used to try his material out on me, his "toughest audience," as a litmus test. If it made me laugh, he starred the entry.

Just as I'm methodical with numbers, he's methodical with words, arranging and rearranging sentences to hit the punchline right, organizing material so topics flow into each other. There is a science to telling good jokes, and he is constantly experimenting. He works hard at what he does, but unlike pouring fourteen hours a day into a job he abhors, this is his passion.

When I turn around to show Marsh the journal, I notice he's actually taking the game seriously. He's a one-man assembly line, filling his box up, his arms almost robotic in their laser focus. He tapes the box shut, pushes it against the wall, and collects his cookie reward from the stairs. That's when I notice there's three boxes against his wall.

Marsh - 3. Data - 0.

"Delicious," he says, winking at me, his mouth full of Mallomar.

Oh, hell no. I can't let Marsh eat the entire box of Mallomars. Neither his cholesterol nor my pride can handle it.

I slip the joke journal in my back pocket and get to work. If he's a packing assembly line, I'm a packing Terminator. I pack as feverishly as I can, leaving no stone of clutter unturned in my half of the basement. I don't have time to fall into nostalgia traps. Hasta la vista, memories.

"Question," Marsh calls from his side of the basement. "What tastes better: victory or Mallomars?"

"I'll let you know when I win," I say, pushing a box against my basement wall and racing to the stairs for my reward. I take a bite and smile at Marsh, showing off the half-chewed graham cracker and chocolate in my teeth.

Who's twelve now? Me.

I open a new box and shove who-knows-what inside. We can deal with it back in the city.

Time speeds by as the clutter of the basement is replaced by neat stacks of boxes against the walls. I find an old radio and turn on the local station. "All music, all the time" is their tagline, which really means they have no budget for anything more than a randomized playlist of ancient mellow hits. Yes, this was a waste of precious packing time, but we need background noise. Marsh takes the game so seriously, he's not making his usual quips.

I hear the rustle of the Mallomars box. Marsh pops another one into his mouth.

"There's only one left," he says. "And I'm almost done with my side."

"Your items were less bulky and easier to pack," I say with a smile. "Rigged."

"See if there's a participation trophy in your stack that you can cry into." Marsh rubs his fist against his cheeks, mimicking a crybaby.

"I demand an audit of your box to make sure they're sufficiently packed."

"We're supposed to be packing, not bantering, Marshall." He wiggles his eyebrows at me, knowing how that turns me on, but I refuse to be distracted.

I zero in on my final box, my mind locking into focus as if I'm staring at my four screens at work. I pack with such ferocity my arms begin to tire, but I can't stop. I won't stop. In relationships, most times you want to see your partner succeed. But then there are times when you want to kick his perfectly plump ass. Lovingly, of course.

I scramble to throw in books, posters, a picnic set, an old pack of gum that I should toss but the garbage is too far away. Excitement lights my body on fire when I fill my box. I launch the tape over the top, pressing it shut, as I hear Marsh jump up from his spot.

I shove the box against the wall, leap up, and dash to the

stairs, the finish line in my sights. Our hands jam into the Mallomar box at the same time.

"I got here first," he says.

"But my hand was on the Mallomar first."

We keep our fingers wrapped around the treat. No tug of war. We don't want this delicate creature to break apart.

And then Marsh, in a most unsportsmanlike move, tickles my side.

I let out a yelp but manage to hold on to my precious prize.

And I, in an equally unsportsmanlike move, whack him on the dick. I'm laughing so hard from the tickling and the adrenaline, tears pool at my eyes. Marsh doubles over, loosening his grip on the Mallomar. I jump off the stairs. This time, it's my turn for a victory dance.

"Cheater." He rushes at me, laughing just as hard, face all red.

He pulls me close, tries to grab my reward, but I won't let go. I evade his grasp as we find ourselves shuffling backward. I trip over a rogue ski and fall back into the pile of cushions for our outdoor furniture. Marsh tumbles on top of me.

Miraculously, the Mallomar stays intact. It's me who's on the verge of falling apart.

His lips hang inches from my face, his eyes two deep pools entrancing me, his body heat searing into my flesh.

"I win," I gasp out. I'm about to cram the Mallomar in my mouth in a surge of victory, when Marsh grabs my wrist. Silence blankets the room and my heart beats so fast I worry it might escape my chest. The mood in the basement shifts instantly.

"If you're going to eat the last Mallomar, you gotta savor it," he says, a raspy undertone in his voice. He opens my hand, his grip firm, my fingers powerless to resist.

Marsh takes the confection and hovers it above my face. He

stares directly into my eyes, producing more fire than our stove could ever provide.

"Smell the sweet chocolate shell. Savor it," he commands.

I lift my head up to sniff, the scent of chocolate swirling up my nose, filling my head with pleasure.

"What do you smell?"

"Chocolate. Sweet. Tasty." Breath rattles in my lungs.

"Good," he says. "Lick it." I open my mouth and he pulls the cookie away. "Just the tip."

The chocolate-covered marshmallow part is shaped like a dome that comes to a point at the top. Marsh used to joke that Mallomars have nipples.

My tongue slides out slowly and slithers up to the Mallomar in his hand. The tip of my tongue swirls around the pointed end of the cookie, much like how I would on Marsh's nipple. The sweetness mixes with his warm breath as he lowers the cookie to give me better access.

Like tractor beams, his eyes have not left my gaze. They light up as I lick. While the chocolate melts under the heat of my tongue, my cock hardens in my pants.

"How's the chocolate?"

"So good," I gasp out.

"Lick around the base."

My dick throbs at his order and I slick my tongue around the rounded dome, covering every inch, letting it melt on my taste buds. The sugary hit of marshmallow floods my senses. I lick across the dome, sucking on it gently, hitting the tip again, showing Marsh exactly what I'd do to his dick, my restraint and resolve dissolving as fast as this chocolate shell.

His bottom lip quivers as he studies me. There's a sparkle in Marsh's eyes as a low rustled groan vibrates in my chest and escapes my parted lips. He brushes the Mallomar over my top lip, then my bottom lip, then back inside my mouth.

I moan as the sweetness hits my tongue again.

"You know, you really whacked me hard before. You should apologize."

"All's fair in love and packing wars," I snark back, but his gaze doesn't falter. "Sorry."

"Why don't you make it feel better?" He guides my hand to his crotch, where his cock is a fucking hammer trying to escape. I groan with a guttural want as my fingers caress over his bulge.

He circles the Mallomar around my lips with agonizing slowness as I slip my hand into his sweatpants and grip his fat cock. Even though I enjoyed it yesterday, waiting still feels unbearable.

Marsh unleashes groans above me as I stroke him. The heat from his dick warms my palm and I moan into the Mallomar that dips into my mouth. My other hand shoots into his pants.

I jerk him harder, faster, lost in a spell of sugar and heat. I lift my head and take the whole Mallomar and the fingers holding it into my mouth. Sucking. Swallowing. Savoring every morsel of sweetness and Marsh.

"Fuuuuck," Marsh lets out in a low, blissed-out moan. He fucks his cock into my grip and my breath hitches as his stomach presses me down in place.

"I'm gonna come. Fuck, I'm gonna come."

I nibble his skin in my mouth, his thick fingers on my tongue, my breath unable to keep up, lust coursing through my veins.

I bite into the cookie as hot jets of cum blast over my fist.

"Data, fuck." Marsh's face is a knot of red, eyes rolling back as he unloads.

He holds himself up, although I can tell he wants to tumble onto me.

"How does it taste?" Marsh asks, catching his breath.

"Amazing. But it needs one more thing." I pull my hands from his sweatpants and take the Mallomar from him. My cum-soaked fingers coat the cookie. I take another bite, relishing the icing he's given the treat. The bitterness mixes perfectly with the sweetness. Marsh's jaw flops open in shock and lust.

"Eat it." I place the last bite into his mouth.

Our eyes lock as we chew and swallow. My entire body tingles with satisfaction as the last bit of Mallomar-Marsh deliciousness goes down my throat.

"Delicious."

"Hmm." Marsh rolls off me. He looks down at the soaked spot on his sweatpants and chuckles to himself. "If this is my last Mallomar, it'll be one I'll never forget," he says, licking the last crumbs from his fingers.

Chapter Fourteen

Marsh

Here's the thing you need to know about Data: When he has his mind set on something, he doesn't give up. Case in point: he's called seven different snowplow companies so far with no luck, yet he soldiers on.

After we, uh, finished in the basement, we came upstairs, baked another pair of bland TV dinners in the oven, and Data went to work searching for a plow company to clear our driveway and access road. There's a chance we could be stuck here for days.

I go into the bedroom and sit on the bed, my head still spinning from what happened in the basement. That was very undiplomatic behavior. I would definitely get expelled from the UN for that.

Technically, that wasn't break-up sex because there was no penetration, so the loop remains closed. The loop in my mind, replaying that scene, in addition to our sexytimes in the bathroom? That's going nonstop.

I'm not a religious person, but the fact that my phone buzzes with a text from Preeti seems like a sign from God. I call her back immediately.

"If you were about to leave me a voicemail, I was going to stage an intervention."

"Good callback," I say.

A calm instantly comes over me when I hear her voice. It quiets the confused voices in my head for a moment.

"Which file has the new flier graphics for the show? Our shared Google drive is a shitshow. Also, have you been working on material up there?"

A queasy feeling hits my stomach whenever our show comes up. Preeti is a persistent person, and I know she'll keep nudging me to perform.

"The file name is FinalFlyer underscore revision 3 underscore final final," I tell her, proud of myself for remembering the whole name. I don't answer her other question.

"You could've texted that."

"I wanted to hear your voice."

"Bullshit. What's up?" she asks.

"I kinda, maybe need to talk?"

"What happened, sweetie?" she asks, thrown off that I would be so directly earnest. Our love language is sarcasm, not heart-to-hearts. "How's the weekend going?"

"It's interesting."

"Ahem?"

"You were right. I'm on Data's shit list," I answer.

"Oooh. Awkward City."

"Uh kinda."

"Marsh, I'm not a fan of the live vaguebooking. I have a waxing appointment in twenty. Now make like an oil tanker and spill."

"Eh, I don't love the oil tanker analogy. It's a little dated."

"Big corporations fucking up the planet will never be outdated. But fine: now make like Prince Harry's memoir and spill."

I poke my head from the bedroom door to ensure Data is still on the phone, before launching into it with Preeti. I tell her about the break-up sex in the bathroom, Data wanting to close the loop, and then the sex-by-Mallomar. I have to catch my breath at the end of things.

A beat of silence hangs on the line.

"You still there?" I ask.

"With a Mallomar? What kind of *Call Me By Your Name* bullshit is going on up there?"

"It just happened. There's a lot of tension in this cabin, and unfortunately, there's no Peloton where we can burn it off, so we have to improvise."

"Hmm. Well, I've been to countless improv shows, and I've never seen two people fuck on stage. Also, can two guys really improvise sex? Don't you need lubricant?" she asks.

My desire years ago to tell Preeti how painful the spit-lube sex must've been in *Brokeback Mountain* is coming back to bite me in the butt.

"I bought a tube of it at the general store."

"You brought lube to a weekend with your ex? That's premeditation."

Damn Preeti's parents convincing her to take the LSATs *just in case.*

But she's right. The second I plucked that bottle of lube off Maddi's shelf, my mind went to a place it wasn't supposed to. And it's been going there all weekend.

"Two ex-boyfriends can have sex a few times over a weekend. It's like being on a diet and cheating at a friend's wedding," I say.

"And how many diets have you kept?" she shoots back.

Touceé. And not untrue.

"Marsh," she asks, her tone softer. "Do you want him back?"

I sit on the bed. That's the million-dollar question. The easy answer is yes. Of course I do. I want to spend the rest of my life with him, but my fantasies curdle quickly. Sure, the sex will be great, but does he want to spend his life supporting a struggling comic? What if that stress drives him to develop Alzheimer's in thirty years? Does he want to introduce me at office Christmas parties as his partner *who's really funny, he just hasn't gotten his big break yet?* Does he want to look back on his life and think about what could've been if he'd gone with Evan the hunky ENT and Maxwell the Instagram-famous corgi?

The real question isn't if I want Data back. It's *does he want me back?*

And right now, I get the sense this is all one last hurrah for him. Maybe it's best just to settle for him on his back.

"Hey, Marsh!" Data calls from the living room, a lifeline from this conversation.

"I gotta go, P. Any final remarks?"

"Yeah. Stop having sex!"

I click off the call and join Data. He tosses his phone in his hand, the look on his face a harbinger of bad news.

"None of the plows are able to get out," he says.

"Isn't that their job?"

"They're either booked, or the snow is too deep for their trucks."

Even men with their big, bad, overcompensating trucks can't get us out of this mess.

Data puts his hands by the woodburning stove to heat up. While the draftiness of earlier has subsided, it isn't totally gone. There's a faint chill that seems to cover our cozy cabin.

"The snow is tapering off, so maybe later today I'll try again, see if one of them can come out in the morning," he says. Sunday morning. So he can head out. The ticking clock on this weekend makes my insides crumble a bit.

"I can't believe we packed up the whole basement," Data said, his pride glowing on his face. "I have to hand it to you, Marsh. Your game idea worked."

"All of it?" I ask, leaving the hottest parts unsaid. The tackling? Willing you into chocolatey, marshmallowy, and graham crackery submission?

Data's ears burn red. Instead of giving me an answer, he takes something from his back pocket, wraps his hand around it like he did to my dick not too long ago. "I found this."

"Marshall Not-Mathers, I didn't think you had a nostalgic bone in your body," I joke. "What is it?"

He hands it over. The notebook sits heavy in my palm, comforting and taunting me, the feelings switch back and forth. I don't know how to feel about this blast from the past. It was used by a guy who had a lot more enthusiasm and optimism than the one currently holding it. What would the me who scrawled in this journal think of the me today? What would the Data of back then think of me?

"Cool." I flap it against my other hand and place it on an empty shelf. "Thanks for saving it."

"There's some good jokes in there. A few still make me laugh."

"Well that explains why I kicked your ass at the packing game. You got distracted."

"We tied." Data grabs it off the shelf and flips to a page in the middle. "This joke about Tom Hanks is gold." He clears his throat, about to read said joke. Panic surges through me, putting my body on high alert the same way a car swerving into my lane would.

I snatch the journal from him, adding a laugh to hide my shooting anxiety.

"Maybe later," I say.

"It's a good one. Oh, and there's one about—"

"We don't have to go through all my old material. There's a reason why it stayed in the notebook." I let out another laugh, hoping to dispel the awkwardness filling the room.

"Oh," he says, deflating slightly. "You know, despite everything, you're still the funniest person I know."

The compliment lands like arrows through my chest. Letting down people who believe in you is a gut punch like no other.

"Thanks."

"How have your recent shows gone since … ?"

"Since my on stage implosion? They, uh, haven't." I decide to hold my head up high, refusing to be a kicked puppy about this. "I'm quitting. Laughingstock was my final show."

Data blinks at me, taking in the update. His reaction reminds me of when I broke up with him. Another crushing blow.

"I can start the new year fresh, focus on helping my dad, and getting things in order." All the things I said I needed to do when I broke up with him. Maybe I can finally stop fucking up my life. "I gave it a good go, but … "

"But what?" Data's eyes widen, full of the same caring that supported me for all those years. "People think you're hilarious. You *are* hilarious."

"You're just saying that."

"I'm not. As your ex-boyfriend, I'm under no obligation to boost your ego. In fact, I should be doing the opposite."

I crack a smile. "That was good."

"You've worked so hard. And you are funny. You can't just give up. You were making progress. You even said it yourself last year. You said you could feel yourself improving. Getting bigger laughs. Jokes hitting with more frequency. People recognizing you and wanting to come to your shows. Landing more auditions."

"I was the laughingstock of Laughingstock." Just saying the name makes my throat go dry. "Comedians bomb all the time, but that was nuclear."

"Marsh, your dad was just diagnosed with Alzheimer's. You obviously weren't in the right headspace with a lot of things."

The last part breaks through my coat of humorous armor

for a second, hanging heavy in the air. "No do overs, unfortunately. Look, people give up on things all the time. You gotta know when to leave the party."

"I don't think it's time yet," he shoots back.

Sometimes, I couldn't tell if Data was my boyfriend or my manager. His hype man act could push into overeager, like I wasn't allowed to do anything but keep moving forward. There's being supportive, and then there's being a stage mom.

There was something about his unwavering support that left a sting in my chest. For a man so dead set on stability, his dedication to my decidedly unstable career didn't track.

I look for an exit from this rocky conversation, and my eyes glance into the bedroom. Little Marsh and Little Data sit on the dresser, staring back at me.

A question pops into my mind, one that had been lingering for a while in our relationship. And since this may be the last time we hang out, I figure it's as good as any to ask it. If this is our grand finale, then better get it all out there.

I run into the bedroom and scoop up the two figurines.

"Why did you stop?" I ask, holding them out. Little Marsh and Little Data stare him down.

"What are you doing with those?" His eyes cut to me, as if he got caught somehow.

"I found them while packing. You used to make stuff like this all the time. You even carved a breakfast-in-bed tray, even though you hate eating breakfast in bed because of crumbs. And you were good at it. Really good. As good as you say I am with comedy. When I worked at Harmony, co-workers would always pick up one of your figures from my desk and admire it, and I got to brag that my boyfriend made them *from scratch*."

"I got busy. Working. Paying bills. Adulting. Life—the ultimate obstacle."

That was his answer for everything. I began to wonder whether it was an answer or an excuse. Now that I'm not his boyfriend, I feel a freedom to push back. Why did I let our relationship be so one-sided about my career? I regret being so wrapped up in my own shit and not asking these questions years ago.

"Were you really so busy that you couldn't take any time for yourself to pursue something you obviously love?"

He shrugs, unable to provide an answer.

"You could've done it full time. You could've been a furniture maker with a store, a line of quality goods. You still can."

He shakes his head no and laughs at the suggestion. "And do what? Sell my stuff at flea markets? I can't make a living that way."

"How do you know for sure? You're a really good woodworker. Give me one second. Half a second." I scoot into the kitchen. I dig through the bottom shelf until I pull out the aforementioned breakfast-in-bed tray. I run back to the living room and hold it out to him like I'm presenting evidence to the jury. "Look at the craftsmanship. This makes Pottery Barn look like Ikea."

I keep holding it out until he has no choice but to take the tray and admire what he created. He runs his fingers over the latticed border and the MM insignia, a nod to Marshmallow Mountain, etched in the center, lost in the details for a moment.

"And there's something else I never understood. Why were you so supportive of me quitting my job to pursue comedy, and yet you won't support yourself doing the same, *Marshall*?"

It hadn't occurred to me how much of a *Do as I say not as I do* situation we'd found ourselves in as a couple. Maybe that was the heart of my frustration.

"It's different. There are a myriad of examples of comedians and comedic actors who have been able to make a living. There are several ways to generate income for oneself, between performances, acting gigs, commercials, traveling improv troupes, writing for late night."

My stomach churns—each example a dig of something I haven't accomplished.

Data puts down the tray on the loveseat, and its weight indents the cushions. "Those are still in the cards for you, Marsh. You're putting in the work, and it will bear fruit."

"Why can't you speak to yourself like this? Who says there aren't avenues for you to make it as an artisan?"

He had put his nickname to use and helped me research the feasibility of a career in comedy. While it was difficult, it was doable. And yet we never did the same for him. He never let us broach the subject.

"Do you know any successful furniture designers? Can you name one?" he asks, crossing his arms.

"Uh … yes. Yes I can." A grin gallops across my face. "Aidan Shaw."

He rolls his eyes. "Carrie's ex-boyfriend on *Sex and the City* does not count."

"Ex-fiancé, technically."

Data's face shifts to a patronizing smile, as if I'm a child who suggested we move to Mars or something. "It's not a realistic career path for me. It's a hobby."

"A hobby that you never do, even though you love it. Did you ever look into pursuing it more seriously? Instead of staying in a job you hate."

"Here we go again. I don't hate my job."

"Yes you do, Data! I mean, Marshall." I force a smile. "I was your boyfriend for eight years. I saw you every night when you came home from work, and I saw you every morning when you had to get up and do it all over again. So don't sit on my face and tell me it's raining."

"I don't think that's how the line goes." He scratches at his neck, his eyes stealthily looking for the exits. "I appreciate your concern, but it's a moot point."

I can't stand when he gets like this, deflecting any tough

question with layers of passive-aggressive politeness that would take a jackhammer to break through, thinking that he wins an argument merely by staying calm. It was always okay to analyze my career path, my relationship with my dad. But Data never turns those powers of perception on himself.

My chest thumps as I retrieve a card I've been hiding up my sleeve for years. It's a card I didn't feel comfortable playing when we were together, but we're not together anymore. So fuck it.

"Maybe it's time to admit the truth: You're almost forty years old, and you're still a scared boy afraid to disappoint his mother."

There will be no explosion of hate sex this time around. Just hate. Data's face hardens into a steely glare, his coat of armor disintegrating.

Without saying a word, he gets up and calmly walks into the guest room.

I knew I crossed a line the moment the words left my lips. Guilt washes over me, but not enough to make me apologize. In our relationship, I was the one who smoothed over arguments, who used humor to pull us back from the brink. But it's time for Data to be called on his bullshit.

I pluck the tray off the couch and am about to retreat into the kitchen when he yells from the guest room.

"Shit!"

I race in and see that our argument is the furthest thing from his mind. My naturally overheated self immediately begins to shiver.

"Shit. Shit," I say.

Our relationship isn't the only thing that's broken. So is the guest room window.

Chapter Fifteen

~~Data~~ Marshall

Impromptu weekend with the ex who shattered my heart six months ago? Check. Surprise snowstorm only Maddi's chickens knew about? Check. Trapped in a cabin with the ex packing up memories of the life we built together and he threw out like day old news? Check. Said ex reminding me my entire life is a farce because I repeatedly take the safe route in life and am a boring pencil pusher? Check. Broken window in the guest room that really *is* more of a closet than a room even though I'd never admit that to Bryce? Check. While I do love a list with items to check off, this isn't doing it for me. With every breath I take, I'm feeling more like the ultimate schlemiel.

"What happened?" Marsh asks. He tends to ask questions when I clearly don't know the answers.

"The window broke."

"Yeah, I see that, but how?" Marsh stands behind me. Peering over my shoulder, waiting for something to happen. Perhaps the window fairy will magically appear and fix the damn thing—me, I'm the window fairy. There's a small crack in the window, maybe an inch, but with the storm raging, cold air blows in, and a small pile of snow resembling powdered sugar has accumulated on the sill.

"I have no clue. Probably from the storm. The windows are old. We should've replaced them years ago. Nobody's been here all winter. Maybe the glass gave out? How do I know? Do I look like Bob Vila?"

"You wish. Bob was a total daddy. A daddy with a tool belt."

I sigh. Even when I'm frustrated with his inopportune jokes, Marsh still finds a way to lighten the mood. But right now, we have bigger problems than his Bob Vila kink.

"We'll need to fix it before we can sell," I say, searching for the piece of broken glass on the floor. "And we need to at least do some sort of impromptu repair in the meantime."

"Thank god you're here. You can fix anything."

Except us. Not like that's been the goal of this weekend.

"Hey." Marsh nudges me on the shoulder. "I'm sorry about what I said out there. Things got heated and—"

"It's okay. It sounds like you've wanted to get that off your chest for a while. And you did." I don't have the energy for another argument. I'd rather focus on what I can fix: a broken window. "Can you bring me an empty box and a roll of tape?"

"Yes, sir!" Marsh salutes and darts off. I need to tell him to stop the adorable gesture. Later.

The shard of glass is missing, which means it probably fell outside. I could gear up and go search for it, but finding a transparent piece of glass in feet of snow probably isn't prudent. I eyeball the hole and figure tape and cardboard can keep it secure enough to last the weekend.

Growing up with a financially struggling single parent, I became resourceful at a young age. I had to. My dad walked out on us when I was six. Mom told me he remarried and started a new family in Georgia, which stung. I never attempted to reconnect—abandoning us was his loss.

Mom was busy working two jobs to make ends meet, so there was nobody to show me how to fix things when they broke—and they broke often. I had to figure it out on my own. At the public library, I discovered these enormous, comprehensive home improvement books that I would borrow and read for enjoyment. Turns out nobody ever checked them out but me. They became my go-to resource whenever something needed fixing in our frequently troubled old apartment, at least until YouTube came on the scene.

Over time, I needed the books less and less—but more importantly, I realized working with my hands could bring a sense of joy and fulfillment I didn't know I missed. And I became quite the handyman. Mom bragged to the neighbors about my skills and soon everyone in the building was calling on me to fix broken doors, clogged garbage disposals, and broken bathroom tiles.

When I saw Shop as an elective freshman year, I immediately signed up. I was the stand out student, the pride of my teacher Mr. Foley. Yet with each project I came home with, Mom's enthusiasm waned just a touch, a hint of hesitation in her voice as she saw me get more active in woodworking projects. She complimented my work, but caveated that electives were meant for fun, not for earning a living.

"Your supplies, sir!" Marsh stands back stiffly, holding out the box and tape.

"Please stop calling me sir."

His face falls, and then he shakes his head. "Sorry, just trying to be … "

"Adorable," I say. "You can stop it right now." I take the items from him. "Please."

Marsh leaves me alone with my indignation. Am I being too hard on him? Knowing that he got that bad news about dad just before his big show makes everything that came after make sense. Or at least a little more sense. Humor was a lifeline for Marsh, but it couldn't work on an Alzheimer's diagnosis and he bombed on stage a day later. But still, did that completely explain why he needed space from us?

I'd like nothing more than to grab him and squeeze his

scrumptious stomach. Wrap my arms around him and kiss every inch of his handsome face before throwing him down and having my way with him. But he made it clear he needs space. He's quitting the thing he's passionate about and good at. I tried to go in the opposite direction of Mom, encouraging him to follow comedy. And yet still, it backfired. Maybe she was right all this time.

Well, Mr. Space Man can launch himself into the stratosphere and stop confusing me. I turn my attention to the broken window. It will be a quick fix, unlike the lingering fracture Marsh left in my heart.

With the window securely patched, my stomach roils at the thought of facing Marsh again. I need to be anchored. Resolute. Reaching into my pocket, I pull out my phone, hoping for a signal. With only a single bar of service, I quickly dial Bryce's number before the cell gods revoke my rights.

"Marshall? Are you alive? Did a bear eat you?"

"I wish."

"I said eat you. Not eat you *out*."

My ass tweaks remembering Marsh buried chin-deep in my hole at the General Store. Lapping me up. Tongue fucking me. Getting me ready for his thick, long …

"Marshall? Are you there? Can you hear me?"

"I'm here. Service is spotty. We're snowed in." I use a small towel to wipe the water on the windowsill where the snow has melted.

"But I thought the storm wasn't coming until next week."

"It wasn't … but the fucking chickens."

"Chickens? The reception is awful. You're breaking up. Chickens are fucking?"

"It's a Maine thing, apparently."

"That tracks," Bryce says. "Well, if you're stuck, you can finally have that breakup sex you need to move on." I move to the bed. A piece of wood I saved in my pocket from outside falls onto the comforter, like a small gift.

"About that … " I pick the timber up. When I was chopping, small shards splintered off with each cut, but this one was larger than the others. When it landed in the snow, it looked … lonely. I carefully slipped it into the safety of my pocket while Marsh was inside.

"Already? It's been a day, you sly skank." Bryce makes a kissing noise. "I've never been more proud of you."

"It just … happened. He fucked me like a madman in The General Store bathroom." My fingers glide down the smooth side of the hickory, avoiding the rough spots sure to cause a nasty splinter. The wood is hard, strong, and it would take a firm hand to carve it. I turn the wedge over in my hand, imagining the cuts I'd make. A little here. A longer push cut. Flip it, a paring cut.

Look at this craftsmanship. This makes Pottery Barn look like Ikea. Marsh's words echo in my head, taunting me with unrealistic possibilities. *You could've been a furniture maker with a store, a line of quality goods. You still can.*

Was this how Marsh felt whenever I encouraged him? Like a soothing hug curdled into suffocation? Warm support mixed with a jolt of ice cold fear?

"Good. You got some. I'm too much of a germaphobe to do it in a public toilet, but you do you, boo," Bryce says. "Now you can pack up and sell the shack."

"That's the plan. But it's been, I don't know, awkward since."

"Define awkward," he replies.

"Awkward. When something is hard or difficult to deal with. It's *awkward* how Bryce's dog loves me more than his owner."

"I know what the word means, smartass." There's some shuffling, and I picture Bryce repositioning himself on his sofa. "What's been awkward between you two? Do you think maybe you want him back?"

"It doesn't matter if I want him back, he … "

"Invited you up to your love nest for a weekend of snowed in slap and tickle."

"Not exactly. To pack. To sell. To move on. But he's been … " I put the wood down and watch the snowflakes outside the repaired window, momentarily hypnotized by the white blur.

"What?" Bryce asks, snapping me back to attention.

"Flirty? Charming? Adorable?" Marsh's face appears in my head, his sheepish grin and sexy smile once again distracting me.

"You've always thought so," Bryce says. "You love the whole hilarious himbo vibe. We all have our kinks."

"It's over though. It's just hard seeing him again. Spending time together. So close." My palm massages my stomach, and butterflies flutter as I remember it brushing up against Marsh's when he was on top of me in the basement. "I thought it would close the loop, but it hasn't."

"Ah, that's the problem. The break-up sex at the store was a start, but you need to fuck him to seal the deal. The loop is not closed. You vers boys have to fuck and be fucked to appease the breakup sex gods."

"That's not a real thing."

"Isn't it though?"

The hickory takes shape in my mind. An image revealing itself in its full beauty, and it's up to me to bring it to life. Yes. Of course, that's what it wants to be. My hands itch for my tools.

"I should go. We have packing to finish. Say a prayer I'm able to escape tomorrow." I look out the broken window. As I survey the woods, the snow seems to pick up. Awesome.

"You got it. Prayer to the breakup sex gods coming your way."

Even though he can't see me, I roll my eyes. Hard. "Bye, Bryce."

The thought of more sex with Marsh, me on top, thrusting into him, his eyes rolling back as his body falls under my spell, sends an unwanted bolt of heat from my toes to my head. Or heads. Sex has already made this weekend even more uncomfortable, despite how exhilarating it was. The breakup sex gods will have to appease themselves.

Marsh is just on the other side of that door, more awkwardness and adorableness waiting to confuse me. My whole body is jumpy, twitchy. I need to calm down before I have another sexual slipup with my ex.

Laying on the floor, I extend my arm under the bed. My fingers grasp for the case holding my carving tools hidden in the darkness. The moment I touch the supple leather, a wave of relaxation washes over me, muscle memory doing the rest.

Chapter Sixteen

Marsh

Here's the thing you need to know about Data: the man takes his time when he wants to.

Whether it's slowly eating his food while I scarf mine down, not leaving a museum exhibit until he reads every plaque, or not moving from the guest room until the window is repaired, he won't let anyone rush him.

It's been over an hour, and I can't fault him for being diligent. If it were me, I'd stuff a pillow in the opening and call it a day. I keep the door shut to block the draft that's still coming from the room.

Night begins to descend on the mountain. A dark glow shines on the fallen snow, which despite throwing a wrench in this weekend is still very pretty to look at. Nature looks especially peaceful at dusk, as if all the trees and little creatures are waiting to be tucked in and read a bedtime story.

I find a forgotten frozen pizza in the bottom of the freezer. Holding it up to the light, it doesn't look particularly appetizing, but it does look edible. I sigh. It'll do, as most of our other food falls in the snack category. I could cook us a decent meal, but dinner is not a battle worth fighting when I've insulted his line of work and his mother.

I slip the pizza into the oven so it can do its convection

magic. Who am I kidding? Even when pizza's kinda gross, it's still delicious.

I glance behind me at the guest room. Still closed. I could go in there and see what's going on, but the door is almost giving me a vibe that it should stay closed. To pass the time, I make a list of the food that's left and what can be eaten in the fridge. My list is not long. Is ketchup considered a vegetable?

"Do I smell pizza?" Data emerges from the guest room, his body relaxed as if he spent the past hour plus reading poolside with a margarita in hand. He rolls his wrist and stretches out his hand. Um … what was he doing in there?

No judgment, of course.

"I found a pizza. Did you fix the window?"

"I made a stopgap. It's still cold in there." He scoots past me, his spicy scent doing its usual thing to me. He washes his hands in the kitchen sink. "To conserve heat, we should keep the door closed."

"I guess that means we're bunking tonight." My heart speeds up a touch, a rebellious tap of the accelerator. I blame his scent and strong hands.

"It does not." He dries his hands on a dish towel, his relaxed vibe fading quicker than the heat in the guest room.

"Where are you going to sleep? There's only one usable bed left." I nudge my chin at the main bedroom. Our bedroom.

"The couch will be fine," he says.

"It's a loveseat. We barely fit sitting and you're going to sleep on it?"

"I've napped on it. I'll make it work."

"You're not a twenty-five-year-old crashing on a couch. You're going to wake up with a bad back. Trust me on this. Sleeping on a couch isn't enjoyable," I tell him.

Data scrunches his eyebrows together in that quizzical way that makes my stomach flip.

"I've been crashing on Preeti's couch since we … since I moved out."

"Marsh." He puts his hand on his heart. "I've been to her apartment. That's not a comfortable couch."

"You don't need to tell me." I shrug.

"And it's a studio," he adds.

"We thumbtacked an old tablecloth to the ceiling for privacy." Sadly, tablecloths aren't soundproof.

"Good Lord, that sounds depressing."

"It's a roof over my head. And it's only temporary," I reply with a confident nod. I want him to know I'm okay.

"Babe." The word slips so easily from his lips. It catches Data off guard, and I don't correct him. "If you need money, I …"

I hold up my hand, refusing to go down that path. I don't deserve his sympathy, and I sure as hell don't deserve his money. I made my uncomfortable couch, and I must lay in it.

"Once we sell this place, I'll be able to get my own apartment."

"Yeah. Right. That's good. I'm gonna … " Data points to scoot past me once more. This time, I create ample space to let him pass. No spicy scent sniffing.

"How is the apartment? What's the scoop on The Bigby?"

"Same old. The steps between the second and third floors are still shaky. Mrs. Krumholtz is continuing her crusade to ban people from using the rooftop for parties. Horton's parrot won't shut up no matter how much Mrs. Lee yells at it from her balcony. Carl thinks being the super simply is a title and doesn't mean he needs to actually fix anything. And Bryce and Anthony are being very Bryce and Anthony."

The updates tug at me unexpectedly. Kooky neighbors are like family. Annoying as shit, but forever holding a place in your heart. I didn't just lose a boyfriend and a place to sleep when I broke up with Data.

"Bryce says hello, by the way."

"No, he doesn't." I know Bryce. The man never met a piece of drama he couldn't find a way to insert himself into. As I was moving out of the apartment, he stopped me in the hall, and whispered "I wish you well" into my ear, exactly as Gwyneth Paltrow did to the man who sued her and lost.

"What's Bryce saying about me?" I ask. "Let me guess: something about the breakup gods enacting revenge."

Data's eyes bulge open, a deer caught in some kind of headlights.

"You okay?"

"I'm going to pack up some more books." He turns to the waiting piles on the floor. I packed up some earlier today, but there's always more.

I was never a book person until we bought this cabin. A cozy stove and lots of chunky blankets make for a perfect reading environment. After a leisurely hike in warmer months, I'd make us fresh lemonade, and we'd sit out back, reading, and sipping our drinks. In colder months, we'd snuggle on the small couch or just stay in bed, alternating between canoodling, reading, and other physical activities. It was the perfect antidote to a stressful week in the NYC grind.

"Why do we have so many books?" Data flips through a used Emily Henry book likely picked up for a quarter from the thrift shop.

"Because you didn't want a TV up here. You thought it would kill the romance."

"Yeah, we managed to do that on our own," Data says with a loaded sigh. If only a breakup could kill the romance between two people. Too bad love is stronger than we think.

The oven dings. I retreat to the kitchen to pull out the pizza. The warm aroma of the cheese makes my stomach growl. Yep, totally edible.

"Another thing," he says, when I bring it to the living room on plates for us. An accounting textbook sits on his lap. "Maybe accounting isn't my passion, but I don't hate it. I like figuring out problems and finding order. There may be no art to it, but I'm proud of the work I do."

"And you're damn good at it. I should've said that before." I wave behind me. Before meaning earlier today, and years ago. "I think I took out some of my job frustration on yours. Anyone who's able to justify my Chipotle lunches as a legitimate business expense is a master at their craft."

Data flashes me a supportive smile, one full of long-wanted appreciation. "Speaking of food, this is the least appetizing pizza I've ever had."

As soon as I take a bite, I have to agree. It's the flat cola of pizza. The ingredients are there, but the taste is not.

"Maybe we can try to go to the General Store for another food run tomorrow," I say. "Maybe Duffy is selling eggs. I could go for a good omelet."

"Marsh." He shoves my shoulder.

"Ow."

"That's it! Duffy!"

"Duffy? What about Duffy?" Aside from the fact that he gets all of his news from the bulletin board in the store, Maddi's husband is a sweet guy. He co-runs the store with her and sells eggs and meat at local farmers markets.

"Remember when we were last here over the summer, and Duffy was talking about getting a plow installed on his truck to make some extra money?"

"You remember that?"

"Yes, because all the way home, you kept making jokes about how much you love plowing and getting plowed. Ha ha, we get it. Plowing. Double entendres. Honestly, I think those jokes were beneath you."

"Fair, but if I recall correctly, later that day, so were you."

Data's cheeks go red. My pants get tight. Fortunately, I have Emily Henry to shield my erection.

"Anyway, if Duffy has a plow, he can clear our driveway and access road, and we'll be able to get out of here." Data paces with possibility. "Maybe we can even get out on schedule."

"Sweet." I jam half a slice of cardboard pizza into my mouth, a familiar twinge tightening inside me.

"First thing tomorrow, we're going to The General Store." Data is like a kid who can't wait to wake up on Christmas morning.

I give him a salute, even if my heart's not in it.

Chapter Seventeen

~~Data~~ Marshall

For such a small cabin, you'd think we'd be able to pack everything up quickly. You'd be completely wrong. That's the thing they don't tell you about relationships: you accumulate a lot of crap. Every time we wanted something that wouldn't fit in our tiny city apartment, we rationalized buying it by hauling it up to our tiny mountain cabin. Over the years, as our city dwelling remained organized and tidy, the cabin became cluttered. And now we have to wrap it all up in Darren Criss' beautiful face and shove it into a box.

Standing in the kitchen, I'm overwhelmed by just how much we have left to do. After our pizza dinner, I suggested we squeeze in a touch more packing. The more we do today, the less we'll have to do tomorrow, the more likely we'll stay on schedule. I hope that my Duffy plan works. Bryce's breakup sex part two idea lingers in my head. It'd be a bad idea to act on it no matter what he says.

We pull out every unturned stone in the common area, emptying every last drawer and every last closet. The mess of our relationship piled before us.

"Do you want this?" Marsh holds up a beige and powder blue metal tin. I think it came with shortbread cookies wrapped in delicate paper we ravished like dogs after fucking in the woods like rabbits.

I shake my head, hoping he doesn't remember the carnal memories attached to it. He glances at the tin, rubs his fingers over the lid, and tosses it in the trash pile. A hollowness burrows in my chest as I survey the chaos scattered across our once cozy living room. The finality of throwing everything away hits me like a Mack truck.

"Hey, I have an idea," Marsh says.

"That's never good for me." I mean it as a joke, but in our current situation, it falls completely flat.

"For everything we pack, we have to share a memory about it."

Our eyes lock onto the abandoned cookie tin.

"PG stories," I say.

"Or at least PG-13." Marsh kicks the tin, and a broken umbrella from the pile falls, thankfully, finally concealing it.

"I'll go first," he says, grabbing a brightly colored pitcher. "We bought this at a flea market in Massachusetts on the drive up." Marsh runs his fingers over the smooth surface. "You loved the colors. And thought it would be lovely for parties."

"Which we never have here."

"Because there's barely room for us, let alone a party." He pulls his lips in, surveying the back of the pitcher.

"We don't know anyone but Maddi and Duffy."

"And the chickens," Marsh adds.

"Fucking chickens."

Marsh holds the pitcher up. I'm not sure if I'm supposed to say something else about it, or simply decide its fate.

"Keep it," I say. "It's too pretty to toss."

"Agreed," he answers, grabbing some newspaper and wrapping it carefully. "Okay, your turn."

I glance around the room. We've accumulated an excessive amount of possessions. Why we thought the cabin would expand with all our junk is beyond me. The usual messiness has escalated to packing level messiness and I try to find something safe to talk about and store away.

"Ah, here." I pick up the pen set my mother bought me when I landed the job at Baker & Gray.

"Your mom bought you that." Marsh takes a step closer. "She was so proud of you."

"She was. After working at a small firm for years, her son finally was hired by one of the Big Four. She knew I'd be okay." My eyes flick up and meet Marsh's. "At least financially."

"Data. Marshall. I'm … " He bites at his lower lip.

"What?" I ask. Slowly but surely, he has been revealing the cards he holds close to his chest throughout the weekend, and I'm eager to uncover the next one.

"I'm sorry."

He's sorry? For what? For breaking my heart? For hauling me up to the cabin to pack and sell the last vestige of our relationship? For telling me he missed me while fucking me silly in The General Store bathroom? My eyebrows lift, and as usual, Marsh fills the dead air.

"For what I said … about you … and your mom."

Oh, that.

"I was out of line."

Marsh's apology warms my insides.

"And I'm sorry."

"Thank you." I bite at my lower lip, my whiskers prickling my tongue as I stare at the pen set. My mom thought I'd use the pens for work. Of course, it's all done on computers, but I wasn't telling her that. I should've brought it to my office, but I let my embarrassment stop me. I didn't want to be teased about a gift from my 'mommy' and, like so many lost precious items, the pen set found its way up to Marshmallow Mountain.

"Thing is … " I swallow past the golf ball-sized lump in my throat. "You're not wrong."

He falls silent and I steal a glance to make sure he's still breathing. I cock my head, waiting for his reply, but he remains quiet.

"What?" I ask.

"While usually I'd celebrate the fact that you said I was right, I don't know … I know your relationship with your mom is complicated."

Marsh never got to have a complicated relationship with his mom, just as I never had one with my dad. There's a part of our hearts that the other can never know.

"Well, it's true." I run my fingers over the engraving in the center of the plaque holding the two pens—'Marshall Kaplan, CPA.'

"This had to cost mom two weeks' salary. She can't afford that. I'm going to sell it and give her the money back." I place the set in the pawn pile.

"Data, she wanted to spend the money on her son. She's proud of you."

"I know, but it's silly. On pens? That I literally never use."

Marsh sits next to me, holding a sheet of newspaper.

"Here, let's wrap it carefully." He unfolds the paper on the floor and I place the set on it.

"But you were right. I don't want to disappoint her." I fold the paper over the top, wrapping it tightly. "It's not like your family. I know you lost your mom when you were little, but you have a brother, and family nearby. I'm all my mother has. She's finally letting me help her a little, but we've always struggled with money."

Growing up, Mom always worked two jobs. Sometimes three. People think working as a check processor for a large bank would pay well, but living in the tri-state area, everything was expensive. Mom would clean rooms at a local hotel on weekends and when I was old enough, I immediately got a job scooping ice cream at The Dairy King—definitely no relation to the famous franchise. Unlike my friends who used their money for movies, gas, and clothes, my wages went directly to Mom.

Marsh picks the pen set up, inspects to ensure it's properly wrapped, and places it in a box. "I know, Data."

He gives me a reassuring soft smile and fuck, my heart aches for this. Him. Us. Tears nip the corners of my eyes and I'm not sure if it's thinking about my mom and the damn pen set or missing my partner and the life I thought we were creating together. Mom has always wanted me to be financially secure, but surely she also wants me to have a full life with a loving partner. Right?

In a moment of weakness, I lean my head on his shoulder, and the way my heart thumps at his warmth can't be bought. It can't be replicated with a secure job and flush bank account. Being so close, this isn't like the bathroom at the store. This isn't the jizz-covered Mallomar. This is what I've missed most. Marsh rests his head on mine, his warm breath blowing my hair as he sighs—he has the ability to reset my barometer. Maybe the harsh realities of life caused Mom to stop believing in love, to only focus on what she could control. I wish things could've been different for her.

Being cocooned in Marsh's arms, I realize that I need more. I need the freedom of being vulnerable with someone. I need the security that can only come with a tight hug that crashes my face into the other person's chest. I need someone I can fall apart around and know that he'll catch me every time.

With Marsh's fingers caressing my chin, I tilt my face towards him, our lips close enough to touch.

"Anyway," Marsh says, and he's up, scratching at his neck and grabbing an old ceramic emerald green vase. "You just had to have this. It's kind of ugly, but you insisted we needed something for the wildflowers we picked while hiking."

My throat closes up like a vice grip. With a heavy sigh, I

stand and head for the couch. I can't handle another memory tonight.

"I'm gonna go to bed."

Marsh nods, his jaw tight. "There are extra blankets—"

"Top shelf. Hall closet. I know."

"Right." He turns back to me, as if he's about to hug me but stops himself. "Good night, Marshall."

"Good night, Marshall," I reply. I've never hated the way my name sounds as much as I do now.

Chapter Eighteen

Marsh

Here's the thing you need to know about Data: despite always feeling cold, his body is essentially a human-shaped weighted blanket that radiates warmth.

I never slept so well as I did when we were together. Whether I was big spoon or little spoon, having Data's thick body pressing against mine lulled me into a deep sleep. And sure, there were times where we had a tug of war over the blankets, or where I'd try to sneak his pillow in the middle of the night because it was firmer than mine, even though they were the same kind. But whenever his arms pulled me close, they seemed to shut out the world and quiet all the nonstop chatter in my head.

That's the thing nobody tells you about breaking up with someone: it fucks with your sleep.

I've slept like shit for the past six months. Tossing and turning as if searching for something perpetually out of grasp. Waking up with weird back pain as my body tries to adjust to a Data-less sleep position.

And having him under the same roof as me and not sharing a bed is making my insomnia extra severe. Last night, I barely slept, and tonight looks to be a repeat.

I glimpse the large, red numbers on the clock by my bed. 2:18.

My body is exhausted from a day of packing, but my mind is acting like it mainlined espresso right before bedtime. I stare at the ceiling, the pathetic light hanging above me. Since I arrived, I've had a highlight reel from our relationship playing in my head, and it refuses to turn off. If anything, it's only gotten louder.

I've been doing my best to keep my distance from Data, to act cordially so we can be on good terms. But it's hard. Really hard. Harder than that time I tried to be a vegetarian, which lasted all of six hours.

God, holding him close as he talked about his mom and those fakakta pens, I almost broke. I almost kissed him and refused to let him go. My attempts to resist our sexual chemistry have been, shall we say, lackluster.

Yes, I want to put my hands and tongue everywhere on his body, but I also want to laugh with him, share inside jokes with him, sit in comfortable silence with him, and relish in the feeling of him taking up space with me. I want to tell him that he is the most wonderful, thoughtful son a mother could have. I want to talk to him about how my financial sitch is a mess because he would know what to do. I want to tell him how scared I am that it's never going to happen for me with comedy, and that I've thrown away a family business for nothing. I want to talk to him about how fucking scared I am about taking care of my dad. I want him to hold me in his arms and tell me everything will be okay—my flailing career, my bank account, my dad, and my life. That I haven't completely fucked it all up. That I am the man he still believes in. That there's still hope.

I sit up. No use going through the motions of sleep when it's not happening.

I turn to the clock again and its bright numbers.

2:21.

Why does my spiraling take up so little time?

I throw the covers off and walk to the door. That's another

thing. I'm not used to sleeping with a closed bedroom door. My lungs prefer proper air circulation.

I creep into the hallway, only a few steps away from the kitchen. Immediately, I'm hit by the temperature change. It's a good five degrees colder out here. I tiptoe as best I can, making sure to step on the rug, not the creaky floorboards. Strips of moonlight slash between the trees and through the windows, providing enough glow for me to find the cabinet with the snacks. I take out a bag of Fritos ever so slowly. With the snacks in hand I let out a soft sigh. Fritos have never let me down.

I peek past the kitchen counter into the living room.

Data's up.

Well, he looks asleep, and most people would assume he's asleep. People who don't know him inside and out. He's smushed his body into a ball on the loveseat, legs tucked into his stomach with his eyes squeezed shut. Cat-like. Yet after sleeping next to the man for almost a decade, I can tell he's actually awake.

"Hey," I say when I sit on the arm of the loveseat. Data's eyes spring open and I turn the bag of chips to him. "Frito?" I ask, doing my best to roll the R.

He groans, but winds up taking a chip. "I was sleeping," he says.

"No you weren't." Data reaches in for another chip and I pull the bag back playfully before relenting. "You hate sleeping in the fetal position. You need space to stretch."

"I can manage."

"Your ass was falling off the couch."

"Must you always notice my ass?" he asks.

"It's very noticeable."

Data takes another chip.

"Why don't you just take a handful?" I ask.

"So half of them can fall in my lap like yours?" he shoots back.

I prefer scooping out a handful of chips and resting them on my stomach, whereas Data picks out and eats one chip at a time.

"You're not comfortable here," I tell him. "Why don't you share the bed with me?"

"We are not sharing a bed," he says adamantly, a flash of panic behind his eyes. "I will be fine here." He taps the loveseat, perhaps a little too forcefully.

"You've never been able to sleep on it. And it's cold out here."

"It's a little drafty, but I'm all right."

"You're going to get sick." I stand up defiant. I should've pushed for this before we went to sleep. I feel bad that he's tossed and turned on a too small couch in a drafty living room. "You're sharing the bed with me."

"Marsh, I'm f—"

"Nope. You will not use the word fine. The only f-word I'll allow to be uttered is Frito Lay." I hold up the bag. "Maker of these chips."

Data falls back on the loveseat and whips the blanket back over himself. I forgot how damn stubborn he can be.

I stand over him, crossing my arms. "You're not sleeping out here. I may lack upper arm strength, but I *will* find a way to carry you into the bedroom if I have to."

"Marsh … "

I hold up my hands, the chip bag rustling between my fingers. "I promise only sleeping will occur. I will keep my hands to myself. If I spring a boner, you have permission to chop it off."

Data huffs out a breath through his nostrils. Is it weird I find it cute? I don't look at other people and swoon when their nostrils flare.

The struggle hiding behind his eyes is real. I know this will be awkward, but it doesn't have to be. We need rest. He can't sleep in the cold.

I can make it through one night of sharing a bed. Hell, I once went six hours without meat. This will be a cakewalk compared to that.

"Okay." He collects his blanket into a ball and shoves his pillow under his arm. He winces and hisses as he maneuvers himself off the loveseat. Almost fortysomething bodies aren't made to crash on couches.

I extend a hand, which he swats away.

"I don't need help."

"Okay, Grandpa."

Data grabs my hand. I pull back to lift. And maybe my upper arm strength is better than I thought because he launches off the loveseat and lands smack against my chest, our faces and lips perilously close.

He licks his lips, whether from the salty chips, the dry air, or something else entirely.

"Thanks." He steps back and heads into the bedroom before I can reply.

I promised him no boners, and I'm going to do my damndest to keep that promise. Glancing at my crotch I say, "Behave."

I thought sleeping in bed without Data was hell. Nope. Not even close. It was hell adjacent. It was Florida.

The real hell is sleeping in a bed with Data and not being able to lay a finger on him. My heated, human weighted blanket is purposefully out of reach. He's asleep, his back moving up and down in gentle rhythm. I turn away from him and face my alarm clock.

3:04.

I can do this. I've fallen asleep pretty much every single night of my life. I can do it again. No biggie. Pretend that Data is a pile of clean laundry that I was too lazy to fold.

I shut my eyes and take deep breaths, avoiding the tightness in my chest. The peaceful lull of sleep begins to drag me under, but like a wave retreating back to the ocean, it's gone just as fast.

Shit.

I flip around to my other side wondering if that'll do the trick. When I do, I find Data staring at me in a cold, unblinking gaze, almost making me wonder if he's sleeping with his eyes open.

I study him for a moment, trying to gauge where in his REM cycle he might be, when he grabs me by the shirt and pulls me to him. His mouth covers mine, fills me with his hot Frito breath. As his lips meet mine, he groans, his primal grunts of lust filling the air, his fist clenching my shirt tightly.

I don't dare speak. Following his lead, I take everything he's giving. I grab his love handles and pull him flush against me, feeling his erection press into my thigh. Fluttering overtakes my chest and travels down to my stomach, landing in my groin where it sends a jolt of blood to my dick.

Data reaches down my pajama pants and wraps his fingers around my cock like it's a set of car keys he'd been searching for.

"God," I moan against his lips, wondering how I made it six months—fuck, try six minutes—without the feel of his hot skin.

I wait for him to be the one to pull back, to say something, to comment about what's going on, to slam on the brakes, but he's silent. Only our huffs and moans and smacking lips fill the empty air.

I run my fingers through his hair, thick strands mussed up

from bed. The pads of my thumbs prickle over his beard, that beard I could set up permanent residence in. Our tongues slide over each other as I pull his face closer to mine.

My greedy fingers travel down his chest, pinch at his nipples, bump over the lumps of torso and through the grainy hairs. I savor every inch of him. The weight of him on me. The indulgence and *more*ness of his body, that it's all for me in this moment.

He strokes me faster. I hump up to meet his fist. His hand is dry and it's a little rough, but I ain't complaining. I wrap my arms around him and pull him close, smashing us together.

Data wrests from my grip just as fast. He sits up on his knees. I meet his gaze, and that same fixed stare is on me, as if he's forcing himself to stay in the zone and keep this as "just sex" as he can. He is a man on a mission, and there will be no detours.

He pushes down his pajama pants and underwear and scoots closer to my head. His cock is slick with precum and engorged, bobbing from the quick movement.

"Suck," Data commands, his jaw tight.

I only have to sit up a bit to meet his dick. My throat practically throws it a damn homecoming parade. I lap up its salty taste. My tongue slips around the head and slinks down the shaft. I take him all the way down, my head bumping into his furry stomach each time he fills me up.

He says nothing, only unleashes unabashedly loud grunts that echo with as much pain as pleasure. His fingers dig into the back of my head as he pushes me down on him, his bulbous cockhead filling my throat like a cork. I moan against him, wanting all of this.

I stroke him as fast as I suck, my hand-mouth coordination so in sync you could set the atomic clock to it. I'm determined for this blow job to live on in his memory. When he's ninety and surrounded by his twenty grandkids, he'll remember he once dated a failed comic with a mouth of gold. I have my faults, but giving mediocre head is not one of them. My neck aches from the odd angle, but I power through.

Data lifts his cock and presents his balls, all for the taking. I swirl a tongue around one, let his musky scent swarm my nostrils. My face is fucking full of him, but still it's not enough. It'll never be enough because I know it's only temporary. I clamp a hand on his thick thigh, fluttering my fingers over his hair.

"Fuck. You taste so good. Want your cum," I sputter out, my lungs claiming each new gasp of air as a victory.

"Not yet," he says, his voice deep. "Lift your legs."

The *take off your underwear* part was implied. My cock throbs even harder at the instruction. Data pulls back, giving me space to feverishly tear off the clothing rudely covering up my manliest bits. I hurl my boxers into the corner of the room. Fuck you, boxers!

I throw my legs in the air and hold them, the draft from outside suddenly hitting me. My hole is exposed, and I'm desperately counting down the seconds until it's fucked full of Data. He pulls the lube from the bedside table and slicks himself up. Moonlight slashes through the window, cloaking him in a milky glow. His eyes flick to me with a heavy-lidded stare drunk with lust—and only lust.

"Yes," I moan out when he leans down. He hasn't even made contact with my ass, and I'm already giddy and begging like a dog at the dinner table.

And then the scruff of his beard hits my most sensitive area. Data knows how this makes me squirm in all the best ways. He rubs it up and down my taint in a slow, controlled rhythm, eliciting an unending current of electricity up my spine. It's coarse and dirty and manly in a way I can't describe. If I was able to grow facial hair like him, I'd totally reciprocate.

"God, Data. Don't stop. Please don't stop." Only I'm lying because I want him to stop so he can fuck me into Canada.

His tongue makes contact with my hole, circling the rim, sliding up my crack, sending a new rush of feeling to flood my nervous system. He pulls back and spits on it, presses a thumb inside me to open me up. He slips his digit in and out a few times, more for practical purposes than foreplay. Data can be very attentive when he wants to be, but there is a momentum happening between us that neither of us want to slow. Sometimes sex is making love, and sometimes it's fucking. This is fucking.

He coats my opening with lube. I pull my legs closer to my stomach, dizzy with anticipation. It's like I've moved up in line and am next to ride the roller coaster.

He kneels over me, his big, beefy chest heaving for air. I meet his eyes. Behind the lust and mission-focus, there's warmth hiding way in the back. He's so beautiful I can't stand it.

"Data, I ... "

He pushes his fingers against my lips. "Don't. Don't say it, Marsh. Don't say it." His voice is trying so damn hard to be firm, but it wobbles at the end, and it comes out as part-command and part-plea. "This is break-up sex part two. Closing the loop once and for all."

And with that, he presses inside me with ravenous thrusts that are painful for both of us. He grabs my legs and slams into me, his cock plunging in all the way. I arch my back to take him even deeper. Sweat drips down his chest. I love the way his gut hangs out and proudly takes up space as he fucks me. I love the sounds of our skin making contact. I love knowing he's inside me, filling me up.

My raging hard cock flaps against my stomach as he plows into me. Data gives it a stroke, hurtling me to the edge. My stamina withers in the face of his lust.

"Give it to me," I beg.

I try to meet his eyes, but he's looking down, watching himself rail me.

"I'm going to come," I cry out, my body tensing.

And then suddenly he pulls out. "No," he says, almost in a growl.

He pushes my legs down, and before I can make sense of what's going on, he's slicking my cock up with lube and straddling me. His big torso hangs in my face. He reaches behind himself and gets his ass prepped. My head spins as my cock tingles with need.

Data glares at me, his forehead wrinkled with determination as he impales himself on my cock. He bounces up and down, his beefy chest and commanding stomach right in my face and unbearably hot. There's both too much and not enough of him. I soon realize that my job is to lay there. I am a mechanical bull being taken for a ride, a human dildo fulfilling its owner's needs. He is going to fuck the orgasm out of both of us.

"Yes," he whines each time he falls back onto my dick.

I get him to meet my eyes. He stares back, his face strangled with heat and emotion, refusing to let me in. Our bodies are as close as could be, and yet he's never felt so far away.

His ass tightens around my cock as he shoots his load, cum splattering my stomach. His body loosens up in real time, as if he discovered a newfound peace with break-up sex part two.

"Come for me, Marsh," he says, his raspy voice cutting through the quiet.

The sound of my name on his lips is enough to keep me in the game. It's a thread that keeps us tethered just long enough for me to empty inside him.

He dismounts me and stands up, refusing to spend a second in post-coital bliss. He walks to the bathroom door and turns back. He begins nodding a few seconds before he speaks. "We needed to do that. The break-up sex gods are appeased."

And then he's gone, leaving me alone in the dark, wondering how the hell I'm ever going to get to sleep.

Chapter Nineteen

~~D~~ata Marshall

My back hurts from this damn loveseat. My ass hurts from … Oh my god. What did I do? Why does my ass hurt? And then it comes crashing back, like a vivid dream, except, nope, not a dream. It really happened—Breakup Sex Part Two, The Flip Fuck Fantasy. Apparently, my ability to keep my feelings for Marsh bottled up seems to falter whenever I'm within six feet of him. Over the eight years since we met at Pauline's, the magnetic force that drew me to him has grown stronger. Coming here, spending time alone with him. What did I think would happen?

The muscles in my lower back spasm, and I twist to change positions, but there's only one way for me to fit on this loveseat, and I'm unable to stop the discomfort. Marsh knows I can't sleep on this fakakta couch. Was he trying to be sweet inviting me to sleep next to him or was he hoping I'd attack him like a wolf being fed steak after days of searching for a meal? There was no way I was going back to bed after … that. I grabbed the extra comforter from the bed and made the best of it. Almost forty-year-old back be damned.

I should be embarrassed by my behavior. Ashamed at how I pounced. Commanded. Took control. But I'm not. Marsh does something to me I've yet to experience with anyone else. It's electric. And he was willing. Able. Hard. Begging for it. To be fucked. Slamming into him, my cock throbbing inside his hungry hole, and then riding his fat dick until I finished. All over his broad chest. Oy. Awesome, now I'm hard. My cock throbs under the blanket and why didn't I grab my boxers before escaping to the sofa?

It's still dark out and I grab my phone and see it's almost seven. The sun should be out. I quickly check the weather and I see the snow should let up in an hour or two. But there's another winter storm warning in effect tomorrow. Wonderful. Fantastic. Fucking chickens. They belong on a spit roast at Costco, not bungling the forecast. I pull the comforter under my chin, attempting to shield myself from the chilly air. Before returning my phone to the coffee table, I notice the battery is at thirty-five percent and plug it in. Ignoring my raging boner, I wrap the blanket around me like a giant shawl and head to the guest room for clothes and to check the window.

Unlike my life, the temporary repair seems to be intact. There's a slight draft, but nothing that would account for the cold in the living room with the door shut. Hmm. The hickory I began carving yesterday morning sits on the bed. My tools are strewn about like lost toys waiting to be found. I gather them into the carrying pouch, tuck the wood under my arm, and head back to my uncomfortable home on the sofa with thoughts about the piece's next steps.

Carving the hickory yesterday helped clear my head. Maybe I'll have the same luck again.

"Morning." Marsh stands by the couch naked from the waist down, doing his best Winnie the Pooh impression. He yawns and stretches, and his shirt rises, exposing his smooth, sexy belly. His semi-hard dick taunts me and, for a moment, I'm tempted to throw him back on the bed, toss his legs over his head, and repeat the beard on taint activities from last night.

"You're naked," I say.

"I'm wearing a shirt. I'm cosplaying as Winnie the Pooh." Marsh scratches his belly and how is he able to crawl inside my brain and know exactly what I'm thinking? "And anyway," he continues, "so are you. Unless wearing blankets as skirts is a new fashion trend I missed."

Marsh nods to my cock. With a mind of its own, especially around him, I'm also hard. Fuck.

In an alternate universe, this is where we'd have amazing morning sex. Marsh would have his way with me, the two of us moaning and wailing with pleasure—not a neighbor for miles to disturb.

"And you seem to be … excited," Marsh says, taking a step toward me.

"No, it's morning wood. It's a natural bodily function."

"So is fornication."

I grab another blanket and throw it over my crotch.

"Well, that solves one problem." Marsh rolls his eyes and sits on the couch. "We have a bigger one, though: the power's out."

"What?" Panic sends my jaw to the ice cold floor. "Shit. That's why my phone didn't charge." I retrieve it and unplug it from the wall.

"And why it's so cold in here," Marsh says, tugging at my blanket skirt. "Sit. Share, please."

The two of us naked, with semi-hard cocks under a throw, probably isn't wise. "Get your own."

"Okay, not in a sharing mood. Noted," Marsh says. "You didn't seem to mind last night. For the record, I kept my promise. I did not make a move. That was all you. You were like the titular alien from *Alien* lurching at me and suctioning your tentacles to my face and … other regions."

"Do we have to talk about it?" I ask, even though I'm pretty sure ignoring the hot-as-hell porn sex we had isn't an option. At a minimum, he'll want to joke about it.

"I mean, we haven't had porn sex in a long time, so … yeah, we probably should."

"Get out of my head!" I shout. Keeping myself covered, I'm like an actress trying to walk down a red carpet in couture. I march into the bedroom, yank the rumpled comforter from the bed, return to the loveseat, and throw it at Marsh. "There."

Keeping as much distance between us as possible, I sit, cover myself, and tuck my blanket under my legs tightly, doing my best to create a makeshift chastity belt.

"You good?" Marsh asks.

No, I'm not good. I'm stuck in a cabin with my ex who broke my heart six months ago and is now attempting to pick his way inside to do more damage by having amazing sex with me multiple times before we pack up and sell the damn place. I should write a country song.

"I'm fine." I glance out the window. The snow is thicker than the comforter Marsh is currently adjusting himself under. The certainty I had in my plan last night falters in the harsh white light of day. "Marsh, we're snowed in. Our driveway hasn't been plowed. The access road hasn't been plowed. We're not even sure if the main roads have been plowed."

Marsh grins and opens his mouth, but I interrupt him. "I swear, if you make a joke about plowing me, being plowed, or use the word plow in any form, I will scream."

With a firm nod, Marsh closes his mouth.

"Let's have some breakfast," I say. As I stand, I tightly wrap myself in the warm blanket, tucking in the loose end securely before making my way to the kitchen. "Then we'll figure out when or even if we can head to The General Store. We don't even know if they're open."

"Breakfast. Yes. Food first. That's my Data." He bites his lip, a human record scratch.

"'That's my Data' is actually an ancient Hebrew expression that means 'breakfast time.'"

With this, I take a deep breath, holding it for a moment, grateful I'm not facing Marsh and he doesn't see the complete frustration on my face.

"Are you feeling magically delicious, or do you prefer a monster for breakfast?" Marsh's eyebrows pop up and he holds both boxes up for me.

"How do two grown men only have cereal options fit for a nine-year-old?" I ask, even though I'm secretly glad we were never a Cheerios or Corn Flakes couple.

"A monster it is," he says, handing me the Franken Berry. "You always steal the strawberry marshmallows from my Charms, anyway."

"You don't have to make a joke out of everything."

"Right. Because it's better to eat breakfast in awkward silence."

I take the box and sit. Of course, Marsh is right. Again. Are we sure he's the one that's usually wrong about stuff? He begins pouring cereal, the smell of sugar making my stomach grumble.

I do prefer the strawberry marshmallows and when forced to eat Lucky Charms will pilfer all of them from his bowl. But he always lets me. He usually helps me gather them up, saying "Strawberries for my peach." My eyes sting for a moment. Marsh. Who literally gives me the strawberry marshmallows from his cereal, the best ones, the gold standard, the epitome of marshmallows, and yet thinks we're better off alone. He sure didn't seem to think so when my beard and tongue were tickling his taint last night.

"So, about last night," Marsh says, already harvesting the strawberry marshmallows out of his bowl for me. "*Are* we gonna talk about it?"

I take a deep inhale. "Breakup sex."

"Part two. The Empire Breaks My Back. Part two. 2 Butts 2 Furious."

"Marsh."

"If we do it again, then part three should be called Fuck Hard: With a Vengeance."

I try not to laugh, but I'm too tired, too hungry, and too cold to hold it in.

Marsh picks at his cereal, searching. "You know, if we keep having breakup sex, we'll eventually smash our relationship to bits. I mean, if that's what you want."

"What? No. Wait, yes. I mean smashed to bits. Not more sex." Heat consumes my neck, crawling up to my face. "Stop confusing me."

Marsh and his jokes. He's playing with my head. I'm supposed to be furious with him. He insisted we end things. Insisted on selling the cabin. Asked for help. And now we're going to freeze to death up here. Without pants on.

"We need to pack up and get out of here," I say. Finally finished with his marshmallow excavation, Marsh pours milk for both of us. "So we can sell."

He says nothing—not even a joke.

"That's what you want, right?" I ask.

"Right." He shovels Lucky Charms in his mouth, milk dribbles on his chin and my fingers twitch with the desire to wipe it for him.

"We should try to hike to the store this morning. I guarantee it'll be open. Maddi would never let the snow get the better of her," he says. "Bring backpacks. Charge our phones. Grab more Mallomars."

I swallow back a mammoth-sized lump in my throat. I can still taste the chocolate mixed with his fingers on my tongue.

"I'll go. You can't hike three miles in the snow," I say. His asthma and the bitter cold do not mix well. Even during warmer months, our longer treks made me anxious.

"Oh sure, I'll stay here like a damsel in distress," Marsh covers his head with his napkin, a makeshift wig, "while you go out for provisions." He shakes his head back and forth, swaying the napkin like a valley girl tossing her hair. "You're not going alone. I'll be fine."

I sigh, knowing there's no arguing with his stubbornness.

"Fine, but we're taking it slow."

"Yes, sir!" He salutes, knocking his cotton wig off. "Crap."

I fight back a grin, but I savor this crumb of nostalgia for the good times we had so easily.

"We could stand another bag of Fritos." I spot the open bag on the counter. "I may have eaten more last night after … ."

"Burning tons of calories from the amazing porn sex we're still not talking about?"

I drop my spoon and the pink tinged milk splashes onto the table.

"What exactly do you want to talk about, Marsh?" I jut my head forward. "It was hot, and it happened. We had to get it out of our systems completely. It's over. Just like us. You made that perfectly clear." Unconsciously, I wipe the remnants of cereal from his chin. Like all messes, somebody has to be the one to clean it up.

"Data … " He reaches for my hand, but I pull it away. Being comforted by the person who caused the pain makes no sense. Does a tiger console the gazelle it's mauled?

"Finish," I say. "I'm going to brush my teeth and get dressed. We should try to leave within a half hour." I march off to the bathroom, my blanket-skirt falling, exposing my plump ass before I yank it up to my chest.

"It's fucking cold out here," Marsh says.

We're bundled up like two adult versions of the kid from *A*

Christmas Story. With our backpacks strapped on, we clomp through the soft snow, packing a path toward the access road.

"Thanks for the weather report," I reply. He either doesn't hear me or chooses to ignore my sass.

"How far is it?" he asks, leading the way. I do my best to follow his tracks.

"A mile or so to the main road. Then another two to the store."

"We can do that." Marsh raises his hand to block the sun. It's attempting to peek through the clouds, the snow taking a reprieve, perhaps to ease our trek.

"We've hiked further," I say, moving next to him. Snow seems to blanket the entire universe, and the quiet is palpable—the sound of our breathing and soft snow crunching under our feet is the only noise. Marsh and I used to love taking hikes. Not so much in a blizzard, but daily walks around the property—finding new landmarks and quiet places to rest, eat, and make out—were a significant part of our time here.

"We have." Marsh pats my back and my chest warms. Even through long Johns, sweats, coats, and mittens, his touch sparks something deep inside. I'm tempted to pull away, attempt an escape, but, at least for now, we're in this adventure together.

"Ah, the rock." Marsh nods towards a spot off the access road. An enormous boulder near the iced over pond looms. It's covered in snow now, but in warmer months, after a dip in the pond, the giant stone provided a place for our suits to dry. Plastered against the warm rock, we'd lay naked on towels. Snacking on chips, Mallomars, and … each other. The verve of sex on a towel in the woods was something special, nothing between the balmy breeze and our bare skin. We knew there was nobody within earshot, but having that slight chance of being caught while we ravaged each other with only the wildlife to witness the action somehow made it all the hotter. Almost like … last night.

"Yeah, good times," I reply, wiping my brow. Somehow, in the frigid air, I'm shvitzing.

"So, you really are okay at work?"

I trip on something. Perhaps a root. A branch. My ego.

"It's fine." My heart races the moment the words leave my mouth. Marsh knows me better than anyone. "I go in. I do my work. I leave and do my best to not think about it when I'm not there."

"How's that working out for you?"

"Would I like to be doing more for the company? Have more responsibilities? Be on a partner track? Of course. But it takes time. You have to put in the hours. Days. Months."

"Years," Marsh says.

"Exactly. It's no different than all the time and energy you're putting in. I'm also waiting for someone to give me my big break in a way. It will pay off. Someday. For both of us."

The thing you need to know about Data … is that he's a coward. Marsh would never say it that way, but it's the truth. At least in my professional life. My chest tightens under the weight of existing. But this is the bed I've made for myself. Sometimes being an adult means fulfilling responsibilities that aren't particularly enjoyable.

"I just want you to be happy," Marsh says, and the moment the last word leaves his lips, he winces. "I mean at work. And life. Happy, in general." A forced, feeble laugh echoes against the frozen trees.

We walk in silence for awhile, the peace of Marshmallow Mountain blanketing us.

"We made it," I say, my legs wobbling.

"Huh?"

"To the main road." The pavement is within view. It's covered in a few inches of snow. The trucks were here. Maybe not for a while, but at some point. "This is great. If the main road was plowed, all we need to worry about is Duffy plowing our access road and driveway."

Marsh raises his right hand. "Let the record show that I am not responding with a plowing joke, even though you've cruelly set me up for one."

The moment our boots hit the road, our pace picks up. Yes, there's still snow to tramp through, but it's more manageable. We still have almost two miles to go, but it feels closer. Within reach.

"Do you think it's safe to walk on the road?" Marsh asks.

"We've got our backpacks on," I say, turning to show him. "There's a reflective patch. Plus, the roads are shit. Nobody will be out. And if they are, we're hitching."

"Good call."

We walk side by side, in silence, and somehow, even on the main road, out here in the sticks, there's not a car in sight. The snow has slowed, but we're still trekking in a complete whiteout —everything is colorless. People seemed to have gotten the memo. Stay home. There aren't any buildings on the road, so it's hard to tell if the power outage is widespread or confined to our section of the mountain. Tranquility shadows us as we walk. We cover a good clip before Marsh pierces the silence.

"So, again. Just want you to be happy. With your job. Work," Marsh says.

"I know," I say, focusing on the canopy of snow-covered branches sheltering the part of the road we're on. "But also, what you said ... about me not loving it ... you're not completely wrong."

"Excuse me?" Marsh stops in his tracks. "Did you just admit I'm right?"

"No, I said you're not completely wrong. That doesn't mean completely right, either."

"Oh."

"But this is my life. I need to support myself. I need health insurance. And my mom … she has nobody else. It may not be glamorous or creative or fun, but it's reality. People have to work to live. Not everyone is as talented as you."

"I know that, but also it's not the only thing you're good at." Marsh pokes my hand, tugging at my mitten, and then takes it in his.

"You're fantastic with these."

I know he's talking about my carving. He always loved my pieces. And while this would be the perfect opportunity for him to crack a joke about finger banging—he doesn't. He simply holds my hand in his.

"Thank you," I reply. "But that's never going to happen." I gently drop his hand. "It's just not sensible."

"In a perfect world, you could do both." Marsh huffs, an immense cloud of condensation creating a massive puff on his lips. "We may not be together, but I'll always be your biggest fan."

"I appreciate that," I say, pausing to wait for him. He really does care about me, even if his actions show otherwise. My head swims with the conflicting sides of Marsh Goldberg until a vision in the distance distracts me.

The buzzy neon of The General Store lights up in the distance like the Las Vegas skyline. Leave it to Maddi to have backup generators upon backup generators. The store looks close, only about a quarter mile away.

"Yes! Are you seeing this? They have power. We're almost there." I wait for him to celebrate with me, but there's nothing. "Marsh?"

When I turn around, Marsh, a few feet back, hunches over. If I didn't know him better, I'd think he was searching for something in the snow, maybe a lost contact, but Marsh doesn't wear contacts. He has perfect vision. No, I recognize this posture and my breath catches. With a mind of their own, my feet move into action. My heart races as I dart to him and kneel. He's wheezing, his chest expanding and contracting heavily under his coat.

"Marsh, I'm here. Where's your inhaler?"

He points to his backpack and I immediately rip it off him, digging in the small outer pocket. When I find it, I pop the cover off and place it near his lips. Marsh reaches up, takes it from me, and begins pumping and inhaling.

"There you go. Deep breaths." I put my hand on his back, waiting to feel the return to steady breathing.

Marsh pulls the inhaler out of his mouth and stands. His pale skin appears damp and I can't tell if he's warm or if it's the asthma.

"Marsh? Babe? Are you okay?"

His eyes find mine. There's a glimmer. I see him in there. Searching my face. He shakes his head and shoves the inhaler back in his mouth. After a few more puffs, he pulls it away and holds it up, scrutinizing the pink plastic.

His mouth forms the word "Out" but no sound can come out over his gasping for air, his lungs hanging off a cliff digging into the rock for dear life. It fumbles out of his fingers as he attempts to hand it over, sinking into the snow.

I grab it, searching for clues. Fuck. The dose counter is at zero and I wonder how long it's been that way. A tiny surge of anger bubbles, because, of course, Marsh would forget to refill the medicine imperative to his existence. I was the one who picked up the prescription refills when he forgot. His big, fear-drenched eyes search my face and my throat tightens with worry.

"Stay here. I'm going to run to the store and refill it. I'll be back in a few minutes. Okay?" I squeeze his hand to reaffirm that I will be back.

Marsh nods. His breathing appears to be calmer, but he needs more medicine before he can walk.

"I'll be right back. Don't move," I say, and even in his

condition, a goofy smile flickers on his lips, warming my heart even in the freezing snow-covered landscape.

Turning toward the store, I break out into a slow jog. Running isn't in my DNA, but in this instance, walking won't cut it. Marsh needs his medicine. Needs me. Now.

Chapter Twenty

Marsh

Here's the thing you need to know about Data: he's one of those people who reads the obituaries. For fun. We'd be eating breakfast, and I'd look over and find a tear rolling down his face onto the newspaper.

"Darryl Washington died," he'd say.

"Who?"

"Seventy-four. Father of three girls. Grandfather to five. He was in the crowd when Martin Luther King Jr. gave his I Have a Dream speech. What a life."

He'd stare at the page intently, a sense of melancholy glazing on his eyes, perhaps wondering whether his life would ever be worthy of a *New York Times* obit.

At the moment, I'm sixty-five percent sure I'm dying. My body is rising up from the ground to the sky, to meet my maker. What will they write in my obit? Will it make Data cry? Will they misspell my name on my tombstone like poor Elvis?

I thought this would be a more profound moment, that I would use these final seconds on earth to flash back on my life. But instead, all I can think about is that something is digging into my back. And there's a loud creaky noise ringing in my ears.

I also thought I would be greeted by dead loved ones like my Grandma Anita and my old dog Kahn—named after

Madeline Kahn, not the Star Trek guy. But it's Data's face that's hovering over me. I'm pretty sure he's still alive because he doesn't have that serene look that people in heaven must have.

I blink twice and realize that I'm not dying, but that I am being raised into the air. Data sticks an inhaler into my mouth and shoots my lungs full of slightly sweet, powdery medicine.

"Again." His fingers comb through my hair and it's damp, either from almost dying, the snow, or both.

He shoots another whoosh of medicine from the inhaler into my mouth, which quite literally gives me life. I begin to sit up but can't feel the ground under me. I'm floating in the air. Wait, *am* I dying? I'm so confused. Is God gaslighting me?

"What's going on?" I look behind me and see Duffy at the controls of a forklift. Once the oxygen hits my brain, it clicks that I am the thing being lifted.

"What the fuck?" I try to sit up, but my huge ass is precariously balanced between the prongs of the lift.

"A few more seconds and we'll put you down," Duffy calls out from the controls. No matter the weather outside, he has on his trusty University of Maine baseball cap. He smiles at me, his fuzzy chinstrap of dark hair curling as well.

Data jogs alongside me as if this forklift is the presidential motorcade. Duffy backs us up out of the woods, The General Store parking lot a few feet away.

"You collapsed. I had to run to the store and get you a new inhaler."

"You left me on the side of the road?"

"You didn't fill up your inhaler!" Data shakes his head, cheeks red. Oops. My bad. "We were almost to the store. It was faster to run there myself than try and carry you. Time was ticking, Marsh. You were turning blue."

We roll over a bump in the path, and the forklift prongs lance my back. I suppose I deserve that for not staying back.

Even though I've had asthma for most of my life, I don't like to admit that it has a hold on me. I'm very much my father's son. Stubborn is as much in our DNA as our big bones.

Fortunately, I was very close to the General Store's parking lot before I gave out. It only takes another minute for Duffy to back us into civilization, a sigh of relief coming over Data and me when we reach pavement. I'm not sure why Duffy owns a forklift since he runs the General Store with Maddi. People in the sticks tend to scoop up big, unnecessary machinery the way urbanites are perpetually obsessed with collecting the latest Apple products.

Duffy lowers me to the ground. Data takes both of my hands and helps me up, our stomachs bumping against each other in the process. Being this close to Data is perhaps the nearest I'll get to heaven before finally kicking the bucket.

He puts his hands on my hips to balance me, and hangs on for an extra moment, staring into my eyes. His lips pout, making them eminently kissable.

"You okay?" he asks softly. "That was scary."

I nod yes. Concern rings his pupils, but also a touch of something else, a flicker of a feeling that's been skirting around the edges of the weekend.

"Thank you," I say. No smirk. No tacked-on joke. Just a terse nod to underline my genuine appreciation. The realization of how close I came to death hits me.

And then, because I'm me, I tack on a joke, because real life is really scary.

"You're the wind—" I stick my inhaler in my mouth and give it a puff as I wink at Data. "Beneath my wings."

"Lord, you're gay." Data chuckles to himself, then turns to Duffy. "Thank you so much."

"Duffy the Asthma Slayer!" I give him a thumbs up.

"Of course. I'm glad you're okay, Marsh." Duffy dips his

head and taps the brim of his hat. "It's not easy walking through knee-high snow."

"The power's out at the cabin," Data says.

"And we needed Mallomars."

Data rolls his eyes at me in that way that gets my dick hard. "And to charge our phones."

"Huh." Duffy wiggles his finger between us. "Maddi said you boys had broken up."

"We did," Data interjects more quickly than I'd like. "We're getting the cabin ready to be sold."

"Oh." Duffy's face drops. His bushy hair curling up from under his hat makes him look like a sad dog with floppy ears. It's funny how people can feel like family. We've been coming up here for years, spending summers and winters getting to know Maddi and Duffy. Consistency breeds friendship. Without the cabin to bring us here, they'll likely dissolve out of our lives.

"We'll come back to visit," I say, my voice cracking as I throw an arm around Data. "Just not together."

I drop my arm, realizing that's not selling our not together-ness. My gaze shifts to the mountain of snow taking up a parking spot, remembering why we're here. "Your parking lot is cleared already. Did you do this yourself?"

"Yeah. Thanks to this sucker right here." Duffy backs up and pats the snow plow attachment on his truck with a sense of pride not unlike when I got my first pair of AirPods. "It can take a while for the regular plow to come through. I swear, plowing can be a real pain in the ass."

Data elbows my side to preemptively shut me up. He knows me so well.

"The plowing service that we usually use is going to take days," Data says. The access road to a single cabin owned by non-billionaires is the lowest of low priorities for street plows. "I don't know when it's going to come."

"They might wait until the snow is done." Duffy sticks his

hands under his armpits Mary Catherine Gallagher-style to keep warm. His flannel shirt and puffy vest are clearly not doing the trick.

"Done?" I ask Duffy.

"Yeah, the weatherman says we're getting another doozy of a storm sometime on Tuesday."

"Fucking chickens." Data's face goes cold, and I watch his eyes fill with anxiety. "I need to get out of here."

I know Data has a life and a job back in the city, but still. It can't help but sting to have a guy clamor to get the hell away from you the morning after mind-blowing sex.

"Duffy, can you plow our road today?" he asks.

He responds by scratching his head under his hat, really digging in there. "I'd like to. I don't know if this baby can handle your twisty, windy road and pushing through all that snow."

"But you did the main road," Data points out.

"I was able to clear it when the snow was still coming down, so it wasn't as bad."

"You sure? We trekked all the way here in the snow."

"Yeah, I know other customers have been doing that, too. I really wish I could help you guys. I do. But I think it's too big of a job for this girl." He gives his plow a loving fist bang. "We can call around to other plow companies inside."

"Yeah. I see." Data's jaw goes tight.

I was the one who dragged him out here in this storm. I'm not going to leave him in the lurch.

"Duff. Dufftacular. Duffy Day-Lewis. The Great British Duff Off." I nudge his elbow with mine and stroll toward his newest pride and joy. "Your snowplow is gorgeous. That is a beautiful piece of equipment. I can see you not wanting to tarnish it. Is it new?"

"No. I got it off a guy in Waterville."

"Whoa! What a steal. You have a great eye." I do a chef's kiss to his snowplow.

"We can call around to plowing services, see if there's anyone who can help you out sooner," he says.

I squat down and admire the metal of the snowplow. Or at least pretend to because I'm not sure how one admires a snow plow.

"Usually, I'd say you were right. Our access road *is* tricky. If only we knew the guy who once drove up Great Bear Mountain in a torrential rainstorm because Maddi left her favorite sweater up there, who once floored his truck through Owego Pond on a dare. That guy would think one puny access road was nothing. That guy didn't let nature stand in his way. That guy would be a hero to his woman, saving two of their friends. I'm *positive* the schmuck in Waterville couldn't do that, but I think I know somebody who could." I shrug, playing up the moment, my minimal acting training coming in handy. "Or, I thought I knew."

Duffy's eyes widen. I can hear the triumphant music playing in his head—maybe a banjo version of "Lose Yourself." I walk around him in a compelling circle. It's not every day one gets to improvise a monologue.

"If there's one thing I know about Duffy Monroe, it's that he powers through where others are afraid to travel and that he looks out for his fellow Mainers. Actually, that's two things, but the point still stands."

Duffy claps my shoulder and squeezes. "I'm going to get you boys back to your cabin."

"Really?" Data asks.

"I sure will. You hang out in the store, and I'll swing up there right now and clear it out." Duffy licks his hand and smooths it over the brim of his hat. He pounds his plow with two more loving fist bangs. "We got this."

"Thanks, buddy. You da man!" I clap his back as he hops into his truck.

I rest my arm on Data's shoulder as we watch him pull out. He glances up at me, his lips curling into a small-but-grateful smile. The littlest gestures from him can send my heart into the stratosphere, even if he wants to get the hell away from me. From us.

Duffy sticks his head out the window and looks back at us. "For a pair of guys who say they aren't together, you're acting awfully … together."

Chapter Twenty-One

Data Marshall

"We never lost power." With a warm smile, Maddi hands us mugs of steaming cocoa, tiny marshmallows bobbing playfully on the surface. Marsh's mug says, 'This coffee is almost as hot as people from Maine' and mine reads 'Maine Girl: like a regular girl, but wicked cool.'

"And if we ever do, Duffy fires up our generator. Can't have the meat spoil."

With our phones plugged in, we park on the floor near the back of the store, attempting to warm up as I ensure Marsh's breathing steadies. Behind us, the community board stands tall, while the door of the bathroom, where we had amazing sex just two days ago, seems to taunt me. Inside the tiny stall, Marsh said he missed me. My ass, yes. But also me. Watching Marsh's lips around the brim of his mug, my mind flashes back to cramming the inhaler in his mouth. Yes, I'm annoyed he came up here with it almost empty, but more than anything, I'm grateful he's okay. Seeing him that way, gasping on his back, his beautiful face turning blue, somehow made me miss him even more, and I honestly didn't think that was possible.

"Well, I'll leave you boys to it," Maddi says. "Duffy'll be back in a jiff, but take your time. Do your shopping and we'll get you home safely. Your power should be back on soon. Even in this storm, the crew will get the lines up."

"Thanks, Maddi." I tip my head to her, clutching my Maine Girl mug for warmth, and Marsh nods his thanks.

"How's your chest?" I ask him.

"Stocky. Beefy. Probably a B cup, maybe a C after Thanksgiving, but no complaints so far."

Tears dot my eyes. Not from his joke, but from him joking. He's back to normal. My head dips and I give him my best side eye.

"What? Are there complaints I don't know about? Wait, do you wish they were *bigger*?"

The man will be on his deathbed, the hospital machines beeping, taking his last breaths of life, and he'll manage to get a joke in as his last words. Not that he'd want me around for that, but still.

"Oh, you meant my *lungs*?" Marsh sips his cocoa, the marshmallows leaving a soft white residue on his upper lip. When he doesn't lick it away, I'm tempted to do it for him. I'm starting to wonder if he leaves food dangling around his mouth as a trap for me. "Fine. All good. Thanks to you."

"Good. You really scared me back there." I hand him a tissue from my coat pocket and tap my lip, signaling to him. "I've never run so fast."

"As your ex-boyfriend, is it inappropriate to say I wish I could've watched your booty bounce as you ran?" Marsh wipes his lip and chuckles at his quip. I try, really hard, to muster up some annoyance with him, but right now, sitting on the floor of The General Store, warm and toasty and safe, it's feeling like old times. Maybe it's okay to have moments like this, a toe dip into the past without fully falling in.

We need to get some provisions and head back to finish packing. Karen won't care I'm stuck on a mountain in Maine when the month end analyses are late. She'd charter a helicopter to fetch me rather than, oh, do any work herself. Being stuck here for a prolonged amount of time with no power and dwindling wood isn't my idea of a fun time. Of course, Marsh could provide a different electricity. Fuck.

"You sit and rest," I say, itching for an escape. "I'll grab the Mallomars."

Mallomars. Double fuck.

"Grab all of them." Marsh winks at me, and I leave him to recharge along with our phones.

The store is empty, which means nothing. It's almost always empty, but the snow and poorly plowed roads make it seem more desolate than normal. I walk up and down the aisles, the brightly colored packages of food all a blur. I grab Fritos as promised, then toss a bag of Cool Ranch Doritos in my basket —Marsh loves them. One time he ate an entire bag in one sitting and, even after scrubbing his hands twice, still had Dorito fingers. I remember sucking them while he pounded me doggy style by the fire. The faint cool ranch-iness filled me up almost as much as his fat cock. I quickly toss the bag back on the shelf like a hot potato.

As I approach the cookies, the bright yellow and black carton beckons. I pop a box in my basket and, peeking at the inventory, notice only two boxes left on the shelf. I wouldn't want them to get lonely. And Marsh doesn't enjoy sharing. Or … he didn't. We should get our own boxes. And an extra. For prosperity.

"You know I only stock those for you boys." Maddi comes around the aisle pushing a dolly with various cookies and crackers, ready to be shelved.

"Nobody else ever requested Mallomars. People up here stick to the standards." She pats a case of Oreos.

I smile, remembering the conversation where Marsh informed her we'd love Mallomars and matzoh ball mix. Not matzoh. Not matzoh meal. Mix. *"We're making soup. There's no need to go all Martha."*

"And we appreciate it. And you," I say with a smile. "No need to reorder."

Maddi smiles softly. "And there's no way you boys might … keep the place."

My chest feels heavy. Tight. "I don't think so."

"But you two seem so … " Maddi doesn't finish the sentence. Instead, she cracks the box, pulls out a bag of chocolate-dipped double-stuffed Oreos, opens it, and hands me a cookie. "I'm sorry."

"Yeah, me too," I say and shove the cookie in my mouth. It's no Mallomar, but I don't want to be rude.

"Duffy can really piss me off. He tries to sing along to songs in the car, but mumbles over the music because he never knows the words. The only line of "We Didn't Start the Fire" he knows is 'JFK blown away.' Everything else is gobbledygook that drowns out poor Billy Joel. I can't tell you how many good songs have come on the radio that've been ruined by his damn mumbling." Maddi chomps into her cookie and rolls her eyes in a way that feels familiar to me. "But when he does remember the words, and we sing along together at the top of our lungs … there's nothing better." She gazes out the window at the forklift, gives out a wistful laugh. "The right person is someone you can't live without, but who you could see yourself murdering too. Love's funny that way."

She hands over the opened package of Oreos and kisses me on the cheek, leaving a lipstick smudge. "On the house."

"Thanks, Maddi," I say through a full mouth, grateful for the gesture. Wisdom comes where you least expect it.

"Y'know, I asked my chickens about you and they scratched up enough dust to make me cough." She turns to head up front, straightening the shelf of cookies as she walks away. "That means you're meant to be. Trust me. My chickens are never wrong."

I nod in agreement because, of course, the chickens know. That plus, my mouth is so full of Oreos and I'm unable to speak or ask her if they know when it's time for fried chicken.

While I still need to find some nourishment not in the cookie food group, I return quickly to check on Marsh, who's in the middle of a FaceTime call. A familiar tangle of anguish twists his face, and I realize instantly who's on the other end.

"Dad, we talked about this. Albie said the contract would be coming over. When I'm back in the city, we can review it together. Don't sign it yet."

I stand against the wall, out of the call's frame.

"Who gave him the right to sell the company?" Joe's gruffness comes through the phone, a wave of nostalgia hitting me. "It's none of his damn business."

"I don't disagree. He's trying to help." A unique type of exhaustion hits Marsh's voice whenever he talks to his dad. "But we can review it together."

"I'll take a look."

"But don't sign anything. Promise me you won't sign anything."

"Don't tell me what to do, Marshall." Joe's stern dad voice strikes fear in me, even though I'm not his son. "I can't believe your brother. What right does a college student have to proffer his father's company to some peckerheads."

"Dad, Albie's not in college anymore."

"Wait till I tell your mother about this. She's going to have a fit."

Marsh hangs his head, but before he can gather up the strength to respond, I squat next to him and wave at the camera.

"Hi Joe!"

"Other Marshall!" He lights up instantly, that smile still a gem. "How's it going?"

"I'm ready for spring, I don't know about you. I'm hankering for more Yankee games."

"Same! Football is for the goyim." He laughs heartily. "Maybe you can knock some sense into your companion, get him to come back to the company."

"Dad! Marshall and I—"

"Have talked about this over and over. Haven't we, babe?" I throw my arm around Marsh and scrunch a hand through his hair, just like old times. "Marsh is doing really well with standup. I'm super proud of him. He's actually planning a huge revue next month that's attracting a lot of attention."

I saw fliers for the show at a coffeehouse. *Out with a Bang.* Such a Marsh title. Marsh turns to me surprised, touched.

"Marsh is working on new material for the show that's the funniest stuff he's ever written," I continue. It's criminal that he wants to deprive the world of his talent. Maybe I let our relationship slip away without a fight, but I won't do the same with his career.

For an actor, he's having a hard time keeping up our ruse, but I don't break in this scene. I gaze right back at him, my chest tingling. It's like riding a bike. An adorable bike.

"Marsh, you didn't tell me about this show," Joe says.

"Yeah … we're having agents, managers, producers come. Preeti and I are planning it. It's going to be big." Marsh plasters on a smile for the screen. Joe's eyebrows lift with interest, taking both of us back.

"Very good," Joe says.

"Marsh is incredibly diligent. He's constantly working on new material, writing new jokes, and networking. I'm really proud of him." And then, to seal the deal or maybe because I've lost touch with reality, I kiss Marsh. For his Dad. For old times sake. For the chickens. His lips, dotted with drops of hot cocoa, send a sugar rush into my mouth and a jolt of contentment straight to my heart. "You're doing it, babe."

"I'm doing … it. Yeah." His cheeks redden as he looks to me, then back to his dad, then back at me, unsure what to say next. "Maybe you can come and see it."

"You should!" I echo. "I can pick you up."

Did I just offer that? Chauffeuring my ex's dad? I blame the sugar high from Marsh's lips.

"That sounds great."

"Joe, we have to go. Get back to our cabin before more snow comes. See you soon!" I wave at the screen.

"Okay. Well, have a good weekend, gentlemen."

Marsh clicks out of FaceTime and stares at the screen, still in a bit of a daze. "You kissed me."

"That … was not a real kiss. I was helping an elderly man."

A sly grin slides onto his face—that damn punim.

"And now you have to do that show." I arch an eyebrow back at him. "You asked your dad to come."

"I was blindsided by the not-real kiss."

That's not a yes, but it's also not a no. I'll take it.

"What was that call about?" I ask.

Marsh sighs. An enormous sigh. The good news is his lungs seem to be efficiently transmitting oxygen. The bad news is, he's upset about something. "What?"

"Fucking Albie. He sent Dad the acquisition agreement for Harmony Pianos."

"Oh." Marsh's family business. The cabin. Our relationship. Everything's being sold or dissolved.

"Dad is in no state to make these types of decisions, let alone read and sign a contract like this." He ruffles a hand through his hair. "I've thought about asking for power of attorney, but if I do that, then that means … "

"That things are really bad with him."

He nods.

"With how things are … progressing, it's probably best he's

selling sooner rather than later, right?" I put the cookie-laden basket down.

"Yeah, it's just these guys he's selling to ... I don't know. I'm sure they're fine, but they're not family. More than anything, Dad wanted this to stay a family business."

I can practically see the weight digging into his shoulders, the tiredness in his eyes. I throw an arm around him and pull him close.

"Has he thought about handing it over to a non-family member? A friend?"

"All of his friends are retired." He takes the last sip of his cocoa. "Maybe I should go back. I'm sure the books are a mess, but we have a good relationship with the suppliers. Nobody's buying pianos like they used to. It feels a little like taking the helm of the Titanic."

I take a breath, but before speaking, I brace myself, knowing that a joke is about to be cracked.

"And nobody's offering to paint me like a French girl."

There's my Marsh. No, just Marsh. Not my Marsh. His jokes are for everyone, but they're also just for me. Or used to be.

"Do you want me to look anything over? The books. The contract. I mean, I'm not an attorney, but I have some experience with legalese. And lots of experience with numbers."

Marsh was the face, the frontman, the salesman. Selling pianos was easy for him; he studied people every day as a performer, forever interested in what made them tick. If you walked into a Harmony store, you were at least thinking about a piano, and that was all Marsh needed to close the deal. It was the back-end, businessy part of the job that never gelled with him. Unlike me, he's not built for spreadsheets.

He heaves out a sigh, a million different thoughts pinging back and forth in his eyes. "Maybe this is just how it goes, y'know? Businesses end all the time."

"Just because something ends doesn't mean it's gone. We carry pieces of it, memories." A tightness tugs at my chest, the push-pull of wanting to fight for something but knowing some battles just can't be won. "There are people who will continue to play on the Harmony Piano that they've had for decades. There are adults who still have the muscle memory from years of practice as a kid. There are musicians who will never forget their first instrument, sold to them by you. Your company is no longer manufacturing pianos, but that doesn't mean it will cease to be remembered. That doesn't mean what your family built hasn't changed lives."

He turns to me, his green irises eclipsed by the deep black of his pupils. "That was … beautiful."

I nod, because I suddenly have lost the ability to speak, because I realize I'm still in mourning for something that ended but never left.

"You're still a really good kisser," Marsh says.

He pockets his phone and attempts to stand. I rush to offer my hand and Marsh takes it, grunting as he lifts himself. Pulling harder to assist, he pops up with a force neither of us expects and falls into me.

"Woah." I wrap my arms around his broad torso, catching Marsh as he regains his balance. "Easy does it."

Marsh's face comes dangerously close to mine. My breath hitches at the closeness.

"Hey," he whispers. Our chests collide, and I feel the strong, rhythmic thumping of Marsh's heartbeat against my own. His face looms inches from mine, so near that I can scrutinize every detail of his features. He hasn't shaved since we've been here and the light stubble on his face draws my gaze. My hands have the urge to push Marsh away and barge off, but also to grab him closer, gather him up, and capture his lips with mine.

"You boys ready?" Duffy says behind us. "Plow's all ready for ya."

Marsh's gaze lingers on me for an unnerving extra second. I want to stay in this moment completely, seal us off from the cold contours of the outside world.

He grabs the basket from me, holds it up, and eyes the cookie haul.

"That's my Data. I mean, Marshall." He pats my back and walks off, sending my heart tumbling all over again.

<u>Chapter Twenty-Two</u>

Marsh

Here's the thing you need to know about Data: The man wears the hell out of a watch.

There's something about a man in a nice watch that's sexy, like a gay Clark Gable. I got him a fancy one for his thirty-fifth. I'm glad he didn't get rid of it post-break up. It's thick with a big head, and oozes charm. Like another part of him. The timepiece makes his wrist and forearm bulge with strength and assuredness. Sometimes, I'd glimpse it while he pushed my head into his crotch and get turned on even more.

Data taps the watch as he scans the cabin, sending a quick jolt of heat down my spine.

"Okay, we have approximately twenty-three hours to pack up this place and get the hell off this mountain."

The heat dissipates as soon as I stare out on what remains of Marshmallow Mountain. Maddi was right about the power coming back on sooner rather than later. Or maybe it was the chickens. The cabin is in a state of hellish disarray that comes with packing. If the gods really wanted to punish Sisyphus, they'd force him to pack up his apartment anew every day.

Data heaves out a breath through his inexplicably sexy nostrils. "We can do this."

Fortunately, after plowing our road, Duffy helped Data

shovel out our cars. I offered to help, but he insisted I hang back and avoid another near-death moment.

According to the weather app—and Maddi's chickens—the next blizzard is scheduled to start late Monday afternoon. Twenty-three hours left to pack. Twenty-three hours left to put a final, permanent stamp on this relationship. Twenty-three hours left with Data.

Can we be one of those couples that transitions to actual friends? It's a very common thing in the gay community. Gay guys get each other in a way the rest of the world doesn't, and we also want to jump each other's bones. It's a feature, not a bug. But I don't know if I can be only friends with Data. Meet up for coffee or hang out at a game night knowing that we won't be going home together?

I know I chose this, but that doesn't mean I have to like it. People choose to eat salad to be healthy, even though it's salad. Keeping our relationship kaput is me being healthy. I can't let myself get tempted to eat Data's salad.

I should've picked a different metaphor.

Data claps his hands in front of my face. "Focus. We haven't made efficient use of our time this weekend. Time is ticking."

I don't need the reminder. "We got this. I once wrote, directed, and performed a play in twenty-four hours."

"*A Fire Island Rumspringa*. I remember." He laughs to himself. "That was the weirdest show I've ever seen of yours, and that's saying something."

I'm so grateful that he hasn't lost his sense of humor throughout this manic, hot, emotionally draining, life-threatening weekend. When I needed him on short notice, Data stepped up, something I won't forget. He's a real mensch.

"Thanks again for coming up here. I appreciate it." I take my phone from my pocket and put it on the kitchen counter. Less temptation to scroll.

Even though the power's back, there's no sense in wasting perfectly good candles, so I light the cabin with candles and the crackling fire of the woodburning stove.

Nothing romantic about that.

"Yeah, no problem." Data places fresh logs in the fireplace and gets it roaring. "If I'd known that you were in … if your financial situation … you didn't have to feel forced to sell the cabin if you didn't want to."

"There's no sense in keeping it, right?" I say with a shrug. "It's time to let this place go."

"How bad are things for you right now?" He squints at me as if I'm a ledger with a logical solution.

"I'm good."

"Marsh." He tips his head at me. It's very hard to lie to someone you love. I should've gotten an Oscar for making it through my crap break-up excuse six months ago. Or at least a Golden Globe. Hey, if Madonna could win one for *Evita* …

My shoulders slump. "I've been getting by with temp jobs until I figure out my next move."

"So that's it? You're just done with comedy entirely?"

"My big break came and I blew it. Time to move on." The hard truth with a career in the arts is that some people launch into stardom on a rocket ship, and others muddle along waiting for their rocket to arrive. Sometimes it has to do with talent, but not always. I've seen comedians that I think are doing next-level stuff on stage, like Preeti, but they can't break through. I try to stay positive in front of Data because nobody likes a Debbie Downer (unless it's Rachel Dratch, of course).

"What if Laughingstock wasn't your big break? What if it was just another bump in the road? Not every successful comedian is discovered at the festival. In fact, I'd wager that statistically, the majority of big breaks don't happen at Laughingstock."

"I love that you managed to bring numbers into this

conversation." I chuckle at his analysis, but there's a kernel of truth that stimulates something in the back of my head. A pilot light clicking on. His math *is* mathing. There are a million different ways to breakthrough. Laughingstock was simply one option. What if it was just meant to be a bump? A test to see if I have the fortitude. And I'm bailing.

"I really admire you, Marsh."

"The backbreaking labor of trying to make people laugh?" I ask.

"You've worked really hard."

I shrug my shoulders. "Am I going to find my rocket, or am I one of those people destined to fade into obscurity? I wish I could know that in advance."

"Everybody wishes they knew that in advance. That's not how life works." Data begins opening a box and taping the bottom. I take one and join him. For the life of me, I am incapable of rolling out a piece of tape in a straight line.

"Be honest with me: Did you ever think about quitting accounting and trying to give woodworking a legitimate shot? Was there ever a tiny, kitten whisper of a thought in your head that it could work?"

Data scratches at his beard for a moment. I appreciate that he's giving the question honest consideration.

"Yeah. I thought about it here and there. I'll admit, watching you take the leap got the wheels turning for me."

That's news to me. Whenever I broached the topic with him in our relationship, he was a firm no. I guess we couldn't know every thought in our partner's head.

"I actually talked to a furniture designer to fully understand what it requires."

"You did?"

My heart races as he nods. Ever the multi-tasker, he begins packing his box with cookbooks from the small shelf above the sink. No matter what we say, no matter if we use them or not, neither of us have the heart to throw cookbooks with beautiful photos into the trash.

"I ran through scenarios of what it would look like," he says. "But it wasn't for me."

"Why?" I open the nearby kitchen cabinet and wrap glasses in newspaper.

"I don't know."

"That's not an answer. Did you get scared?" I place the glassware gently in the box.

He considers the question. Another beard scratch with his watch-wearing hand. A second jolt of heat fizzles down my spine. Data doesn't even realize all these little moments of his are hot—which makes them even hotter.

"A little," he admits. "Marsh, you don't understand. You grew up differently than me."

"My dad's business wasn't some cash cow. It ebbed and flowed."

"The fact that you can say 'my dad's business' means you don't understand. I know there were tight times for Harmony when you were younger, but did you ever feel it as a kid?"

"I mean, my parents didn't really discuss business financials with me and Albie."

"You never had to worry about food on the table or gas in the car. You never had the landlord personally come to your apartment to hand you an eviction notice. You never went to bed with a sick feeling in your stomach after watching your mom cry." Data looks away and grabs a vegetarian cookbook we really should trash. He doesn't yell, but there is a quiet intensity in his voice that hits me in the gut.

I stop mid-newspaper roll of a wine glass. After eight years together, it's still possible to learn something new about your partner. He always told me things were tight growing up, but he never wanted to elaborate.

"I didn't know things were that bad." My heart breaks for

little Data curled up in his bed. I hate that there's nothing I can do to change his past, that he has to live with those memories for the rest of his life.

"My entire childhood was a rough patch," he says flatly. "I didn't want to talk about it. And you … I mean, you said that when Harmony had a tough year, your parents could only send you to summer camp for one month, not two."

I hang my head, laughing at my insensitive Karen Walker moment. "God, how you never smacked me all those times."

"It's hard to be mad at you. That's one of your best qualities."

"I'm sorry you didn't feel comfortable talking to me about stuff like that."

"It's not your fault. I didn't want to share. I don't want people's pity."

I can't stop thinking about little Data and his mom. She's a sweet woman, but she also doesn't take shit from anyone. I can see how that kind of struggle can wear a person down.

"Now I get why she was so adamant about you choosing a safe profession. I'm sorry for telling you to quit all those times." I swallow past the lump in my throat. He didn't have the luxury to follow his passion. "You've done well, Da–Marshall. She's proud of you."

"You're probably right. I don't like my job, but I don't hate it." He exhales a breath of relief as if it were some big secret he was keeping. "When I looked into woodworking as a career, it wasn't just the uncertainty. There are parts of my work that I enjoy. I like business and working with a team, and I like finding a story in the numbers."

"Plot twist. Data likes data."

"You gave me the nickname because of my butt, and you wound up capturing my whole personality. Go figure." He cracks a smile, then tests lifting his box of books to make sure it's liftable. "We can get a few more in here."

He walks over to a shelf of fiction in the living room and clotheslines a row of smaller paperbacks onto his lap.

He reads the cover of a paperback and snorts. "Do you remember when you bought this?"

Data turns it to me. The familiar pinched face of a man either crying or orgasming catches my eye.

"*A Little Life*!" I swipe it from him. "I'm still planning to read this. I promise."

"That's what you said when you bought it what? Five years ago?"

"I'll get excommunicated from homosexuality if I don't read it." I weigh the tomb in my hand. "We only went into that store because you saw a black cat napping in the front window, so this purchase is partially your fault."

I hand it back, but Data refuses, making the man on the cover cry and/or orgasm more.

"I'm not schlepping it into a storage unit. That thing is a door-stopper of depression."

"Fine. I'll keep it." I might read it … or I might use it for the wobbly leg of Preeti's coffee table. "But if I'm forced to keep this, then you are taking these back home with you."

From the back of the kitchen cabinet, I pull a six piece set of little blue-and-white tea cups and coasters. They are covered in dust because they have never been used.

He bursts into a wild gale of laughter. "They're nice!"

"You made us drive all the way back to that antique store so you could buy these. So we could have high tea with a quilting bee, I'm assuming. Even though I reminded you multiple times that we don't drink tea and we already have coffee mugs." For some gay men, like Data, old lady antiques were as addictive as poppers.

Data puts his hand on *A Little Life* as if about to go on the witness stand. "I swear to take this lovely tea set home with me."

I put my hand over his and take a similar stance. "And I swear to take this book home, read it, and cry my eyes out."

I rub my thumb over his pinky. His pinky wraps around my thumb, gives it a squeeze, melting my heart. It's one of those perfect fleeting moments that I'll randomly flash back repeatedly and smile to myself while riding the subway.

"Hey. I have an idea." I quirk an eyebrow. "We've already had le breakup sex. But we haven't had le breakup meal. The stove's working. What do you say, for old time's sake? I'll make your favorite."

Data doesn't even try to protest. I may be a so-so comic, and a so-so ex-boyfriend, but I make a damn good matzoh ball soup.

Chapter Twenty-Three

Data Marshall

I may be stubborn as a mule, but there's something about Marsh's balls that completely flood my basement. His *matzoh* balls. Much like his actual balls, they're simply perfect. Delectable. And he knows it. About both. But stuck here in the snowy tundra that's enveloped our mountain, with only a little time left on the ticking clock that's become a slow crawl to the finish line of our relationship, I'll happily lose myself in Marsh's Magnificent (Matzoh) Balls—his name for them, not mine.

"See, now aren't you glad I bought the ingredients?" He piles carrots, celery, and onions on top of the maple cutting board I made him for our first anniversary. His love for cooking combined with his passion for my hand-crafted pieces made it an easy and special gift. I rescue his favorite knife from an open box on the kitchen floor and hand it to him, handle first.

"I'm certainly not mad about it. I mean, it would be a crime to let that box of matzoh ball mix go to waste," I say.

"Criminal," Marsh says, cracking eggs into a small metal bowl. "We wouldn't want to break any laws. Someone might need to be handcuffed. Taken away. Punished for being a bad boy." Marsh smirks and my face flashes hot, remembering the previous time we were here months ago. Our last time here together … when he slapped my ass so hard he left a red mark and I begged for more. *Who's been a bad boy?*

"No, we wouldn't want that." I turn away, attempting to hide my rosy cheeks and prevent more teasing from Marsh.

"Do you know what box the oil is in?" he asks, washing his hands after cracking the eggs.

"Oil, hmm, yes," I poke through the open boxes, appreciative for the distraction. "Dry goods, it should be … " I poke over a few boxes of angel hair, and a bag of rice, and the small bottle appears. "Olive oil, at your service."

"Am I Popeye or Bluto?" Marsh cocks an eyebrow as he takes the bottle from me. His thumb brushes mine. After the Thumb Pinky Summit while packing books earlier, my stomach should be calm, but nope, the butterflies are swarming from a simple thumb touch from Marsh. I offer him a soft smile, sigh, and pull my hand back.

"We don't have any spinach," I say, doing my best to play along with his joke. "So Bluto."

Marsh pops his sweater over his head, pulls the sleeves of his T-shirt up, and flexes his meaty biceps. "Well, blow me down!"

"That's Popeye."

"They're both hot." Marsh's arms taunt me and I do my best not to stare. "They should've canned Olive Oyl and just hooked up."

"I'd watch that movie." My mind fills with images of the two beefy cartoon men in compromising positions.

"I am what I am, and that's all that I am," Marsh scowls, attempting his best Popeye face. "I mean, come on, that's totally the predecessor to 'I'm here. I'm queer. Get used to it.'"

Even when his humor misses, even when the joke doesn't quite land, I still want to smash our faces together. Somehow, the ones that don't really work, while maybe frustrating as hell to him, make him even more charming—which isn't helpful when he's gone and broken my heart.

"Do you want me to chop the onions?" I ask, knowing his disdain for tears in the kitchen.

"You don't mind?" Marsh takes two onions and attempts to juggle them. His tongue juts out in concentration and once again, without trying, he's too fucking cute for words.

"Nope. Bring on the forced emotions," I say. Peeling the first onion, the vapors quickly take over and I welcome the excuse to cry while being his sous chef one last time.

"That's my … " Marsh's eyes meet my already damp ones, and he waits. Pursing my lips, I give him a gentle nod and he says, "Data."

I'm his. His Data. Nobody else will ever call me that. Nobody will ever have my heart like Marsh. A tear falls from my right eye. Damn onions. I'm stuck here for at least another day, making my favorite soup with my ex-boyfriend, who I'm still madly in love with, even if he made it crystal clear he needed to be alone. Mr. Space Man hurling through the cosmos. I do my best to dice the onion into small pieces the way he likes. My heart mimics the knife, with rapid fire thumps against my chest.

"It's fitting this will be our last meal here," he says, peeling a carrot over the Wildlife Bin. It says 'compost' but we simply toss it out in the woods and the animals devour it.

"Yeah, we're lucky Duffy could clear us out," I say. "If we can finish packing by tomorrow, we can beat the next storm."

"We got this, Data." He flips the carrot, catches it, and places it on the cutting board. "We're a good team. Like celery and carrots."

"I think it's peas and carrots that go together," I say.

"Yeah, but peas in matzoh ball soup? That's like casting a shiksa as Fanny Brice. Blasphemous."

Carefully, I set aside the carrot and celery, making room to continue chopping the onions.

"We wouldn't want blasphemous soup," I say.

"Absolutely not. Soup is comfort food. And … " He returns to peeling, his soft green eyes seem to search for the right words. "You love my balls."

I sniff and chuckle, the onion finally overpowering my senses, barely allowing the laugh in through the tears.

"Some people's are too big. Some are tiny." I blink hard, trying to eradicate the onion. "Yours are … "

"Delicious."

"I was going to say just right, but yes, delicious works, too." With the last onion chopped and in the pot, I scrub my hands, working the soap in between my fingers, doing my best to wash away the snivel-inducing juices and aroma.

"Let's get them in the fridge," Marsh says. He sets the carrot aside and mixes the packet of matzoh meal into the egg and oil mixture. "The longer they sit, the easier they'll be to form."

I take a seat at the small table smashed against the wall. The cabin doesn't have an eat-in kitchen or dining room, so this was our solution. "We'll make it work," Marsh said when we found the tiny table antiquing. "Maybe you'll make us a new one someday." I run my hand over the knot in the wood, imagining what I could have made for us.

This is my spot while he cooks. We chat, he tells me stories and jokes, and I bask in the Marshness of Marsh. He's performing. For me. Just me. Like I'm the only guy in the world.

He places the bowl in the fridge and returns to the cutting board. Knife in hand, he's about to make the first slice, the innocent carrot waiting for its fate when it happens. My mouth, apparently hell-bent on causing trouble, overrides my brain and I blurt, "Why did you dump me?"

Marsh's eyes go wide. The knife wobbles in his hand slightly.

"And don't give me the bullshit space and time excuse. I know that you were upset about the showcase. I now know that you received that horrible news about your dad right before. But why was your response to shut me out?" Bottled up for months, the words pour out of me. "I was your boyfriend, your partner. I wanted to be there for you, and you wouldn't let me. I don't get it. So please, I want to know the real reason." I straighten my back against the stiff chair. "After eight years, if nothing else, I think I deserve the truth."

Marsh puts the knife down, and I take it as a good omen as he moves to the other chair, which, given the size of the table, puts him about two feet away from me.

"You're right," Marsh says. His lack of a smart-ass comeback catches me off guard.

"Why Marsh?" Tears prick at my eyes. Maybe it's the lingering onion fumes in the air, or maybe it's my heart cracking open.

He sighs. His entire torso puffs up and then deflates like a horrible hot air balloon disaster imploding in our tiny cabin. "You really want to know?"

That's the kind of question an ex asks you that instantly sends your stomach into a tumultuous earthquake. Violent shaking. Rocking back and forth. What horrible thing have I done? How can someone possibly throw another hurtful log on the devastating fire already blazing inside me? But I want to know. Need to know. All the breakup sex and matzoh ball soup in the world won't help me move on without knowing the truth.

"Yes."

Marsh's gaze lands on the table. My insides burn and churn, waiting for the final nail to be hammered into my heart.

"You deserve someone better."

His voice is quiet. Soft. Almost a whisper. This isn't how Marsh speaks. I'm not positive I've heard him correctly.

"What did you say?"

"You deserve someone better." This time his eyes find mine and his voice approaches his typical vim and vigor volume. "Better than me. Someone who isn't closing in on forty and still figuring out how to be a functioning adult. Someone who can support you the way you supported me—emotionally, financially, all of it."

Tears well up and this time, I'm fairly certain the onions aren't to blame.

"Oh." A sigh of relief escapes my lips as my heart pounds like a bass drum. "I thought maybe it was … me."

"You?" he asks, complete confusion overtaking his face.

"I wasn't sure what you were going to say, but a lifetime of feeling responsible for anything wrong happening around me made me think maybe it was something about … me." My hand covers my face. "I don't know. Maybe I became too annoying. Too controlling. Too … everything."

Marsh reaches out and removes my hand from my face. His fingers rub mine, and he gently massages my palm with his thumb. Even a gesture as small as this settles me in a way only he's capable of doing.

"Oh, my Data. No. This was all about me. Not being enough. Wanting more for you. You deserve the sun and the moon and I'm barely a meteorite."

It finally hits me. Marsh dumped me for … me. Or at least that's what he thinks.

"But you don't get to decide that." My voice trembles. I'm careful not to raise it.

"You'd never … " Marsh says, but then stops.

"No, I wouldn't. Because you don't get to make that decision for me. Without my input. Because now, I'm … I'm … " My eyes clench closed, and my shoulders tremble.

"What? You're what?"

"Ruined. You ruined me, Marsh," I say.

My words slap a sting of pain across Marsh's face. "Ruined you?"

"For anyone else. I'm trying to move on, but all I want is … you."

His fingers stop massaging mine, but he doesn't let go of my hand.

"Why didn't you tell me this six months ago instead of insisting we break up?" I ask.

"Because I know my stubborn little mule wouldn't have listened."

A half chuckle escapes my mouth. "You're right, I wouldn't have." Sometimes I wonder if Marsh knows me too well. Wait, did he just call me *his* stubborn little mule? "Because that's not what people who love each other do. Give up when they're scared and insecure. They lean on each other."

Marsh scoots his chair closer to mine, the wood scraping on the ancient linoleum. He shimmies down, and leans his gigantic head on my shoulder. The big lug.

"Like this?"

His voice vibrates against my body, and goosebumps scatter across my skin.

"Yes. Like this." I cup his chubby cheek, and his warmth transfers to my palm. It's been a long time since I've felt this close to him, and the absence of any sexual tension somehow makes it even more intimate.

"My balls," Marsh says. He pops upright. "Let's make them."

He retrieves the bowl from the fridge, and I sit and watch him create the most delicious, comforting salve for us. We may be over. We may be selling our love nest. But at least we have Marsh's Magnificent (Matzoh) Balls.

Marsh

Here's the thing you need to know about Data: the man knows how to set a mean table.

Even though we're packing things up, he finds a pair of plates, cloth napkins, and silverware and arranges them beautifully on our coffee table. Rather than eat at the smushed-in kitchen table, we choose to have our soup in the living room near the crackling fireplace.

I bring the pot of soup and a trivet to the table. Two candles are lit in the center.

He sits on a throw pillow on the floor. "If we use up the candles tonight, that's one less thing we have to pack."

That's my Data. Ever the romantic pragmatist.

I put down the trivet and soup and spoon us out two bowlfuls. There's something homey about the smell of matzoh ball soup that makes me feel like everything will be okay. It's like the warm hugs my mom used to give me when I was little, the ones that made me believe that the worst the world could throw at me was no match for Mom. God, sometimes I wish I could call her.

I take a moment to find my butt balance on the throw pillow. Sitting on the floor is something typically meant for preschoolers and melodramatic twentysomethings. Not grown-ass adults. But I power through the back and leg strain until I find the right position.

"Ah, there," I say.

"I also found this." Data pulls a bottle of champagne from off the loveseat.

"Whoa! We have champagne?"

"The realtor gave it to us when we moved in." He gives a far-off chuckle. "I kept wanting to save it for a special occasion."

"It *is* a special occasion. Our final night on Marshmallow Mountain." It almost sounds magical.

He pours two tea cups of champagne, hands one to me. "I told you we'd find a use for these."

I hold my tea cup, pinky proudly out. "Cheers."

He wears a bittersweet, lopsided grin as we clink cups.

"Hmm. This is good," I say as the bubbles tickle my nose. "In my unprofessional opinion. And my thumb fits perfectly inside the tea cup handle."

Data laughs, but still has that far-off look on his face. We all like to think we're more inscrutable than we actually are.

"Hey." I try to bring him back to the present. Whatever he's feeling, I'm feeling it too. We've gone from a quick, unsatisfying breakup to one that keeps getting dragged out.

"Marsh, I'd like us to stay friends. I didn't mean what I said when I first arrived."

"Me too." The lump in my throat that's been there all weekend gets a little bit bigger. "To quote God herself, my life would suck without you."

"I have something for you." Data's eyes twinkle as he pokes around in his pocket. Before I can speak, he holds it out. The most perfectly crafted, tiny replica of our cabin sits in his palm. I suck in a quick gulp of air before remembering to breathe. "I made it for you."

My heart freezes. No, it's pounding. All the blood in my

body seems to rush to my ears and I open my mouth, but nothing escapes.

"It's not sanded. Or stained. And I kinda messed up the front steps at the end." His fingers brush over the roof. "But, I thought you might like a mini version of Marshmallow Mountain. To help remember … things."

"It's perfect." The words come out like a devotion. "And I could never forget … things."

A grainy highlight reel plays in my mind. The first time we entered the cabin, joking about who got to carry who over the threshold. The first time we plunked down into the loveseat. Adding yet another worn paperback to the shelf. Stealing kisses on his neck in the hall. Frisky Fridays and lazy Saturdays. The A/C that never worked as well as we wanted. The one picture on the wall that refused to hang straight. The laughs. Tears. Meals. Board games. Data screaming my name before he came. Data screaming my name when I broke a dish. The moments of contented silence that never had to be filled.

I squeeze the figurine in my palm so hard the edges dig into my hand, branding itself on my skin and in my soul.

It's going to be hard as fucking hell to stay friends with this man and not have my heart gash open every time I see him. What the fuck am I going to do when he starts dating someone? Am I really going to do bar trivia with Data and Evan the ENT? Am I going to dog sit Maxwell the corgi while they take a romantic long weekend to Provincetown?

Getting to stay in his life, despite the way I ended things, is a gift. I'm not going to shoo it away.

The heavy moment lifts, and we're able to enjoy our meal. The champagne helps loosen us up, as does the fresh stock of Mallomars. I found a loaf of rye bread in the freezer, and I toasted a few slices for us. Eating soup without bread to dip is against human nature.

Data gives me a review of the new Mexican brunch spot

Bryce and Anthony have been dragging him to. I update him on what Preeti is cooking up for *Out with a Bang*, and as I tell him about the show, my body hums with excitement. The rush of performing comes back to me. The flutter in my stomach when I walk out onstage. The way vibing with an audience feels like riding that perfect wave. Not just doing graphics, but up there, putting myself out there. Taking a leap.

We talk about cute contestants on this season of *Survivor*. I forgot how fun it was talking with Data about the most arbitrary stuff. Finding the right someone to talk about nothing with is what makes life enjoyable.

Eventually, we eat every last matzoh ball, every last Mallomar. The candles are burned down to half masts. We clear off the table and tag team clean up: I wash, he dries. I grab my phone to play some music. We sing along to Billy Joel's "Piano Man," a song ingrained into every Jewish kid who ever attended a youth group event. A cozy twinkle sparkles in Data's eyes as he watches me mumble through the last verse, the hardest one to remember. After, I share the theory that the song is a gay anthem because it's about a piano player who doesn't realize he's playing at a gay bar, and all the men are flirting with him. Data rolls his eyes, but doesn't disagree. He makes me play the song again.

"You sure you want to sleep on the loveseat?" I ask him a little bit later when it's time for bed. He tucks the sheet into the cushions.

"It'll be fine. With the fire and the heat from the kitchen, I'll be warm enough."

No, you won't. You will only be fine if you sleep spooned in my arms. This is gay science. The words stay in my mouth, even though they're dying to break free.

"Will the fire burn through the night?" I ask.

"I can always add a few logs." He continues to make up the loveseat.

"Yeah. Okay." My tongue is thick in my throat. How the fuck am I going to sleep knowing he's so close, yet so far, knowing that after tonight, everything will change forever.

I let Data go because he deserves a man who can give him the fucking world. And yeah, my career is on life support, my family unit is falling apart, I'm sleeping on a rigid sofa in a shitty studio apartment, and The Gap no longer carries my size.

But maybe … what if I *could* be the guy who gave him the world? Why *not* me?

"Here's the thing you need to know about Data: the man cannot sleep in an unmade bed. We're talking top sheets, dust ruffles," I say as I watch him tuck the sheet firmly under the cushion.

Data snorts. "I used to be embarrassed when you'd use that in your routines, but I love how it became your calling card."

Dating a comedian means that your relationship is creative terrain. Fortunately, he never objected. I couldn't get enough of his quirks, and neither could inebriated audiences.

"Here's the thing you need to know about Data: he doesn't 'trust' dishwashers." I use emphatic air quotes. "He thinks they don't clean plates well enough, and he believes they were behind the Tide Pod craze."

His eyes crinkle in a silent laugh as he fluffs his pillow. "Here's the thing you need to know about Marsh: the man doesn't like using towels because he prefers to air dry and because he claims they scratch his precious skin."

"True and true. I'm too cheap for nice towels, so it's air drying all the way." I take a step closer, shove my hands into my pockets. "Here's the thing you need to know about Data: he actively chooses to go to Times Square for some reason."

"That was one time, and I thought it would be fun."

"Times Square is never fun unless you're from Nebraska," I say.

"Here's the thing about Marsh: he made me watch every episode of *The Simpsons*."

"Only the first ten seasons!" We're cackling so hard we can barely catch our breath. "Here's the thing you need to know about Data: he gave me the third degree when I merely suggested we get an Alexa."

"It literally spies on you in order to sell you products," he replies.

"It also tells me the time when I'm too lazy to look at my phone." I take a tentative step toward him. "Here's the thing you need to know about Data: he insisted we purchase a snowy cabin on a mountain even though he doesn't like to ski."

"It's for the ambiance." His eyes squeeze shut as the laughter makes him vibrate. When they open, they're watery and clear and staring right at me. "Here's the thing you need to know about Marsh."

But there's no punchline. Only the sound of our breath attempting to fill the dead air. He closes the space between us and gets on his toes to meet my lips. Unlike the hungry, angry kissing of last night, this kiss is soft, tender, infused with significance.

I bury my fingers in his beard, feeling his jaw open and close as we kiss. I rummage up to his ears, gliding along the soft drops of his earlobes, then to the prickly hairs on his neck, savoring each part of him. The sounds of our lips smacking and the crackling embers of the fire fill the room. He purrs into my mouth and I relish the vibrations against my lips.

"My Data," I say, his big, round face in my hands. I trace his bottom lip with my thumb. He gives it a peck.

I pull him close, wrap my arms around his thick frame, smell his musky scent on his sweatshirt. All I want to do is hold him and kiss him and never let him go.

Data slips me some tongue, its warmth filling my mouth. I slide my tongue around his, making him shiver at my touch.

My hands go back to his beard, then up to his hair. I remember how much he loved when I would wash his hair in the shower using hypnotic circles into his scalp. My fingers repeat the motion now and he tilts his head back into my touch.

Slowly, I lower us onto the loveseat. He lays down, and I lay on top of him.

"Wait." I struggle to maneuver my legs in between his. I toss the throw pillows on the floor. "Big guys. Small couch."

I lean over him, but gravity pulls me off the loveseat.

"Shit." I catch myself before I tumble into a full-on pratfall.

"I can make more room," he offers. He scrunches himself deeper into the cushions so I can put my knee on there for balance, but there's only so much he can scrunch. It's kind of like tilting your body as you watch your bowling ball go down the lane hoping that'll change your inevitable gutterball.

"Is that better?" he asks.

"Yeah," I lie. My knee can't get onto the loveseat, but I'm not about to derail this hot makeout sesh.

Fuck. Data is under me, all for me, cute as anything. His face is flush with color. His cock digs into my thigh. I want him so bad. I'll see a million chiropractors after this, I don't care. I plant a foot on the ground and a hand on top of the loveseat. I'm free soloing this goddamn piece of furniture.

"You are so beautiful." I tip his chin up for another gentle kiss, pressing my tongue into his mouth, his hot panting breath sending tingles through my body.

"Are you comfortable? Your face is very red," he says.

"I'm great." I slink my hand under his sweatshirt, shutting him up. My fingers graze over the soft hair on his big belly. I travel up and pinch his nipple, eliciting a gasp of lust from my Data. He lifts his hips, a subtle reminder that he's very hard.

I attempt to pull his sweatshirt off, but I can't do it one-handed. And if I lift my other hand, I will tumble off the couch and pop a kneecap.

I thrust my hips, letting him feel how much I want him.

"Oh fuck," I grunt as he undoes my belt. My heart races with the same excitement and greedy anticipation as if this were our first time. He shoves his hand into my boxers and grips my aching, leaking cock.

I respond by tugging at his chest hair, delirious with lust. I push through the pain shooting up my leg and down my arm.

He undoes his pants and suddenly our dicks are mashed together in his sweaty hand. He jerks us together, his heat blazing through my core, our balls rubbing against one another. I rut against his cock, my mouth struggling to keep kissing him while gasping for air. He bites my lower lip, digs the fingernails of his free hand into my back.

My tender cockhead pulses against his touch, jabs against his hairy stomach.

"I miss you, Data," I say, no taking it back. "I miss you."

"Oh, Marsh." He throws his head back, pinches his eyes closed. "Fuck."

"Oh babe."

"No. The arm of the couch is digging into my head." He tries to sit up, and that throws me off balance. My foot and hand lose their grip, and I flop onto him before falling off his body entirely. My fat ass knocks into the coffee table as I hit the floor, making the candles do a precarious shimmy. I save them from toppling over without burning myself.

"Why did we get this tiny ass couch?" I ask.

"Because we wanted to be cozy?"

I stand up, cock still hard and pointing at my man. I hold out my hand. "Let's continue this on the bed."

As I pull him toward me, we kiss again, our cocks sword fighting below, before venturing into the bedroom.

Chapter Twenty-Five

Data

Here's the thing you need to know about Marsh: when he says "My Data," his voice completely changes. Two words. Three syllables. But, there's a softness. A yearning. Something about the way those sounds come together produces a unique reaction in his vocal cords. And I'm the only one lucky enough to hear it. My Data. My Data. My Data.

Those words, from his lips, melt my insides like a thick dab of butter on a warm biscuit. Not the cheap ones they sell at the grocery in a six-pack, but the hefty, flaky ones you get at the Portuguese bakery on fifty-fourth street. The ones that cost six dollars a biscuit, but are worth every penny. My stomach flips at the thought of his voice. Or maybe it's a hunger pang from thinking about those damn biscuits.

After freshening up in the bathroom, I find Marsh sprawled out on the bed. Even though the room is colder than we'd like, he's lying naked on top of the comforter. Standing in the doorway, I realize this is the first time I've seen Marsh naked since we broke up. Unlike our recent encounters, the lights are on, I'm fully awake and able to take him all in.

Marsh exudes a confidence in his skin I found sexy from the moment I laid eyes on him. With his hands behind his head, his cock, rock hard and ready, lies pointing at his round stomach. Light peach fuzz starts just below his belly button until it meets the barely there bush above his dick. He wants so badly to be a bear, but he's almost hairless. The one time he tried to grow a beard, he ended up looking like a naked mole rat.

Marsh spots me, and a smile overtakes his delectable face. My entire body hums with anticipation. There's no denying it. I love everything about this man. My Marsh.

"Come here often?"

I chuckle because even when his jokes delve into dad territory, his charm somehow buoys them.

"This Winnie the Pooh cosplay you're doing is everything."

I glance down and yup, only wearing the red U.S. Open T-shirt I bought solely because the fit was right, and while those men look delicious smacking a ball back and forth over a net, I look like a certain bear who wears a shirt and nothing else.

"Do you want me to take it off?" I ask, tugging at the hem.

"No, keep it on. You can be my Data the Pooh Bear."

I'm fairly certain he isn't interested in a Hundred Acre Wood fantasy, but right now, I wouldn't even object. I'll be the Winnie to his Tigger anyday.

Laying next to him, my hands immediately land on his belly. Something about it attracts my fingers like bees to honey. The words almost escape my lips, but I'm hesitant to encourage his A. A. Milne kink.

"My Data." He moves his hand around me as I snuggle into his burly chest. His smell, a mix of that ridiculous body spray and his natural scent, slightly sweet and ripe, intoxicates me and I have the desire to crawl inside him and stay there forever. Except, right now, I want him inside me.

I tilt my head so my eyes find his and hope I'm able to convey just how much I want to be his. Now. Tomorrow. Forever.

"Did you mean it?" I ask.

"About you being my Pooh Bear?"

I chuckle. "No. About missing me." I kiss Marsh's chin and study his beautiful face.

"Data Bear," he says, this new nickname flowing over me like sweet honey, "I've missed you every second since … "

The corners of his eyes prickle. There's nothing but sincerity in his voice. I rescue him from having to say it, craning my head to capture his soft lips. He still tastes like matzoh ball soup and I'm not mad about it. My tongue juts between his lips and Marsh lets out a quiet moan. There's miles between us and the closest neighbors, but years of living like sardines in the city have him on guard. I'm determined to untangle him.

Reaching down, I palm his dick, taking my time to let my fingers remember the landscape. Every line and curve comes flooding back as my thumb traces his shaft. Skating up to the head, brushing over the tip, his precum alerting me to his excitement.

"God, I've missed this," he says.

"Me grabbing your cock?"

Marsh laughs, and a wave of satisfaction washes over me, knowing I've tickled his funny bone.

"That's not what I meant, but yeah." I gently clutch him, and then slowly stroke, my fingers falling back into the familiarity of all his favorite spots.

"Did you miss me sucking it?" I ask.

He reaches up and traces my bottom lip before slipping his finger inside. Instantly, I'm sucking, swirling my tongue around his finger, giving him a preview of what I'm about to do to him.

"My Data and his magical mouth."

I chuckle and lightly bite down on his finger, a slight snarl overtaking my lips. Being this close on the bed, the intimacy not rushed, but treasured, part of me hopes Mother Nature unloads ten feet of fresh powder and we're trapped in the cabin together for all eternity. We can arrange for pizza and Mallomars to be airlifted in.

He pulls his finger out of my mouth. "Let's see if I've still got it," I tease, snaking down to his chest. He tickles my back as my tongue flirts with his nipple.

"There's my Data," he coos. "Oh, lord."

My tongue traces the perimeter, slowly flicking, bringing Marsh to full attention. My left hand joins the right on his cock. He's so fucking hard, and the nerves on my fingertips crackle under the heat.

Kissing his chest, I steal a glance at Marsh's face before resuming my journey south. He's staring at me with eyes like two giant emerald pools I want to do a massive cannonball into. Eight years of togetherness comes crashing back in that look. He can tell me he misses me until the end of time and I wouldn't tire of it. Those eyes. Marsh's missing me sends tingles rushing over my skin like a tsunami.

"I missed you too," I say. "So fucking much."

A half smile tugs at his lips, and he sighs. There's no quip. No punchline. Just him waiting for me to service his glorious cock.

Marsh reaches for my face, his thumb tracing my jawline. As he rubs my beard, he finishes with a sweep of my lips and I kiss his finger.

"I love you." The words fall from my lips like shooting stars.

He replies by pulsing his dick in my palm. He once joked he could send me the complete works of David Sedaris in Morse code with his cock. Science should study the man's erections.

"My sweet Data," he finally says. He doesn't need to tell me he loves me. His eyes do all the talking.

I push myself down and his beautiful package finally comes close enough to taste. Marsh really has a gorgeous dick—when I wrap my fist around it, my fingers barely reach my thumb. It took me months to get the majority down my throat, but one thing about me, when it comes to blowing Marsh, I'm persistent. I once tried to whittle a replica out of basswood, but I couldn't get the curve right.

"Why would you want a wood dildo of my dick? That's a nasty splinter waiting to happen," he said.

"Marsh, it deserves to be honored with a sculpture and I'm the only one qualified for the task."

Holding the real deal, inches from my face, I whisper, "Hey, you."

"Are you talking to my boner?" Marsh asks.

"Hush," I say, turning toward him. "This is a private conversation."

"Now, you," I say, turning back to his erection, "I've missed you almost as much as him." I nod at Marsh.

"What's that?" I ask, pulling the head toward my ear.

"Oh sure, a kiss first?" I gently brush my lips on the tip.

"More? Of course," I tease and pop his cock into my mouth.

My tongue brushes the head, back and forth, as my hand assists, covering more real estate and giving him the magical experience he always raved about. Marsh lifts his hips, thrusting up, and his cock fills me, but my gag reflex, still training to take him all after all these years, kicks in and small gasps and gurgles escape my lips.

"You okay, babe?"

His eyebrows are drawn together as he makes strong eye contact. The man doesn't have a mean bone in his body. Even as he jams his tastiest bone down my throat, he's concerned about my comfort, which makes me want to devour him more.

"Yeah, I'm just a few months out of practice," I say, waving his hard cock and slapping it against my beard.

"Oh fuck. The best tickles." Marsh's barrel chest shakes with laughter as I attempt to bury his dick in my whiskers, covering it from every angle. It's my secret weapon to titillate and torture him simultaneously.

"You love it," I say, massaging his dick into the thickest hairs, right below my cheek.

"Guilty."

"Now, before you pound me … " I lift his balls and spread my beard on his taint like a kitten marking his scent. His thighs shiver as I paint him with my facial hair, and a mischievous smile slithers onto my lips.

"Data. Oh, oh!"

I grab his ankles and lift. Marsh hoists his legs in the air, giving me better access, and my tongue glides down and slips right into his hole. With added pressure, my beard prickles the perimeter as I plunge into his opening. Nothing gets him harder than a pre-fucking rim job.

With my tongue darting in and out of him, his cock surges over and over in my hand. If he could deliver/I could read Morse Code, I imagine he'd be tapping out "I'm going to fuck you so hard."

Each throb in my palm is a teaser of what's about to come. My hole twitches in anticipation, knowing how much we both want this. Need this. Every rom-com I've ever seen has taught me two things: Julia Roberts can do no wrong, and the only thing better than breakup sex is makeup sex.

"There we go," I say, tugging at his erection. "You're so ready. Do you want to fuck me?"

"Um, does the Academy love comedians in dramatic roles?"

I grin at his joke.

"Except for Jim Carrey."

"You'll never get over that, will you?" I ask.

"Criminal oversight."

My face stretches and sends whiskers flying across his entire rump. Marsh trembles and mumbles, "Oooh."

"How do you want to do it?" Waiting for his reply, I lick up to his balls, continuing to his shaft and kissing the head of his cock for good measure.

"My dick. Your ass."

"Yeah, I figured, but how?"

"Data, I don't fucking care. I just want to be buried inside you." He reaches for my chin and lifts my head so our eyes meet. "Soon."

I kiss my way up to his face, peppering as much of his skin as I can until my lips land on his. Wrapping his paws around my torso, he pulls me close, our tongues playing chase inside each other's mouths until I fall on him with a thud. I may be a big boy, but he's bigger. Taller. Broader. Stronger. Inside and out. Marsh shelters me. I never have to worry about crushing him. He takes every ounce of me like a pro, welcoming my weight on his sturdy body.

Pausing the kiss, Marsh keeps his lips brushed against mine. "My Data."

My legs straddle him and his cock, already poking at my hole, lurches against me. Now it's Marsh's turn to deliver a sexy as fuck mischievous grin.

"You ready?" I ask.

"Baby, I was born ready." He slaps my ass and smiles.

He always has a plan—especially for sex. When I was in the bathroom, he smartly planted the bottle of lube from The General Store on the bedside table. No scurrying or searching when the moment hits. Grab and go.

He hands me the bottle and I squirt a generous amount on my palm and slather it on myself. When I'm ready, I warm a little more up for him and reach back and apply it on his hard-as-a-diamond cock. Marsh's face lights up like I've just told him he's opening for the late George Carlin. The way he's looking at me like I'm the only soul in the universe, I've missed that more than anything.

Leaning forward, his cock finds its target, and I slowly ease back, only taking the tip. After the hammering in The General Store bathroom and riding him like a mechanical bull in the middle of last night, my ass is more than ready. But I'm in no rush. I want to savor him. Sneaking a peek, I find him staring at me.

"What?" I ask.

"You. Who gave you permission to be this perfect?"

Here's the thing you need to know about Marsh: Yes, he can land a whip smart joke quicker than a wink, but he also can put a sentence together that takes my breath away. How am I supposed to answer him? Marsh sees me. All of me. He always has. And he's always made me feel like the sexiest, most desirable man on the planet.

Unable to reply, I rest back, allowing his cock to slide in. I reach back and caress his balls. The barely there hair always elicits a smile, and my fingers travel up the base of his dick, relishing feeling the point of our connection.

"Feel good?" he asks, running his hands up my stomach and landing on my chest.

"Phenomenal. As always." I continue alternating between gently massaging his balls, adding some pressure underneath, and feeling his thick dick sliding inside me. The pleasure from my ass travels outward and frissons of pleasure ripple through me.

"You missed me, right?" I ask.

"So much."

"Fuck me like you missed me."

He does his best to thrust up, but I want him deeper. Closer. More connected.

Leaning over, my lips land on his, and he slips out of me, the popping noise causing us both to giggle as he nibbles my lips.

"Oops," I say. My legs are tired and I fall next to him. With the lube still slick and sticky in my palm, my hand takes over, jerking him slowly.

"My Data." He kisses my nose. My cheek. My chin. His lips ruffle the small hairs in my beard and I catch his eyes studying me.

With a mix of sadness and urgency, he says, "Fuck, I missed you."

"Me or my ass?"

"Data, I missed every inch of you."

He rolls toward me, reaches behind, and slaps my ass, the sound and sting sending a jolt of passion to my core.

"But mostly dat ass. Dat ass. Dat ass." With each utterance, he slaps me.

I shift my position, allowing him better access and Marsh slips two fingers in my eager hole.

"Slide it in."

I roll away from him and lift my leg, bending and pulling it toward my chest.

His fingers spread me open, and he guides himself in. His arm wraps around my torso, clutching me close as he fucks me. Picking up speed, his lips find my ear and he whispers, "My Data. My Data. My Data."

With each declaration, he plunges into me, finally giving me the pounding I'm craving.

"There you go," I say. "Harder. Harder. Fuck me harder."

His fingers grip my chest, pulling and tugging at the hair, but I don't care. There's no way I'm asking him to stop. He's clinging to me like his life depends on it, and I'm determined to stay as close as possible.

I reach back, running my fingers through his hair, pulling his lips toward my neck. Seeking another point of contact, Marsh nibbles, kisses, and licks. This is the moment I wish could last forever. No stopping. No separating. Just us. Here. Connected.

"Data. Babe. I'm close."

But that's not how sex works. Its fleeting nature is part of what makes it so fucking amazing.

"Okay. Like this?" I ask.

"Yeah, this. Close. Fuck, I missed you."

I laugh because Marsh may never stop telling me. And I'm perfectly fine with that.

With my free hand, I reach between my legs, feeling his balls again, his cock sliding in and out, waiting for his tell. When his sack contracts, I pause my fingers, waiting for it. Before he utters a word, I feel his cock throbbing, shooting, filling me up.

"Lord, Data." He pulls me even closer, attempting to fuse our bodies together as he ravages me.

His body slows, but he doesn't pull out. Instead, he draws me to him with both arms now, kissing my upper back, whispering over and over, "My Data. My Data. My Data."

Even after he's come, Marsh's cock stays hard for a good fifteen minutes. He doesn't know why, but it has proven useful on multiple occasions. Again: science community, get on this.

"If you wait a few minutes, I can keep going," he offers.

"Marsh. You're not the Energizer Bunny. Let's not give your asthma an excuse to flare up." I scoot forward, the familiar pop of his erection leaving me echoing in the room. I lay on my back and pat his smooth chest.

"But I have my inhaler." He pulls it from a drawer in the bedside table. "Locked and loaded."

"Babe. I'm good. Truly," I say, palming myself, ready to release the first not break-up sex orgasm since we arrived on the mountain.

"Okay, but let me at least … " Marsh shimmies down and takes me in his hand. After a few strokes, he's sucking, the small room filling with the sounds of his enjoyment.

"So much fucking better than matzoh ball soup," he says,

licking down my shaft to my balls, Marsh tongues them, covering as much surface area as possible.

"Don't knock your soup," I say. "It's delicious."

"Yeah, so are these." He laps at my balls.

After eight years together, Marsh knows how to make me come fast. First, he takes my cock in his mouth, rolling his tongue around the head, swirling and slurping, putting his all into getting me off. Next, he reaches up with one hand, pinching and flicking my left nipple. He's researched them both and finds the left more efficient. Finally, with his other hand, he slips two fingers into my hole. After the hammering he just gave me, I'm open, ready, desperate for his touch. With his patented three-point system, hints of my orgasm appear quickly.

With my breath deepening, Marsh picks up speed. Alternating between my chest and shaft, one hand strokes and squeezes, while the other fucks me deep, hitting my spot. My entire body shakes, my lips part, and gasps and moans reverberate off the tacky wood paneling we never replaced.

"There's my Data. Come for me, babe. Give it to me."

And that's it. My orgasm cracks me open. I'm split in two, allowing him right back into the vacancy he left in my heart. The first spurt hits his face, but he doesn't recoil. Like a firefighter running toward the danger, he lunges his face forward, swallowing me whole. My cock shoots down his throat and Marsh's gulping joins my sighs of pleasure as he takes me all in.

"Fucking scrumptious. If only I had a Mallomar with it." Marsh licks his lips and lies next to me.

Panting heavily, I say, "Maybe next time."

Marsh cuddles into my chest.

"Covers, please," he says, and we scurry under. He's immediately back, plastering himself against me. I do my best to gather him in my arms, rolling him slightly and drawing his back toward me. Even though he's bigger, Marsh always finds a way to be the small spoon.

"I missed you," he says. "So damn much."

"I know, babe."

"And I'm sorry. Again."

"You don't have to keep apologizing," I say.

"I was an idiot. A scared, insecure idiot."

"Talk to me next time. This." I pat his chest, right where his heart beats. "This is what I care about."

"Deal."

Marsh always had this ritual before bed. We had to kiss exactly three times. He swore he couldn't sleep well otherwise. The first two are soft and quick, but on the final one, he presses and stays a little longer. He says, "It locks the first two in place."

"Kiss, please," I say.

Marsh turns around, kisses me twice, short and sweet, and then finally, the last kiss comes. He lingers longer than usual, and I breathe him in. Grateful to have him back where he belongs. In my arms. My Marsh.

Marsh

Here's the thing you need to know about Data: the man has a beautiful snore.

It's a persistent hum with a little bit of wheeze thrown in for good measure. Kind of like the staticky breathing of astronauts in space, or astronauts practicing tantric sex. I wonder if the lack of gravity helps or hurts. Anyway, Data's snore is my personal sound machine, and I didn't realize how much I missed it until it was back in my life. No wonder I'd been sleeping like shit for the last six months.

I'm up, but I don't want to get out of bed. Data's arm is draped over me, his staticky astronaut tantric sex breath rustling against my shoulder. I could stay like this forever.

You can tell if you're meant to be with someone by how you sleep with them. Are you able to fall asleep and stay asleep with this person next to you? Sleep chemistry is real. I'd dated guys where I tossed and turned all night and kept thinking about how much I wanted them out of my bed so I could get some decent shut eye.

With Data, I slept like a baby from the jump.

"Good morning," he utters in a growly whisper as he pulls me against his warm teddy bear body.

"And good morning to you," I say back, grinding myself against his very good morning wood.

It feels good to have Data's hands on my body again. His fingers travel through the tiny wisp of chest hair God gave me. I feel like my naked, hairless body needs to come with ID.

"We can't stay in bed all day," he says.

"No. We mustn't," I agree, slipping into a British accent for no reason. I then burrow my bum further against his knob.

"We can't, Marsh. We have to finish packing and leave this afternoon before the storm comes."

"Do we?" I sit up. An idea that'd been kicking around in my head over the past day rushes out. "Do we really need to pack this place up?"

I study his face, trying to gauge his reaction. His big, dark eyes fill with hope and give me an idea.

"What are you saying, Marsh?"

"I think I made it clear last night. This whole weekend has been one big blinking light telling me that I made a huge mistake. To quote The Jackson 5 and NSYNC, I want you back, Data." I interlock my fingers with his.

"You really want to give things another shot?"

"No." I shake my head confidently. "I'm not giving this a shot. I'm not here for whims. I'm doing this for real. My life is pretty much incomplete without you, and it's very hard functioning as an incomplete human being. Not even the best coffee can help with that." I tip his chin up to meet my eyes. "I love you."

"I love you too." Data bites his lips and I know he's holding something back, but I can't tell what it is.

"Talk to me."

He leans back on the solid oak headboard, which is the champion of West Elm headboards for handling all of our rigorous lovemaking without splintering into pieces. They really should market it that way.

"Well, you used to tell me you loved me all the time. Until you didn't."

"I never stopped loving you, Data. Never. I just got scared. And embarrassed."

"Embarrassed? I am the last person you need to feel embarrassed around."

"You deserve—"

He presses a hand over my mouth. I can tell this isn't one of those times to lick his fingers in protest.

"Nope. I decide what I deserve. I don't care that you're not headlining Madison Square Garden or doing stand-up specials on Netflix. What you do is a small part of who you are. Your job doesn't define you. Or shouldn't." His features suddenly go still and I can almost see the wheels turning in his adorable head. "You're smart, caring, funny. You're looking after your father in an impossible situation. Without being asked, you watered Mrs. Krumholtz's plants downstairs for a month when she was in the hospital. You're already a success to me."

Data frees my mouth from his clutches.

"I'm just trying to be the kind of man worthy of you."

"Well, I'd say you're doing a good job. Aside from the whole dumping thing."

I'll be kicking myself about that for years to come. Fear and self-loathing can make us do some really stupid things.

"You're pursuing your dreams, which most of us are too scared to do." Just as I'm about to chime in with my usual refrain, he presses his hand back against my mouth. "Until now."

He stares at the comforter bunched around us.

"I think it's time that I follow your lead. When I get back to the city, I am starting a job hunt." He pulls his lips in and nods. "I'm not sure what I want exactly, but for the first time in my life, I'm going to let myself decide."

"You can do anything. You're the smartest person I know."

"Didn't your cousin go to MIT?"

"Yeah, but he smells like cottage cheese."

He breaks into a laugh. The kiss I plant on his lips is a promise. I'm not going to fuck this up again.

"To answer your original question," he says, his eyes glimmering with light. "No. We don't need to pack up Marshmallow Mountain."

I crash my lips against his and lower us back down onto the bed. "So that means we have the morning free … "

"Technically, that is true. Although now we have to unpack everything."

I kiss along his neck, tasting his sweet scent. "We can do that next time." There will be plenty of next times.

I palm his hairy chest, savoring the cuddliness of his torso, and let my hand drift down to his erection. We have a six month sex drought to make up for.

"Shit!" he yells as soon as my hand wraps around his cock.

"Are you about to come?" I ask incredulously. Maybe I'm just that good.

"No." Data removes my hand, sits up, and points.

I follow his insistent index finger, which should be up my ass at the moment, but instead pulls my focus to the window.

"Mother of shit," I say.

Heaps of snow come down fast, blanketing the landscape. After this weekend, I'm kind of over the stuff. Maybe we can get a place in Costa Rica. It never snows in Costa Rica, right?

"That's not supposed to be happening until later today," I say. Data was supposed to be the one coming early, not Mother Nature.

He hops out of bed and stares out the window. I can't admire his naked body as I'm too caught up on what's happening outside. (Well, I can a little bit. I'm only human.)

"Marsh, this is bad. Our driveway already has a layer of snow over where Duffy plowed."

As much as I want to spend the rest of my life with him, I'd like to do so outside this cabin. Preferably somewhere with Wi-Fi, reliable electricity, and an unlimited supply of Mallomars.

"We have to get out of here," he says. "If we can't make it off the access road, we're going to be snowed in for another week."

"We can have Duffy swing by again, right?"

He shakes his head no. "Duffy's plow barely made it up the access road the first time. We're supposed to get even more snow this time." He rakes a hand through his hair, spins around, cups my face, and plants a kiss on my lips reminding me that we're a unit. "Babe, we need to get dressed, pack up our essentials, and get the hell off this mountain ASAP."

"Do we have time to take a shower?" I ask.

"A quick one."

"What about shower sex?"

Data shoots me a no-way look. Fair.

"Shower hand jobs?" I tilt my head.

"I will give you all the shower sex you can handle when we get back to the city."

"I'm going to hold you to it." I almost put out my pinkie to seal the promise.

He storms out of the bedroom, and I follow behind. The living room is shining in a snowy glow. Outside, it's nearly a whiteout. Worse than Saturday. The snow is unrelenting, coming down in thick, determined flakes.

I gulp back a lump in my throat. Data's panic is less subtle.

"It could be worse," I say.

"How could this be any worse?"

I shrug. "We could be straight."

Chapter Twenty-Seven

Data

I never stopped loving you.

Marsh's words reverberate in my head during my very quick shower. My mouth curls into a grin because even though I wanted to throttle Marsh for breaking my heart, I never stopped loving him either.

I'm happy to report that make-up sex lands on a whole new level compared to break-up sex. It's the solo Beyonce to Destiny's Child Beyonce. Both are amazing, but only one wins all the Grammys.

The best part? Waking up with Marsh's hands all over me. The man snuggles better than the ridiculous giggling bear being thrown up in the air hocking fabric softener. We belong together—like peas and carrots, we're perfectly adequate on our own, but make so much more sense combined.

My head would love nothing more than to bask in the glory of his declaration of love (and request for shower sex), but Mother Nature (and probably Maddi's chickens) has other plans. The snow seems determined to trap us on the mountain indefinitely. I wrap a towel around my waist when I exit the shower and scurry to the dresser for an outfit to throw on. I'm not sure whether this button-down shirt is mine or his, but it doesn't matter. It fits. The power of gay relationships.

"Can we just leave my car here?" Marsh mumbles when I

get outside, two Mallomars shoved between his sweet lips. His ability to cram so much in his mouth never fails to amuse and titillate me.

"We could, but I'm worried with so much snow it will become completely buried and die a slow death," I say, tossing my bag into my trunk.

"But I hate driving in the snow." Melted chocolate coats his lower lip, taunting me.

"I'll follow you. We can talk on speaker," I say, walking over and resting my hand on his belly. Even through my gloves and his puffy jacket, my skin melts into him. There's something about touching him that instantly puts me at ease, as if my body instinctively knows it's home. "The snow's coming down fast, but it's soft, so our cars shouldn't get stuck. The main roads should already be salted too. We just have to make it down the access road."

We've been apart for almost six months and I'd much rather spend the long drive next to him. Marsh's hand on mine over the gear shift between us. Grabbing his knee to tickle him when he tells a joke. Listening to *Into the Woods* (the original Broadway cast because nobody tops Bernadette Peters. Not even her lovers.) and arguing about who gets to sing the Baker vs. The Baker's Wife on "It Takes Two." But leaving his car in this mess would be foolish. We can disgrace Sondheim once we're safely out of Mother Nature's wrath.

"Okay, but we need at least one *Into the Woods* sing-a-long when we're home," he says, and before I can tell him I was just thinking about that, he blurts, "I'm the Baker!"

"Yes, Marsh, you can be the Baker." He leans down and kisses my nose before I tilt my head up and capture his lips. The snow falls in thick flakes, framing our embrace. In another universe where we're not desperate to flee the impending storm, we'd be the perfect shot for a Hallmark movie. A gay one. With actors that (gasp) have chest hair and weigh more than a wet noodle. And sex. Lots of sex.

"Are you sure we can't stay?" Marsh asks. His lips are still close enough to tickle mine when he speaks and if I weren't so damn … well, me, I'd drag him back inside and ravish him again, but the darkening skies aren't going to wait for Make-Up Sex Part Two: Electric Buggeraloo.

"Yep. We'll be home by dinner if we're lucky."

"Can we order pork buns?"

"I'll text Bryce and have them waiting for us," I say.

"Baruch Hashem. And apologies to our ancestors." Marsh glances toward heaven, then dips his head in reverence. "For the pork." Snowflakes gather in his hair and I realize we need to get rolling before he catches a cold.

"Okay, let's go." I kiss him once more for the road. "I'll call you at the bottom of the access road."

We scrape our cars while they warm up. Then I back up as close to the cabin as possible, and Marsh pulls out in front of me. He drives tentatively, navigating the dips and hairpin turns covered in snow, but thankfully, the thick flakes seem to provide some traction at our slow speed. Marsh's Corolla still has snow tires on from last winter. We typically take it up to the mountain and for once, his laziness and/or forgetfulness prove practical. My Prius still has summer tires because I had no intention of driving up here this winter, let alone in Snowmageddon.

The entire car lifts slightly as I follow Marsh onto the access road. Only a thin layer of snow shrouds the pavement, a testament to Duffy's thorough, um, plowing. Even as the snow continues to plummet, we're able to pick up a touch of speed.

"You're doing great," I say when Marsh picks up the phone. We both have Bluetooth, which is the only reason I agreed to the marathon session. "Don't go too fast. The snow is soft but that doesn't mean you can't spin out."

"I forgot how much of a backdoor driver you are."

"You mean backseat."

"That too." I can hear the smile cross his lips. Well, the joke's on him because when we get back to the city, I'm going to make sure he can't sit down without wincing.

"I'm just looking out for you."

"I got this. I'm the one who remembered their snow tires."

A smile spreads across my face, and I wish Marsh could see me. Kiss me. A sigh escapes my mouth.

"You okay?" he asks.

"That was a good sigh. I'm just happy."

This weird mix of happy and relieved surges through me. He's finally realized we're bashert. The universe—and Maddi's chickens—wants us together, and there's no sense in fighting it. All the other stuff we can figure out … together.

My phone lights up with a text. I know I shouldn't look at my phone while driving, especially in inclement weather, but a split-second glance should be safe. Neither of us have swerved or slipped so far.

"Yes," I say under my breath as I read Bryce's confirmation.

"What is it?" Marsh asks.

"Pork buns will be waiting for us," I say.

"Bryce with the assist. Three points! Coming through in the clutch," Marsh says.

"God, you sounded so heterosexual just now."

"What are you talking about, bro?"

"Gross."

Marsh's car fishtails for a moment. My heart leaps into my throat.

"Shit," he spits out through the crackling connection. "I'm good. I'm good."

I heave out a sigh of relief, but my nerves remain on edge. "Go. Slow. Maybe we shouldn't talk until we hit the main road."

"Oh, we're fine. Nothing's keeping me from sinking my teeth into those hot buns."

"You mean pork buns," I say.

"Those too." Marsh's laugh takes over my car, completely enveloping me in his hardy baritone. "Marshall, stop bantering with me and focus on the road."

"I'm not the one who fishtailed a moment ago." I haven't had this much fun driving in a snowstorm. I didn't know it was possible to enjoy treacherous driving, but chatting with Marsh is slowly cooling my nerves.

"So, do you think Bryce is going to spit on my pork bun?" Marsh asks.

"No! Bryce likes you."

"He hates me. Understandably so."

I can almost make out Marsh's head driving ahead of me, but the snow blurs my field of vision. I keep squinting, hoping to get a glimpse of his lips moving in his rearview mirror as we chat.

"Actually, Bryce was thrilled we … "

"Fucked? Thrice?" Marsh laughs and I see his shoulders shake slightly.

"I was going to say reconciled, but yes, that too," I say. "I think you two will get along once you get to know each other better. But Bryce has a lot going on right now. Auditioning, training, dealing with his boyfriend."

"Dealing with his boyfriend? What do you mean?" Marsh perks up immediately, a shark sensing blood in the water.

"Nothing. It's nothing."

"Don't hold out on me, Data."

"I should keep my opinions to myself," I say.

"No you shouldn't. We're gay men. We subsist on a diet of cum and gossip."

As disgusting as that statement is, the logic is sadly airtight.

I've been wanting to get this off my chest to someone, and who better than my new-old boyfriend?

"Anthony is a nice guy, but he's not the sharpest crayon in the box. And his acting skills … they need work." Bryce made me go with him to an Off-off-Broadway play he was in. The man was less convincing than the lead actress's pussycat wig. "Bryce should be with someone sharper, someone who can keep up with him. But again, he's a really nice guy."

Well, maybe not *really* nice. He borrowed my decanter for a dinner party three months ago and returned it unwashed.

"And between you and me," I lean a little closer to the steering wheel, "it sounds like Anthony only makes the bed squeak for as long as it takes me to microwave popcorn."

"I'm going to tell Bryce you said all that."

"Do not!"

The car fills with his familiar baritone. "I'm kidding." Marsh breaks into a cough from laughing. "I'm fine. I've got my inhaler. Locked and loaded. Thanks to you."

My heart trips thinking about Marsh hunched over in the snow having an asthma attack. Sometimes, the mere thought of losing your most precious treasure makes you realize just how deeply you love it. Him. Marshall Goldberg. Maybe I should've fought harder when he 'needed space.' But the only thing worse than not having Marsh in my life is arguing with him. The man throws barbs like necklaces at Mardi Gras. He needed to come to this realization on his own. With the help of some Mallomars and fantastic break-up/make-up sex.

"Marsh, you there?" I ask, hearing rustling on his end.

"Yeah, I can't find it … I swore it was in my coat pocket. Or my backpack. Maybe it's in my duffel in the back. Shit!"

His car fishtails again as we descend the final, and steepest, part of the access road.

"Marsh, don't worry about it. Pay attention to the road," I

say. I feel like I'm watching a horror movie with all these jump scares. "We can stop at the next rest stop if we need … "

"Whoa!" he shouts.

The back of his car jerks to the side, and I catch a glimpse of his rear tires spinning frantically.

"Marsh! Keep the wheel straight."

He's silent, but his car seems to right itself.

"Fine, all fine." His voice shakes a little, but he sounds okay.

"We're almost to the end. A mile or so to go." I wipe the flop sweat from my brow. As I remove my sock cap, I feel the dampness of my hair and decide to throw the hat in the back seat. When I reach into my pocket for a tissue to wipe my forehead, I feel something hard and plastic. Marsh's inhaler. Well, at least we know where it is.

"Marsh, do you know why you can't find your inhaler?"

Before he can answer, my car hits a patch of ice. My tires spin, accelerated by the downward angle of the road. There's no turning into it or keeping the wheel straight and my heart thumps loudly in my ears.

"Data!" I hear his scream, but my vocal cords, along with my body, aren't able to respond. The world outside becomes a haze of white and gray combined with more screams from the speakers. I can't tell which way is which, the haze becomes a blur. All at once I feel a drop, like a trapdoor opening beneath me, and the world goes dark.

Marsh

Here's the thing you need to know about Data: he's the better driver in this relationship. Always has been. He uses his turn signal regularly, and his parallel parking is a thing of beauty.

Data is a great driver—he doesn't swerve off the road and he doesn't drive into a ditch.

My heart races in my chest as I stop my car and leap out of my seat. Snow is coming down in sheets. I push past the heavy, resolute flakes and run down the side of the road, following the tire tracks to the car. His car. Off the road. It's too quiet.

"Data!" I yell with every molecule of oxygen in my janky lungs.

No response.

Blizzards are eerie because, for all the inclement weather, they don't make noise. There's no howling wind, no tapping of rain on the ground—the silence pounds in my ears.

Snow quickly shrouds his car, hiding it from the world.

"Data!" I bang on the driver-side window and brush away snow, peering inside. His sweet head rests on the steering wheel, sending a deathly chill up my spine.

I'm the funny one, and he is the strong one—that is the axis upon which our relationship exists. If anything, I should be the one in that car. He'd know what to do.

We just got back together. I can't lose him. I block all the worst-case scenarios spiraling in my head.

"Data!" I bang my fist against the window harder, so hard I worry it's going to break. I pull on the door handle, and fortunately, he didn't lock himself in.

I yank the door open. Data is hunched over the steering wheel, his face turned away from me. He almost looks peaceful.

I shake him hard. "Data! I say this with love and respect: wake the fuck up!"

He doesn't move. My throat goes dry as panic arrives to take over. I push him off the steering wheel. His face is soft, angelic, lips pouted. Eyes closed. Almost like he's asleep. I put my fingers by his mouth and nose.

The faint gusts of his breath tingle on my skin. Oh, thank goodness.

"Okay. You're alive. That's a good step. Now, we just have to wake you up." I figure it's a good idea to think out loud. The more he hears my voice, the more his brain will fight to stay conscious. Or at least, I think that's what happens. Dammit. Why did I give up on Grey's Anatomy in season three? (Oh, right. Because Izzy and George fucked. Gross.)

Data is alive but severely out of it. His eyes flutter open, then close again. I spot a spark of fight in his dark pupils.

"Don't go to sleep! Sleep is bad. Well, in this context."

I take a deep breath and think of Cher.

She won an Oscar for slapping Nicholas Cage in *Moonstruck*. She made a man fall completely in love with her with a single slap. Perhaps I could bring my boyfriend back to life.

The power of Cher compels you. The power of Cher compels you.

"Data, before I do this, I want to state that I am firmly against domestic violence, I love you deeply, and I'm only doing this to save your life."

I pull my hand back. My sweaty palm trembles above his beautiful face.

Wait? What if I miss? It's probably wise to do a practice slap. I bring my hand down softly against his cheek to make sure I have the angle lined up. I can do this. I've slapped his butt a zillion times before. This is merely a different cheek.

Okay, enough dilly-dallying. I can feel snow accumulating on my ass.

"Data, I love you."

I shut my eyes, pull my hand back, and take a deep breath, which is getting harder as the panic rises in my lungs. My hand comes down, making contact with his face in a loud crack that threatens to cause an avalanche in the wintry silence. The slap reverberates in the car, echoes in my ears.

As does Data's reaction, a high-pitched yell that could shatter glass.

"What the fuck?" He rubs his cheek.

"You're alive!" I open my eyes and he scowls at me, but I'll take a scowl over passed-out nothingness.

"You slapped me!"

"You passed out. I had to resuscitate you."

"By slapping me? I swear to God, you will use any excuse to cosplay as Cher in *Moonstruck*, you blatant homosexual," he says.

"What? No. She didn't even cross my mind."

Data rubs his cheek, a sly smile beginning to cross his lips. "Thank you, I guess."

Behind his eyes, I spot touches of fear. He looks around at his busted car, the snow-covered trees in front of him. It begins to sink in just how close a call this was. My stomach churns with the same terror.

The snow isn't stopping for us. We have to get the hell off this mountain.

Had his car rolled off the road a bit faster, things could've been much worse. I could've lost him forever. I cradle his red cheek and kiss him on the lips. We gaze into each other's eyes, and the tether between us becomes even stronger.

"I'm okay," he says, reading my mind.

"Let's go home." I kiss him again, because he's alive, because he's mine.

He scoots out of his seat. I pull him out of the car, and a yelp of pain rips from his lips as soon as he straightens his leg.

"What is it?" I ask.

"Fuck," he grits out. "My leg." He reaches for the left one, wincing. "I think I banged it hard against the steering wheel when I crashed." He squeezes his eyes shut when he takes a step forward as he tries to fight through the agony.

"Can you walk?"

"I think so."

We don't have time for "I think so." I throw his left arm around my shoulder and begin to haul us back to my car. Each step is harder than the one before. Snow comes up to my shins. My legs pull harder to take another step in and out of the snow. He tries to walk on his own, but he has to lean on me. Every muscle in my body tenses as I trudge us forward—maybe those guys who spend all their time at the gym are onto something.

"Marsh, are you okay?"

"Yeah, I got you."

"But you shouldn't be doing strenuous activity."

"I said I have you. You're light as a feather. Seriously Data, eat a fucking sandwich." I'm running on adrenaline, imbued with the deep-seated need to save the love of my life. I'd let Data down plenty in our relationship, but I'm not going to let him down here. My legs and arms quietly scream in pain. My lungs roar in my chest. But I keep going. One foot in front of the other.

I pull Data closer so I can feel his warmth and let it power me.

"I see the car!" he calls out.

I grit my teeth as I yank us up the steepest part of the hill back to the access road. My body is slowing down despite my order to keep going. It's like an overheated laptop with the fan going full blast.

Once we hit the asphalt, Data finds a pocket of strength and helps dredge us through the snow the final distance to the car. The blinding whiteness of the snowy landscape begins to darken my vision, the way a cloud passes over the summer sun.

I reach out to the car door, but my fingers just miss as I fall to the ground.

"Marsh!" The cloud darkens my vision more as my lungs struggle for air. Damn, asthma. Couldn't take one day off. Couldn't see the life-threatening scenario we were in and step aside.

My chest heaves in and out, reaching for any available air that won't come.

I have no choice but to collapse backward, my heart pounding in my ears. Snow dots my forehead. The last thing I see before darkness completely takes over my vision is Data, his gorgeous face over me. There's no better final image.

As my eyes close, I feel something enter my mouth. It's cold and plastic. The rough edges tantalize my brain.

My inhaler.

A gust of medicine hits my lungs. My eyes surge open.

Data leans over me, inhaler plugged into my mouth.

The sensation of another spritz down my throat finally snaps me out of it. Data's warm smile welcomes me back.

"Don't worry. I'm not going to slap you." He pulls me up. He grits out an expletive as he stands us up. "Although it's tempting." He shuffles backward and opens the passenger door.

With my strength slowly returning, I squeeze into the seat. He closes the door and limps to the driver's side.

A surge of relief floods my system when he gets in the car.

Data throws the car into drive and maneuvers us slowly through the snow to the main road, which thankfully is clear. I catch my breath and blink the life back into my eyes.

"I love you," I say.

"I love you too," he replies back, a twinkle in his eye that lets me know everything is going to be okay.

"For the record, I was ninety-five percent done saving you."

His lips curl up.

"And you've been saving me since the day we met."

I run my hand over his beard, another tether back to this man, who I'm never letting out of my sight again.

When he turns us onto the main road, he takes his hand off the gear shift and interlocks our fingers together. Data usually would never drive one-handed in inclement weather, but I'm glad he's making an exception.

We drive down the main road, peaceful and blanketed with snow. In the distance, Maddi's chickens squawk wildly as we pass the general store. Duffy is shoveling off and salting the front steps. He gives us a wave. We wave back with our interlocked hands.

"Not a couple anymore, my ass!" he yells as we leave Marshmallow Mountain in our rearview mirror.

Chapter Twenty-Nine

Data

"Cracker! Cracker!"

Approaching the building's stoop, Camilla's tiny, shrill voice trumpets from Horton's apartment window. Even with the mild January temps, it's still barely above freezing, but the radiators in our building are hit or miss, and Horton's always leans tropical, and he let's everyone know.

"I don't have any crackers!" Shouting at a bird in a window isn't my finest moment, but I'm not in the habit of carrying crackers around with me. One of these days, I'm going to stop at the corner bodega and hand her a stack of saltines. A beautiful African Grey, Camilla, a rescue with apparent 'parrot trauma,' has never learned the 'Polly wants a … ' part of the phrase, so now the residents are all her humble cracker minions.

"Sorry about that." Horton appears in the first-floor window, clutching a mug of something steamy, his bald head glistening from the overactive radiators, the vapor from his mug, or both. "Hot as hell in here."

He works from home, although we're not exactly sure what he does. Bryce is convinced he's running a meth lab, but Horton doesn't appear to be the illegal drug lord type—unless he's dealing Xanax. He doesn't go out much and shows no interest in any building shenanigans. According to Marsh, it's high time we played matchmaker and found Horton a complimentary big boy, but he seems completely satisfied with his current arrangement alongside Camilla.

"No worries. I appreciate her tenacity." I give Horton a nod and unlock the entry door.

Marsh and I are on the second floor, which thankfully means only one flight of stairs. When I open our door, I come face-to-face with my face. Lots of them. All over Marsh's ass.

Ever since we came back from the cabin, those damn boxers have been his de facto garment. The whirr of the vacuum fills the room and he diligently drags it back and forth. We dog-sat Bobo recently, and his thick coat made permanent residence on our floors. Marsh does his best thinking in the shower and while vacuuming. This provides me with both a spotless boyfriend and apartment. Lucky me.

I plop my keys in the bowl by the door and shut the door behind me. He's facing the large window, and I'm fairly certain he hasn't noticed me yet by the way he's shaking his perfect, juicy ass. He's singing—almost shouting—"Agony" from *Into the Woods*, attempting to hear himself over the vacuum and music blaring in his ears. Watching Marsh Goldberg put on his almost naked cleaning show for me makes me want to go rooting through his rutabaga, as Bernadette famously sang.

Walking behind him, I thread my arms under his, laying my head on his back and tugging him close.

"Babe!" Marsh shouts. "I didn't hear you." He shuts off the vacuum and pops out his headphones, "My performance will have to wait. The fans will understand."

He turns around and squeezes me, and unable to resist the pull, my forehead lands on his. Our noses almost touch, and I can smell remnants of his late afternoon snack—cheese puffs, still dusting his lips.

"There's my Data." He brushes his lips on my forehead. "I missed you."

Before I can speak, Marsh dips in for a kiss. His soft lips brush mine, and the salty sharpness of the crumbs makes me smile into his mouth. My hands migrate to his sides, massaging his waistline, my fingers delighting in every inch of him.

"Cheesy," I whisper into his mouth.

"But I *do* miss you when you're at work," Marsh says.

"No, I meant you. You're cheesy." My fingers tap his upper lip. "Literally."

"Oh!" He chuckles, and his chest shakes on mine. "I mean, I'm dangerously cheesy."

"You are." My tongue sweeps over his lips, relishing the combined flavor of the cheese dust and Marsh's skin, before jutting into his mouth. We've only been home for two weeks, but it's almost as if we never broke up. After the accident, Marsh stayed with me for the week to make sure I didn't suffer a concussion and never left. Preeti was sad to see him go but happy to have her couch back. Marshmallow Mountain worked its magic.

"Oh, hello," I say, feeling Marsh's cock poke my thigh. Thank you, flimsy boxers.

"You really love talking to my dick, don't you?"

I shrug and reach under the fabric, teasing his growing thickness. "He's always been so good to me."

"He'd love to be good for you now." Marsh pushes down his boxers, and his cock, hot and firm in my hand, throbs, sending a rush of excitement through my veins.

"Would he? And how exactly does he propose to fulfill that promise?"

"Well, how about you … " Marsh's hand glides down my belly, tugging at my khakis.

"Boys!" Bryce's voice shatters our foreplay bubble as he burst through the door. "I brought buns."

Marsh yanks his boxers up and bolts for the bedroom, presumably to procure pants.

"Your buns are always welcome," I say, wishing I'd remembered to lock the front door.

And then the other love of my life gallops over, all fur and slobber. Bobo stops at my feet, sits, and begins pawing at me. I was never much of a pet person and somehow, Bobo continually steals pieces of my heart.

"Who's my good boy?" Bobo nuzzles into my hip, and I kneel, giving him access to my face.

"I was trying to be," Marsh says, returning from the bedroom with sweats on.

"Oh, did I interrupt an afternoon delight?" Bryce sets the box of treats down on the coffee table. "Bobo, we should leave the lovebirds to their nest."

"No, you're fine." I sit on the floor, and Bobo collapses, resting his giant head on my lap. I pet his face, giving his floppy ears extra attention.

Marsh pops open the box, and the sweet cardamom aroma wafts into the room. "Might as well have two of these to tide me over."

"Don't hog the buns," I say, holding my palm out.

Marsh grabs another and gently places it in my mouth. Bobo curiously sniffs near my chest, his nose twitching with interest, but he refrains from any naughty behavior. He's truly the best boy.

"What's the final countdown?" Bryce takes his bun and sits on the sofa.

"Two days. Friday's my last day," I say.

After the weekend on Marshmallow Mountain and the ensuing crash, where I did my best Brian Boitano impression across the ice, I was more determined than ever to give my notice at the firm. The pragmatist in me knew I should probably identify my next career path before quitting. Never leave a job without another one lined up. But I decided to give my inner pragmatist a sabbatical. It's time to embrace a little fear and instability if it can get me somewhere better.

Marsh and I discussed selling the cabin to shore up our savings and help pay for Joe's eventual in-home care. But I did some research and found that short-term rentals in the area were going for four or five hundred a night. We can rent out the cabin on the weeks we aren't going up, and that'll provide us a nice cushion until I land my next job. Like other bears, I'm not thrilled about the thought of strangers sleeping in our bed, but that is why God invented clean sheets.

"But won't you miss Karen from finance?" Bryce asks. Cardamom sugar dusts his chin, and I'm fairly certain Bobo will take care of it soon enough.

"Yeah," Marsh says. "Data will miss Karen like you miss a cold sore. No, wait, a herpes sore."

My Marsh—always self-revising for the strongest punch line.

"She's just upset she won't be able to bully me into doing her work for her anymore," I say.

"Any leads?" Bryce asks.

"Not yet, but I know the right thing will appear."

"You could always come audition with me," Bryce says.

"Have you seen him dance?" Marsh asks. "His two left feet have two left feet"

Bryce snorts.

"Sadly, I don't think a dance career is on my life's bingo card," I say. "I'll leave that to you, friend."

"Well, if things don't pick up soon, I'll be joining you in the job search." Bryce catches the crumbs in his hand and pops them in his mouth. "Selling opera subscriptions during second shift is getting old."

To help make ends meet in between his sparse gigs, Bryce is a telemarketer at the Metropolitan Opera four nights a week. He persuades rich people to buy ridiculously expensive subscription packages and make hefty donations on top of the tickets. With his charm, he's rather successful at it. He thinks of it as being a phone sex operator but with cleaner language. Dancing professionally is his long-term goal, though, even though he's getting up there in dancer years.

"Any auditions coming up?" Marsh asks. He and Bryce love sharing war stories.

"There's a new Broadway show casting soon. A musical reboot of some old seventies rom-com, because apparently, audiences only want limp reboots of old movies these days."

"And there's a part in it for you?" I ask, chewing on my bun. Unable to ignore his pleading eyes, I tear off a tiny piece and slide it to Bobo, who promptly gobbles it up.

"Part?" Bryce laughs, drawing Bobo's attention as he licks his chops. "I'm praying for the chorus. That's where they hide us big folks."

"Baby, they can't hide you," Marsh says. He leans over and wraps his arm around Bryce's shoulders. "You can't shade the sun."

Marsh leans over and gives Bryce a peck on the cheek, and my chest swells at his sweetness. I knew he'd win Bryce over in no time. Marsh knows what the grind is like and his empathy for Bryce smacks of sincereness.

"We'll see. Right now, we need to get this one," Bryce snaps his head toward me, "employment. Having two under-employed people in the same family isn't cute."

"Something will come up. I can sense it in the air," I say.

"Sorry, that was Bobo, I swear. He's had terrible gas lately."

I laugh because, yup, Bobo definitely ripped one. "But with this punim, who cares?"

I dip my head down, and Bobo gently licks my chin.

"Well, we should go." Bryce stands and takes another bun from the box. "Anthony is waiting for dinner. We're going for

Greek food. He just learned that moussaka isn't made from moose, and now he feels okay about trying it."

Marsh's eyes cut to me as we share a knowing smile.

He's really nice, I mouth back to him.

"Come on, Bobo. Quit groveling. You're too good for him," Bryce says as Bobo stares up at me.

"No, we're just right for each other," I say as I lean down to kiss his giant, black nose. "Lock the door on your way out … please."

Bryce smirks and he and Bobo head out. Finally, alone, I join Marsh on the couch, snuggling into his meaty chest. My fingers graze a nipple, lingering. "You're a good friend."

"Hey, he brought buns."

"Yeah, but not the buns you were hungry for … "

"Flip over," Marsh says.

I do as I'm told, and he smacks my ass, the loud whack echoing against the pre-war drywall.

Marsh tugs at my pants, eagerly trying to remove them. "Dere's dat ass."

Chapter Thirty

Marsh

Here's the thing you need to know about Data: yes, he has a great ass, but underneath dat ass is a heart even bigger than dat ass.

"How're you feeling?" he asks.

"Dandy. You don't happen to have a Costco-sized bottle of Pepto Bismol on your person, do you?"

A month after our daring escape from Marshmallow Mountain, we're back in the car on a Wednesday morning for another trip, this time up to Westchester. Data lets me take his hand as I drive. He gives me a squeeze of support, a gentle tightening of his calloused fingers around my sweaty palm. They provide the warmth only found from nesting in your favorite blanket on the couch watching your favorite comfort show on a sick day. That's where Data brings my soul—home.

He gives my hand another squeeze as we pull into the parking lot of Harmony Pianos' modest headquarters. The long row of offices is capped at the end by the warehouse. As a kid, it reminded me of a lollipop, and I'd joke that only suckers worked there. I was still sharpening my comedic muscles back then.

The place used to be more bustling before the days of work from home, but a smattering of cars dot the parking lot still.

The Harmony Piano logo hangs above the front door, causing a vice of anxiety to clutch around my heart.

I park the car and heave out a breath.

"You're scared. That's a natural feeling." Data rubs my hand with his thumb and the pressure attempts to soothe me. Unemployment suits him. He's become more relaxed, a breezier smile flitting on his kissable lips.

"He's going to be pissed."

"It's going to be okay." Data gives me a half smile. "Whatever happens, we're in this together."

We.

Has there ever been a more wonderful word? Those two letters and Data's two bottomless brown eyes provide all the confidence I need. I'm not going through this alone anymore.

Data plants a soft kiss on my lips, firming up my resolve. I rustle my hands through his prickly beard as complete calmness takes over.

"Hey, Marsh," Data says when I exit the car. He nods at the backseat. The manilla envelope sits there peacefully. "You forgot something."

"Right." I grab the envelope. A few pieces of paper have never felt so heavy in my hands.

When we enter the office, Harriet, Dad's longtime administrative assistant, greets both of us with a big, motherly hug. Her maternal warmth is offset by her hard New York accent and raspy voice—smoking a pack of long skinny menthol cigarettes a day will do that to you.

"Always love seeing you boys," she gushes. Harriet holds up the figurine Data carved of her Siamese cat Misty. "See. I still have it."

Data admires his handiwork for a second. Our apartment window sill is filling up quickly with new woodworking projects he's been making in his spare time between applying for jobs.

"How's he doing today?" I ask Harriet. Her buoyancy dampens.

"Today's been an okay day. Some days are better than others." The stress of helping Dad shows in the creases on her forehead, but as a loyal employee, she keeps it to herself. "We hear there's an offer to buyout the company."

Other employees peek up from their desks. Only ten or so people remain on the corporate side of the company, down from years past. Empty desks dot the space.

"There've been discussions," I say.

"Are we going to keep our jobs?" she asks.

I look to Data, nerves getting the better of me. Because of Dad's declining health and lack of replacement, the offer from Albie's friends is looking like our only option. We have to consider it seriously, which is why we're here today.

"Nothing's been discussed yet. It's still very early stages, but we're doing everything we can to ensure Harmony Pianos stays intact." Data swoops in, saving my tongue-tied ass. "Or rather, Marsh and Joe are."

"Is he in?" I ask.

"Warehouse." Harriet nods down the long hall, which ends with double doors.

We march through the office, saying hi to my old coworkers, who also know Data from years of company gatherings and holiday parties. I push through the double doors and into the warehouse. Workers build pianos. The familiar smell of cut wood wafting through the air. Dad talks with one of the team leads. As soon as he sees me, a surprised smile takes over his face.

My breath catches in my throat. This isn't the same kind of nervous I get before I go on stage. That's more adrenaline, nerves that can fuel me. Today, there's a lead weight of fear in my stomach.

"You can do this." Data squeezes my hand. Having him by

my side makes me feel a little better, but still, the lead weight of fear remains.

"Marshall! And Other Marshall!" He gives both of us hugs. "I didn't expect to see you here."

"Hey, Dad. Can we talk?"

Dad tells the team lead he needs a moment, and the three of us walk into an empty office off the warehouse. It has remnants of life. A desk with a few remaining office supplies like pens and paper clips. A broken-in couch by the door.

I gesture for Dad to sit down on the sofa. I sit next to him rather than across from him, so he knows we're on the same team. Data hangs by the windows into the warehouse.

I look to Data, who gives me a supportive nod. He fiddles with one of the orphaned paper clips, a tell that while he's the strong one in our relationship today, he's also a little nervous.

"I spoke to Albie, and he said you're seriously considering the offer from his friends, to buy the company."

Dad stiffens. "I'm considering it. I'm meeting with them on Friday. If you were still part of this company, I would've looped you in."

I hang my head, insides crumbling in real time. Data pulls his lips in, smiles, and dips his chin.

I put the folder on the cushion between us.

"What is that?" Dad asks.

"Dad, I love you. I don't have a funny story to lead into this, so I'm just going to say it. You've been having some trouble lately … remembering things."

Dad heaves out a breath. "It's called getting old. It happens to everyone."

"Dad, it's not that. You'll forget you're talking to me in the middle of a conversation. You can't remember important details or people." My insides twist in knots. This is the shitty part of being an adult, having to have these tough moments, knowing that there's no way out. You just have to suck it up and do them. "It's getting serious."

"It's fine. I have it under control. There are guys my age who can't even go to the bathroom by themselves. I'm doing much better than they are."

"I'm glad I don't have to drag your ass to the bathroom. Thank you for that. But … you don't have it under control." When we're little, we want nothing more than to tell our parents that actually, they're wrong. But now, it's the last thing I want to do. I want Dad to be his infallible, all-knowing self.

I take his hand and squeeze. He's been strong for me my entire life. Now, it's my turn.

"Dad, you're in cognitive decline. And we can go back and forth on this all day, but it's happening." I want to burst into tears, but I can't do that to him. I'm the adult. "You're in the middle of selling your company, of making extremely important decisions that I don't think you should."

"What do you know about it? You quit the company. You couldn't hack it."

He knows how to land a punch. I remind myself that this isn't him. This is the disease making him angry.

I open the envelope, take out the documents.

"What the hell is this?" he asks.

"It's … " My throat goes dry.

"It's a request to name Marsh power of attorney," Data says, again swooping in to save me. "You would still have input on all important matters in your life and with the company. But this is a protective layer to ensure that your wishes are being carried out as you'd like them. Think of Marsh as your backup."

Dad's face drops. He flips open the file. The legalese is stark, a bucket of cold water on him.

I put my hand over his.

Dad side-eyes me, not liking the comparison. "I don't need this."

"Joe, you shouldn't be signing away your company in your condition. Let us help you. We only want what's best for you." My heart sings at hearing him use *we* and *us*.

Data underlines the statement with a nod, but there's something behind his eyes I can't place, a slight weakening in his support that throws me off.

"'We only want what's best for you' is what every child says to their parent before they pull the plug."

"Dad." He starts to open his mouth to object. I give him a firm, gentle clap on the shoulder. "You spent your entire life looking out for me. I am so lucky that I get to call you my dad. I know my life hasn't gone the way either of us planned, but I haven't given up on my dream, and that's thanks to you. You taught me to keep fighting, don't let obstacles get in my way. You made me who I am today, all my best parts. Please, *let* me do this for you. I'm looking out for you the way you looked out for me."

Dad tears up, his resistance fading. I start to get choked up, but I hold myself back. I can see him focus intently, trying hard to stay in this moment, in this timeline so his mind won't slip.

"I wanted so badly to keep this company in the family, something I could share with my boys. Working with you ... "

"It was one of the happiest times of your life."

"I know what these private equity jerk-offs are going to do. They're going to fire everyone in this building, keep the name, and make an inferior product. But ... maybe it's time. Maybe we only have so much fight left in us." A weight Dad has been carrying slowly begins to slide off his shoulders. Behind his stubbornness is uncertainty. Like so many leaders, he's figuring things out as he goes along.

I glance to Data for another shot of support, hoping to actually get one this time. His eyes are a wild swirl of emotions and thoughts, wheels spinning at a furious pace that makes him unreadable.

I mouth *Are you okay?* He doesn't respond.

"I know this isn't how you wanted things to go, Dad. But you built an incredible company. You should be proud."

"I am proud. Of both my sons." He holds my hand and squeezes hard. Nothing gentle about it, though just as loving.

Something changes in his face, a flint of realization that he'd been putting off. Without saying another word, he signs the document.

"I think it's best that we call them and move up the meeting. Get this over with. I don't want my employees worrying about their jobs over the holidays. Whatever happens, I want them to be taken care of."

"I think I have another idea."

Dad and I look up at the sound of Data's creaky, but assured voice.

"Maybe you don't have to sell the company," my boyfriend says. What the hell is he doing? He is supposed to be the pragmatic one here. We talked about this at length and agreed that selling was the best option.

"That's what I love to see. Some ingenuity!" Dad slaps his hands together.

"Okay." I have no idea what's gotten into him, but I guess I can play along for a second. "What's your grand plan, Data?"

I expect an impromptu presentation on profit margins and restructuring, something that would be dry but helpful, and I'd mostly stare at his lips while he said it. Perhaps he would scribble some math on a piece of paper. Yet Data does none of those things nor scribbles a single number.

Instead, he gets down on one knee and holds out a paper clip twisted into a ring. "Marshall Goldberg, will you marry me?"

Chapter Thirty-One

Data

I over analyze. I overthink. I rely on facts and numbers. I weigh pros and cons and do cost-benefit analyses and write out lists and ask myself if I'm sure about something a dozen times before actually doing it.

I don't blurt out marriage proposals.

And yet, as soon as the words leave my lips and my knee touches the floor, a sense of assured calm comes over me. It's like in the movies when a light shines down from the sky, spotlighting the main character and everything clicks into place.

I have zero desire to analyze or overthink a single cost or benefit when it comes to asking Marsh to spend the rest of his life with me.

I just know.

I know that no matter what, the sun will rise tomorrow and fish will swim in the ocean and I will be in love with Marshall Goldberg.

I've known for a while. Hell, I've known for eight damn years, since the moment he stepped onstage in that fakakta Glengarry Glen Coco and my whole body screamed *Who is this man?* A million microscopic cosmic decisions sprinkled across our lives brought us together. In this big, scary, complex, anxiety-inducing world, the gods of fate let us find each other and enjoy a sliver of happiness amidst the darkness.

And so even though this isn't planned, and even though Marsh is looking at me like I have two heads, for once in my life, I don't have a speck of uncertainty weighing me down.

I am in the exact right place at the exact right time saying the exact right thing to the exact right person.

"Data … are you serious?" Marsh's lower lip wobbles as he processes the shock.

"Yes," I say confidently. "Will you marry me, Marsh?"

Marsh is my family. I've known that for a long time. Before the breakup. During the breakup. Ever since our return from Marshmallow Mountain, the clarity has only intensified. I knew this would happen, eventually. Apparently eventually is now.

"You want to marry me?" Marsh asks, clearly confused with how proposals work.

"Yes. Hence why I asked 'Marshall Goldberg, will you marry me?'"

"You do realize that marriage is until death, right?"

I nod yes.

"And that when you ask me to clean the kitchen, it will never be as spotless as when you do it?"

I nod again.

"And that I will never stop making corny, inappropriate jokes about buns and plowing no matter how many times you roll your eyes?"

"Yes!" Joe shouts out. "Now say yes back and kiss the man, you putz!"

Marsh sits on my bended knee and kisses me. "Then my answer is yes."

"Finally, you'll be a Sadie," Joe says. He hums the song from Funny Girl, and both Marsh and I laugh. In the Venn Diagram of gays and Jews, Barbra lies right in the middle.

I stare into his beautiful eyes. They're misty, and I want to take a picture of his face to remember the image of pure surprise and joy plastered on his handsome mug. Taking his hand in mine, I rub my palm up and down his forearm, returning the gesture he's used so often on me.

"I know this is a surprise." My fingers, on his skin, feel home. "Being apart, even for a few months, only made me realize how much I want to spend the rest of my life with you," I say.

I wait for a joke or a song lyric or a line from a crappy movie he's made me watch four times hoping I'll buy into the humor, but Marsh only sniffs, tilts his head down, and says, "But … "

"But nothing. Marshall Goldberg." I raise his chin so our eyes meet. "You are my everything—whether you like it or not. You're an amazing boyfriend. Son. Man. And you help me be a better version of myself. Nobody could ever ask for more in a spouse."

Marsh takes my hand and kisses my knuckles. The pressure of his lips on my skin grounds me.

"And if we're married," I say, "then we're family. Legally. And then, I can … " I turn toward Joe, pulling my lips in and dipping my chin.

"Take over," Joe says.

"If that's something we can discuss. I want Harmony Pianos to stay a family business, too."

"My chips are with you, baby." Joe shoots me a wink. A moment of crystal clear clarity sparkles in his eyes as he delivers his knockout smile. "Other Marshall, you are smarter than every other person I talked to about taking over the company."

Marsh pulls me up so we're eye to eye. "Are you sure? You'd want that?"

"Yeah. I'm sure. I have ideas for Harmony. Continue with pianos, of course, but a line of quality furniture to complement the pianos. Benches. Side tables. Chairs. If Aidan Shaw can do it, why not me?"

Ideas swirl in my head for interconnected pieces. Designing. Producing. Working with the team here. I move to the sofa and put my arm around Joe. "And I want to partner with you, Joe." I give a quick wink to Marsh. "This way Harmony stays in the family."

Joe's eyes focus on me, his brain trying to keep up. We're throwing a lot at him, but he wants to understand. I can see it. He nods slowly, and I lean in and wrap my arms around his broad shoulders. When my face lands on his neck, he whispers, "My boychik." A sigh escapes my lips, accompanied by a smidge of a sob, because marrying Marsh means Joe will also be family.

I turn toward Marsh, and he joins us on the couch. "I've always worked for other people. Endlessly running on the hamster wheel, trying to climb the rungs to success. Someone else's ladder. Avoiding anything risky. But now ... " I take Marsh's hand, "I'm ready to climb my own ladder."

"I can't wait to walk you both down the aisle." Joe pats both of our hands, his wrinkled, rough skin giving me a feeling of home.

"My mom would love that," I say. "She can hold down the mother of the bride spot in the front."

"For both of us," Marsh says. My heart sings, knowing we'll all be connected.

"Other Marshall working by my side. Harmony is staying in the family." Joe grabs my shoulder and squeezes. "Family."

"And you're sure about ... " Marsh asks me, and I'm not sure if he means us getting married, taking over Harmony, or both.

"Yes. I've never been more sure of anything."

I lean over and kiss him softly.

"My boys," Joe says. He opens his arms and does his best to hug both Marsh and me at the same time.

Sitting here with Marsh and Joe, knowing we'll finally be

family, not only in our hearts but legally tethered, a peacefulness comes over me. Marshall and Marshall.

I can't wait to start the rest of our lives together.

"The Kaplan-Goldbergs. I like the sound of that," I say.

"Has there ever been a more Jewish name?" Marsh asks
with a snort. "Might as well make the hyphen out of gefilte
fish."

<u>Chapter Thirty-Two</u>

Marsh

Despite living in New York, I rarely get all my steps in. Perhaps it's a blessing and a curse that my favorite Duane Reade, taqueria, and comedy club are all mere blocks from our apartment. The only time I ever get close to the magical 10,000 steps is on performance nights because I can't stop pacing.

"Seriously, stop!" Preeti grabs my sleeve to physically hold me in place. I've been pacing backstage at Pauline's for the past twenty minutes, running through each word—nay, each syllable —in my act to iron out every last kink. My nervous system is so nervous you'd think it was a Jewish mother.

"I'm fine," I tell her.

"Watching you is giving me motion sickness." When Preeti's nervous, she goes into super Type-A mode. She's been coordinating with every comic on the docket, as well as the stage crew, the lighting designer, and the ticket sellers to ensure everyone knows their role for tonight. "This is just like any other night, any other performance."

"To quote my Passover Haggadah, why the fuck is this night different from any other night? Oh right, because it's my first show in almost a year and my first time back on stage after bombing so hard Christopher Fucking Nolan wants to make a movie about it." I nod as I do another lap, begging my heart rate to come down.

Preeti tugs on my sleeve again, pulling me into place. "It's not good form to sweat before you get on stage."

"Good call." As soon as I cease pacing, a burn takes over my legs. I should've stretched.

Preeti sizes me up. I'm wearing a T-shirt with Catherine O'Hara's face from *Home Alone 2: Lost in New York* when she screams "Kevin!" Everyone knows the second movie in the series is the gay one because that's where Catherine O'Hara slaps Tim Curry across the face. Preeti pulls down one of my folded up sleeves. I smooth out a wrinkle in her red and black dress that's going for Christmas vixen, plunging neckline included.

"We're actually fucking doing this," she says, her voice a little above a whisper.

"I can't believe we pulled it off. Thanks for keeping my ass in line."

"It was a hard job. Y'know, because your ass is so fucking huge."

"Stop flirting with me." I give her a wink.

Relief washes over me when Data and Bryce join us backstage. Leave it to Data to wear a blazer and slacks to a queer comedy event. He said he wanted to dress up for my big show, and his corduroy blazer is giving sexy professor vibes—all that's missing is a desk to bend me over.

"Nobody tell two pair, but it's a full house out there!" Data laughs giddily at his own … joke? Was that a joke?

"Two pair?" Bryce turns to him, utterly confused as the rest of us.

"Because in poker, a full house beats two pair. So if you were two pair, you'd be scared of a full house because you're going to get beat." To complete the subpar dad joke, Data gives it two thumbs up.

I turn to Preeti, who I can tell is straining not to respond with a sarcastic remark. *Forgive Data*, my eyes tell her, *he knows not what he's done.*

Data looks to Bryce for a laugh. "That was clever, right?"

"Well, at least you're cute." Bryce pats him on the shoulder.

I let out a loud chortle to support my husband. My husband. A smile overtakes my face, not from Data's awful joke, but from the knowledge we're married. After the meeting with Dad, we decided to get married the next week at city hall. With close family and friends waiting, we celebrated with a fancy dinner at a small Italian bistro after. It was complete perfection.

"Good one!" I shout for his horrible joke. Hey, if women can fake it, so can men.

"It actually is a full house out there. I think nearly every seat is full," Data says.

"Who's with my dad right now?" I ask, a sudden panic shooting up my spine.

"Anthony. He's giving Dad tips on crypto investing. Dad's a little confused, but I think it's understandable in this context." Data shrugs.

First off, how cute is it that Data calls him Dad now? If I wasn't about to shit my brains out with nerves, I'd swoon. Secondly, to add another layer of tension to tonight, this is the first show of mine that Dad's attending. He actually came. He wrote it down so he'd remember. Now that Data is stepping in to lead the company, that's helped Dad come around to my career. I'll take the wins where I can.

"But that's not why we're back here," Bryce says excitedly. "I got a producer from *Saturday Night Live* to come. He's in the audience."

Preeti and I turn to each other with the same expression of sheer shock, sheer joy, and sheer terror. If our eyes were bulging any more, we'd be Looney Tunes.

"Bryce, please tell me this isn't a joke because I can't handle another crappy joke," Preeti says, her chest heaving with big breaths. "No offense, Data."

Data's about to object, but knows this isn't the time.

"Lady, I wouldn't joke about this. See for yourself." Bryce leads us to the curtain. He pulls it aside and points to a man in the back row checking his phone. He has the no-nonsense attitude of someone with power.

"Shit. Bryce isn't joking," I say.

"There is a fucking producer from *SNL* here. Fuck." Preeti steps back from the curtain. "How the fuck did you pull that off, Bryce?"

"Pre-Anthony, I sucked a lot of dick in this town," he says matter-of-factly.

"So did I, but all that got me was a coupon for a free cone at Yogurt City," Preeti says.

"Good one," I say back, still stunned.

"You're going to do great!" Data gives us both another thumbs up. It's like he's purposefully trying to be corny at this point. Now I know how he feels when I make plowing jokes. "Just think of it as any other show."

"Too late," I say.

"You're the funniest people I know."

"Can you tell the *SNL* guy?" Preeti laughs nervously, but there's a fire burning in her eyes. She's never one to step back from a challenge. Opportunity is knocking, and this bitch is ready to answer. "Marsh, we could … "

I nod back, already imagining us sharing an office at 30 Rock. "This is now officially the biggest night of our career. I'm sweating like crazy. I don't even know if my material is any good."

"Look on the brightside," Data says. "At least you're not straight."

His smile infuses me with confidence.

"You." I cup his bushy cheeks in my hands as I give him a kiss and a million comedy points. "I think I'll keep you."

Preeti swamps Bryce in a monster hug. "I owe you. I'll let you put your hand under my dress at the afterparty."

"Ew," says Bryce. "I'm going back to my seat. Whatever the comedy version of break a leg is, do that." He blows us kisses and flits off.

"Preeti, I'm going to borrow my husband for a pep talk." Data takes my hand and leads us down the narrow hall. "Where's your dressing room?"

"Ha! Good one." Pauline's isn't fancy enough to have a dressing room, a green room, or a coat room.

We weave through the nervous comedians until Data finds the bathroom. "This'll do."

Like most bathrooms in dingy New York clubs, this one is a tight squeeze. The sink and toilet are so close together one can wash their hands while still on the can. Every inch of the wall is covered with signatures and messages of past performers scribbled in different colors and sizes, some of whom went on to big things, some of whom didn't. The mirror above the sink is grayed at the edges.

"Thanks for being here," I say.

"Of course." Data locks the door behind us. "I wouldn't miss this for the world."

I grab his arms and pull him into a kiss, breathing in his scent. "I couldn't do this without you. Any of this. I love you so much."

"All I did was laugh at your jokes." He smiles against my lips, and I can still hear his unique cackle in the darkness from that very first show.

"It's going to be a great show. Being nervous is a good thing. It's adrenaline," I tell myself. I try to pace in the bathroom, but the square footage won't allow it.

"Let me help calm you down, just a tad." Data grabs two

flimsy paper towels, places them on the floor like a tartan picnic blanket in Central Park, and gets on his knees. I quickly realize his mouth will soon be too full to give a pep talk. He unbuckles my pants, my dick instantly sprouting wood.

"What are you doing?"

"Helping you chill for the show." Data pulls my boxers down, unleashing my throbbing cock. The excitement, the nerves, Data, the enclosed space (why is being crammed into tight spaces with him so fucking hot?) it all combines to make me rock hard.

"Hey, you," he says to my dick.

"You really like talking to it, don't you?"

"Hush." He licks up the underside of my shaft, setting my body ablaze. "Don't be nervous."

"Trust me, babe. That's one part of me that never gets performance anxiety."

His tongue circles my pulsing tip. If Data is feeling scrunched on the floor of a too-small bathroom, he's not showing it. He looks up at me, smiling with warmth and a bit of impishness. Watching his beautiful lips stretch around my dick actually soothes my nerves.

"What is it about us and bathrooms?" I ask.

"Easy access to clean up?" He fondles my balls, his mouth following soon after as he strokes my cock. I bury my face in my arm to stifle the moans escaping. The chatter of the audience and the buzz of backstage carries through the paper-thin walls.

"My Data … fuck, don't stop."

His mouth travels up to the head and takes me down, down, down, his hot saliva sending shivers against my pulsing dick. There is nothing more beautiful than seeing the man you love with his lips wrapped around your cock. His thirsty mouth laps up my precum. My legs shake, barely able to stay up against the power of Data.

"Mmmm. You taste good," he says. The sound of his knee ripping one of the paper towels doesn't even register with him.

"What do I taste like?"

"Dick." He smacks it on his tongue, then his eyes catch on his watch. "Shit, we have to hurry this up. You're on soon."

Data gets to work, bobbing up and down on my dick, making me practically levitate from his tongue power. Saliva shines around his beard, glistens in his fist as it pumps my cock.

"I'm doing you when you're done," I say through staggered breaths.

"Not enough time." He tongues my balls, getting his mouth over every sensitive part of me.

"In the basement of the cabin … I … Mallomars … you jerked me off, but I didn't get to … reciprocate … something something Jewish guilt." My brain is turning to mush in real time as he methodically goes up and down my dick, heat rushing through my core.

"I'll make you a deal. After the show, you can fuck the living daylights out of me."

"Deal." I grab a fistful of his hair and push him down to the base as I come down his throat. Not the most romantic way to end this, but Data wouldn't want me risking a cum stain on my pants. *Saturday Night Live* is in the audience, after all.

He falls back against the wall, hitting his head on the toilet paper dispenser. His lips glisten with the fading remnants of the blow job. Our eyes find each other. Love, support, and the feeling of forever transmits between us.

"My Data, indeed."

"My Marsh. Knock 'em dead."

I tuck my dick back in my pants and pull him to standing. As I envelop him in a bear hug, the loud thud of my elbow hitting the empty paper towel dispenser echoes through the room. I can taste myself on his sweet lips as we kiss—my Data.

How did I ever let him go? I spent years struggling to get

my big break, but the whole time, it was him. The best thing that ever happened to me was getting this man to love me, somehow, someway. There's not a role or opportunity that can compare to being his husband. I ain't fucking this up again.

Data opens the door, the light of the outside world shining upon us. We stumble out into the hallway. He gives me one last smile, one last squeeze of the hand, before walking back to his seat.

I watch him go, still swoony over him after eight years. It's only someone clearing their throat behind me that snaps me out of it.

Preeti stares at me, arms crossed. She eyes the bathroom door, then me, one question visible in her playful glare.

"He was helping me fix my collar."

She rolls her eyes. "And you complain that lesbian sex has too much slurping?"

"Ooh. Really good callback." Game recognizes game.

She gestures to the stage, her glare transforms to a warm smile. "You're on, Goldberg."

"It's Kaplan-Goldberg."

I take a deep breath, finding my center, before I push through the black curtain to face a wall of terrifying darkness. Through the lights, I can make out my dad, my friends, and especially my Data. And suddenly, a sense of calm and confidence comes over me. Because no matter what happens in the next ten minutes, I'm going home with the hottest guy here.

"Here's the thing you need to know about my husband, Data … "

The End

Epilogue

Data

Seven Months Later

"It's almost perfect." My eyes take in the chair's craftsmanship as my fingers run down the wood, feeling for imperfections. Heather, one of our master builders, stands, waiting for more feedback.

The chair will be one of six, part of a dining room set from Harmony Housewares. In the months since I took over as CEO, the name change morphed our production into an entire catalog of furniture. We still produce pianos, which were the cornerstone of Harmony's success. They're part of our Legacy Collection of classic, clean furniture.

"Here." I point to the joint on the back, where the leg meets the backrest. Heather leans in, studying. "This needs to be cleaner." A small sliver needs sanding. "It should be seamless. I can come down to the floor and we can do one together if you like."

"No, you can't. It's time for you to go." Marsh stands at the door to my office, sunglasses atop his head. His charming half-smile sends a rush of adrenaline through my body.

I glance at my watch. It's almost one o'clock, and how did the entire morning get away from me?

"You're leaving early. Remember?" Marsh sets his duffel by the office door and walks in.

While *SNL* didn't get the genius of Marshall Kaplan-Goldberg, *Out with a Bang* renewed his commitment to comedy. He's been writing new jokes nonstop and performing regularly at Pauline's since. And last month, *SNL* reached out to Preeti about writing on staff for the upcoming season. I was worried it would upset Marsh, but he's been more excited than her about the opportunity, constantly reassuring her that she deserves a seat at the table. Preeti is talking about connecting Marsh with the A-list performers, agents, and managers she'll meet. They're already planning to write a screenplay together during the show's winter hiatus.

"But, I just need to … "

"I got it, boss. More seamless at the joint." Heather winks, grabs the chair, and heads back to the production floor.

"Thank you, Heather!" Marsh shouts after her.

A heavy sigh overtakes my chest, knowing I'll be away for an entire week. The last few months have been chaotic, but under my direction, the company is doing well. Our sales have climbed steadily, and to top it off, Furniture Today recognized us as one of the top twenty new companies to watch.

"Now, you … " Marsh takes my hand, pulls me close, and his lips brush mine. "You are coming with me. After that shotgun wedding, you promised me a honeymoon, and it's time to deliver."

"Shotgun wedding? Neither one of us was expecting." I pat Marsh's belly, and he cups my chin before kissing me softly.

"I plan to fix that this week," he says, reaching around and grabbing my ass. "Or at least have fun trying."

"Me too." I grab his two full cheeks and we stand there, jiggling each other's ass and the smile on my face reveals my sheer glee standing in my office of the family company I now run.

"Come on, let's go before the traffic descends like a hoard of Laura Derns in Gay Jurassic Park." Marsh emits a high-pitched noise, his best attempt to mimic a raptor.

Between taking over the business and Marsh's booked calendar of gigs, we've barely been up to the cabin since we escaped from the storm. We've made good money from leasing it out in the interim, but with the business doing so well, we're planning to pull the cabin off the short-term rental market. Like Marsh, I want it all to myself.

A full week on Marshmallow Mountain with my husband. We've earned this.

As we approach the cabin, with the car windows down in our new full-size pickup truck, the smell of fresh pine, dirt, and crisp mountain air fills my lungs. There's more than enough room for us to both manspread, but we don't. My palm lies on Marsh's knee and I gently tickle him as his arm drapes behind my headrest. Wildflowers carpet the area on either side of the dirt road and the myriad of colors makes it hard to discern one blossom from the next. There's no threat of getting stranded in a storm now (sorry chickens) and the sound of the babbling brook that empties into the pond in the distance becomes louder as the cabin, now surrounded by the lush greens of both evergreen and deciduous trees, comes into view.

Marsh's hand lands on my thigh, squeezing gently, and I let out a deep sigh.

"Yeah," he says. "It's good to be back."

Entering the cabin, we head straight for the bedroom. I do my traditional backward flop on the bed, bouncing a few times as the springs creak. Marsh lies on top of me, his fingers exploring my beard as he considers my face.

"What? Crumbs?"

"No." He kisses my chin. "I'd gladly gobble those up." He mouths at my whiskers. "I'm just looking at … " Another peck on my chin. "My husband." Marsh exhales and buries his face in my neck.

Pre-breakup, our visits to Marshmallow Mountain almost always started with a bang—as in fucking. Come to think of it, we had Break-Up Sex Part One in The General Store bathroom fairly quickly last time. But now we're together. Married. In our bed.

My cock swells under the weight of Marsh, and I'm excited to have a week of reading, eating, hiking, sleeping, and sex.

"Not here." Marsh lifts his head, and his serious face greets me.

"But … "

"Nope." And he's up, grabbing my hand. "Come."

"I was hoping we both would."

"Good one," he says, tugging me out the back door.

As we walk, Marsh and I trample the tall grasses and flowers that have grown over the trail down to the pond. The sun peeks through branches, and I crane my face to feel the warmth as Marsh leads me deeper into the privacy of the woods. We round a bend and it comes into view. The rock. Not the beefy star of *The Scorpion King*, but our rock. More of a boulder, it's easily five feet tall and the craggy edges provide the perfect place to hang wet bathing suits.

"There." Marsh stops, his breathing heavy from running. I raise my eyebrows at him and he pats his pocket, and the outline of his inhaler comes into view.

"Is that an inhaler in your pocket, or are you just happy to see me?" I ask.

"Both."

Not missing a beat, Marsh unzips his khaki shorts, and his cock, fat and firm, falls out. He's almost fully hard and the moment our eyes lock, his dick pulses fuller in my peripheral vision.

Marsh pulls off his shorts, digs into the pocket, and pulls out the mini carving of the cabin I made for him the last time we were here. He carefully places it on the rock, and turns toward me.

"Why did you bring that?" I ask.

"I've been carrying it around with me until we returned." He taps the roof. "It belongs here. With us."

"You big sap." I grab his arm and kiss his shoulder. "Did you want to go for a swim?" I tease, the calm pond water only feet away.

"Yeah." He tosses his shorts on the rock, and they fall to the ground. "In your ass."

"We don't have towels," I say, looking around for some secret towel stash left by forest fairies.

"Oh." Marsh's face falls, his spontaneous woods sexscapade in jeopardy.

I pull off my polo and throw it on the ground. "That will have to do."

Marsh yanks off his faux vintage Blockbuster T-shirt and carefully lays it next to mine, creating almost as much space as a towel.

"We'll make it work," he says. "Now … " he tugs at the waistband of my pants. "Get these off." Marsh's lips find mine. "Please."

Our tongues dance as we laugh into each other's mouths and stumble, struggling to remove my pants. When they're finally in a pile next to our shirts, we stand naked, with only the birds and the bees (and maybe a curious deer) to witness us.

"Now, if you'd do me the honor." Marsh nods toward the ground, and I know exactly what he wants.

I lower myself to all fours and arch my back. Doing my best to stay on the shirts, the dirt and gravel underneath won't stop what's about to happen. The buzz and hum of insects calm me. I close my eyes, taking it all in, and then Marsh's hands land on my ass. He spreads me wide and I wait.

"Dat ass. It's so fucking perfect."

Another moment of examining his workspace.

"I love your ass, Data, but I love you most of all. All of you."

With that, Marsh spits. He's preparing his canvas. Another lob of saliva and he dives in.

Opening my eyes, I see a chicken—a rooster with a bright red comb of feathers bursting out of his head—completely oblivious to us, saunter by the far side of the pond, pecking at the dirt.

"Cock!" I whisper-shout, not wanting to startle it.

"Not yet, baby, give me a minute."

"No." I laugh and my body shakes. "Over there. A cock. Rooster."

"Ah. Maybe Maddi sent us a welcome party." Marsh kisses my ass cheek and then resumes his masterful rimming as the bird pecks at something in the grass.

There's nothing new about Marsh eating me out, but being outside, surrounded by nature, the quiet noise of the woods, and knowing we get a whole week up here, somehow his tongue lodged deep inside ignites something new in my core.

"You've got five minutes," I say.

"Huh?" He's come up for air. I turn around and his face, wet and sloppy, tilts in confusion.

"Then I want yours."

Marsh nods quickly. "Fair."

And he's back, licking, slurping, and thrusting his tongue inside me. Even though there's no rush, there's an urgency between us. The summer heat, kept at bay by the canopy of trees, weasels its way toward us, and I brace myself so I'm able to push back against Marsh's mouth.

I reach down and palm my cock, hard and ready, and desire rumbles in my belly.

"Okay, my turn."

I flip over and lay on my back. "Back it up," I say, motioning Marsh in like an airport marshaller. "Sit." I point to my mouth.

"Happy to oblige." Marsh squats over me, his cheeks spreading as he uses his hands to balance himself on my thighs.

"Perfect." I grasp his ample ass, and my eager tongue immediately explores the inviting warmth of his hole.

"Fuck, Data, Fuck."

Reaching around, I grasp his cock, making sure he stays hard and ready for what's coming next.

I tug down gently, and Marsh takes my signal to grind on my face, allowing me to bury myself even deeper. With my heart racing, I'm eager to get fucked.

I slap his ass, our non-verbal cue, and he lifts off me.

"You, okay?"

"Lube. Did you bring lube?" My breath is heavy.

"I may have forgotten the towel, but I'm not a troglodyte."

Marsh stands, scrambles over to his shorts on the ground, and retrieves a tiny bottle of lube.

"Is that … "

"Yup," he finishes. "Same bottle. Thank you, General Store."

Kneeling between my legs, Marsh squirts a good amount on his hands, and to my surprise, applies it to himself.

"Wait," I say.

"Don't worry. You're first. I'm just … preparing."

I'm unable to contain my smile. "Smart. Very smart."

Marsh's eyebrows pop up and down. He's so fucking charming. I want to grab his cheeks—the ones on his face—and kiss every inch of him.

"You okay on your back?" He's over me, lifting my ankles on his shoulders.

"Fuck, yes." I do my best to assist by hoisting my feet and he grabs the left one, kissing the top.

"Now … " He places the tip of his cock at my hole. "Ready?"

I nod slowly. "You've opened me right up with that tongue of yours."

"Yeah, I did."

Marsh pushes in and the pleasure of having him inside me, filling me up, completing our connection, takes over. My head falls back and hits something. A rock. A patch of dirt. I'm not sure, and I don't care. I paw at his back and pull him closer, deeper.

"There's my Data." His fingers brush my forehead and I'm complete. Not only because he's inside me, but also because he's by my side. Now and forever.

We finish with me railing Marsh, leaning against the rock. He loves playing a game of shooting on it and seeing how much rock real estate he can cover. My orgasm crawls up quickly, and I pump deep inside him, urging his release. And when he comes moments later, there's no holding back. The poor boulder never saw what was coming. Literally.

"Fuck, Marsh." I'm still inside him, leaning over, peppering the back of his neck with kisses.

"Yeah, baby. Damn that felt amazing."

Being here on the mountain with him, I'm consumed by an overwhelming sense of peace. Marsh may be hilarious. Charming. Sexy as fuck. But most of all, he makes me feel a little more whole.

"Can we swim?" he asks.

"But we don't have towels."

"We'll air dry. My skin is too delicate for a towel." He slaps his ass cheek. "Or use our clothes. Or put them on wet." He turns around, gathers me up, and I nestle into his chest.

"I don't care," he says.

"Me neither."

Hand in hand, we stroll towards the pond, knowing Marshmallow Mountain will be the backdrop for a week of blissful relaxation. But more importantly, I see our future together. Side-by-side until we're old and gray. Like the small cabin lovingly carved with care, watching over us from the rock, we've transformed into a perfectly crafted piece.

Two Marshalls. One heart.

Cut to the Feeling

BOOK TWO COMING IN OCTOBER 2025

For Bryce Derrickson, rejection is nothing new. He's used to Broadway casting directors seeing his size and assuming he can't be a graceful dancer. But getting dumped with no notice is a special kind of burn. At least his sweet dog Bobo still loves him.

As if being left without warning isn't bad enough, Bryce's ex sublets their apartment without telling him, leaving him without a place to live. When his new 'roommate' turns out to be a stuffy, elbow-patches-on-blazer, permanent-frown-on-face professor, Bryce is furious. No way will he give up his bohemian pad without a fight.

Years ago, Emerson Grant was on the fast track to being a preeminent scholar in his field. Now he's stuck teaching at a commuter school in a cornfield. Finagling a guest lecturing spot at a prestigious New York institution could be his way back into the top reaches of academia. That is, if the man and dog blatantly squatting in his sublet don't drive him bananas first.

Sharing a one-bedroom apartment with a stranger is a New York rite of passage. Sharing it with a stranger you might be falling for is something else entirely.

Preorder Now!

Big Boys Small Spaces: The Series

BY A.J. TRUMAN AND M.A. WARDELL

Marshmallow Mountain: Data and Marsh's story is out now!

Cut to the Feeling: Bryce and Emerson's story coming in 2025.

Untitled Book 3: Horton's story coming in 2026.

Acknowledgments

A.J.

I would like to thank the staff at my gym's Kidzone space, where parents get two hours/day of free child care to work out (or sit on their laptop in the lobby in my case), as well as the patchwork of babysitters who watched my son on random weekday mornings when available. My half of this book was written in the nooks and crannies of time I managed to find, and I am grateful to child care professionals everywhere for being the village modern parents so desperately need.

Also, I have to thank my husband for his unwavering support of this odd career I've chosen to pursue. Thank you for believing in me 100% of the time when I only manage to believe in myself like 38% of the time. And as always, thank you for not murdering me in my sleep.

I can't end this book without thanking Matt. From the moment you ended a rambling story on our first Zoom with "Long story short. Too late," I knew we'd be friends. Thank you for your endless patience with me during this process as I learned how to co-write after writing 19 books by myself. Thank you for being the sunshine to my heartless bitch, for putting up with my frugality-borderline-cheapness, for being my social media sherpa, for teaching this old indie publishing dog some new tricks, for cackling at most of my jokes and pushing me to write funnier ones. But most of all, thank you for your friendship. As a gay man writing in the MM romance world, I've felt like a misfit toy for most of my career, never quite fitting in. I feel lucky to have found a fellow unicorn to ride off into the rainbows with, or whatever the heck unicorns do. (And Matthew, if you tell me that you read this and got choked up, I'm going to have you arrested.)

Matt

First, I didn't get choked up. I cackled. Could you hear it from half way across the country?

To my friends and family, thank you for your unwavering continued support. And to my husband, who puts up with all my shenanigans, you're the real MVP.

I would like to thank A.J. for sliding into my DMs, asking a million questions that ultimately led me to ask, "Hey, why don't we hop on a Zoom?" That first chat lasted hours because A.J. had more questions and I couldn't focus and went off on multiple tangents, mostly asking all about A.J.'s son, husband, and cat, who was determined to participate in our call. From there, we began chatting more, both in DMs and on our phones, and continued Zoom calls. Our friendship grew quickly and Marshmallow Mountain directly results from one of those many conversations. People always wonder what it's like to co-write a book, and for me, it's been a little like sex with someone new. At first, there's an overwhelming awkwardness, but once you find your rhythm, everything seamlessly falls into place and transforms into something incredible. So, thank you A.J. (who I refuse to call by his government name) for being the grumpy to my sunshine and helping push me. While I take pride in the book we've created, it's our friendship that truly makes me feel a sense of accomplishment. 🩶

About A.J. Truman

A.J. Truman writes books with humor, heart, and hot guys. What else does a story need? He lives in a very full house in Indiana with his husband, son, and cats. He loves happily ever afters and sneaking off for an afternoon movie.

www.ajtruman.com

Want to stay in touch and be the first to know about my new books? Join my mailing list The Outsiders today and instantly receive a free short story at www.ajtruman.com/outsiders.

About M.A. Wardell

M.A. Wardell lives near the ocean with his husband and cats. When he isn't writing, he's snuggling those cats, reading all the rom-coms, walking to unravel plot points, and taking long hot baths. He loves playing matchmaker on the page and has many more stories planned.

For more information, visit https://www.mawardell.com/

Purchase signed copies here!

For access to exclusive content and merchandise, join me on Patreon.

Also by A.J. Truman

South Rock High

Ancient History

Drama!

Romance Languages

Advanced Chemistry

Single Dads Club

The Falcon and the Foe

The Mayor and the Mystery Man

The Barkeep and the Bro

Browerton University Series

Out in the Open

Out on a Limb

Out of My Mind

Out for the Night

Out of This World

Outside Looking In

Out of Bounds

Seasonal Novellas

Fall for You

You Got Scrooged

Hot Mall Santa

Only One Coffin

Also by M.A. Wardell

THE TEACHERS IN LOVE SERIES

Teacher of the Year - Marvin and Olan's story is available now!

Mistletoe & Mishigas - Sheldon and Theo's story is available now!

Napkins and Other Distractions - Vincent and Kent's story is available now!

Husband of the Year - Marvin and Olan's series finale coming February 2025

Download free bonus stories!

https://www.mawardell.com/freebies